Bookish Meets Boy

A Downtown Divas Romance

Dianna Dann

Wayward Cat Publishing

While inspired by wonderful Historic Downtown Melbourne, on Florida's sunny Space Coast, this book is a work of fiction and all the characters within it are products of the author's crazy imagination. Any similarities between characters in this book and actual people, living or dead, are purely coincidental.

ISBN 978-1-938999-22-2
Library of Congress Control Number: 2015912211

Wayward Cat Publishing
Palm Bay, Florida
www.waywardcatpublishing.com

Cover art © 2015 Wayward Cat Publishing
Illustration of girl with books © Heather McGrath via istockphoto
Illustrations of cats © Daromo via istockphoto
Illustration of brown cat (back cover only) © bortonia via istock photo
Illustration of stack of books (back cover only) © Diane Labombarbe via istock photo

Bookish Meets Boy

Chapter One

Erich Fromm once said," I told the cats, "'love is the only sane and satisfactory answer to the problem of human existence.'" Weesie, the black-and-white tuxedo, sniffed my fingers approvingly. "But then," I said, "we must remember what we learned from J. Geils Band. 'Love stinks.'" I waited for the cats to soak in the deep, profound truth I'd just imparted. *Love stinks*. "Who are you going to believe?" I asked them. "*Who*...are you going to believe?"

J. Geils Band. That's who.

Okay, so I was bitter.

Every morning, I walked east from my apartment, on Manatee Road, to Manatee Park where tourists gather to gawk at said sea cows in the lagoon, then up Mangrove Street to the back of an abandoned storefront on the south side of downtown. The cats—seven left in the colony—lived there. Used to be sixteen. But I trapped the buggers and had them spayed, neutered, and what-not. They loved me for it. Okay, fifteen of them loved me for it. Samson never forgave me. But he still took food from my hand for a year before he took up with my cousin Carrie; he's a proper indoor cat now.

There used to be, I'm told, a sewing machine repair shop in the building. It's separated by a six-inch alley from the Strawbridge Art League. Next to that is an attorney's office. And next to them, Trudy's Treasures—an old house converted into an antique store. Those other buildings back up against grass lots, but the owner of the building that housed the sewing machine repair shop had a concrete parking lot put in along Mangrove Street. Now...I don't know how many years later, it was cracked, weed infested, and crumbling. At the building's eastern edge, where the grass lots began, there drooped an aged and tired oak struggling to shade a warped and splintered picnic table. I'd taken a few large plastic bins, had Hugh saw half-circles on one side of each, and upended them by the building, near the alley, so the cats could get away from the rain. That was where my darlings lived and I did my best to keep them happy there, so they wouldn't feel the need to prowl over to the park, where they were, according to the Strawbridge City Council, not wanted.

The building's been for sale for as many years as I've been feeding the strays, but it finally got an offer last month and I'd like to say I handled it well. The thought of somebody renovating it, which let's face it, would have to be done, and scaring off my darlings, dispersing them throughout the area, possibly lost forever, nearly drove me insane. I might have been shrieking when I accosted Madaline, the realtor, about it. But she told me 'no problem.' Shoe shop, she said. Quiet reno, easy move in. And they love the idea of having some stray cats out back by the picnic table. Who wouldn't? I mean, really? What sort of person wouldn't love to have seven adorable cats in her backyard that someone else takes care of? Still, when she told me the good news, she was giving me *that look*—the one a lot of the people downtown still gave me. It's the 'let's not upset her' look. The 'we don't want her freaking out and jumping into the lagoon again' look.

It's not as bad as it sounds. I wasn't trying to kill myself. God, I hope I'd do a better job of it than that. And I hadn't lost my marbles and tried to ride a manatee—you get arrested for that sort of thing around here. Honest to all get out, I dropped my friggin' comb into the lagoon and before I considered, maybe...buying a new one, I'd jumped in. Fully clothed. And some of the tourists fished me out again...by the feet. Like I was a dead mermaid. Lucky for me, there were some kids there with their phones, taking video and posting to Instagram. Thanks, children of Strawbridge, a whole hell of a lot.

Weesie purred.

I'm telling you: cats *understand*.

"Gotta go." I gave Sugar, the brown tabby, a quick pet and stuffed the small bag of food and the now empty half-gallon water jug into my big book bag—the one with the Margaret Mitchell quote on it: In a weak moment, I have written a book—and headed to Bookish.

I'll give you the quick version, because frankly, I'm over it. I don't even really want to think about it anymore. I'm done with it. *So done*. It's like this: Cal. I loved him. For two years, I loved him more than life itself. I told him I loved him. Three times. First time, he said, "Oooh, babe. A little soon, don't ya think?" The second time, he said, "I'm flattered." And the third time he said, "I love...Lydia." Lydia lived across the landing, nearly my best friend. We were so close, a bunch of her stuff was in my apartment, hence my stalking out and finding myself along the lagoon at Manatee Park throwing those things into the wat—er, I mean, trying to comb my hair when I tripped and fell in. She doesn't live across the landing anymore. Nope. Now she lives with Cal.

I crossed Mangrove to the little alley next to Fiona's, into the breezeway, exiting onto the main street, Strawbridge, and sucked in a breath, ready to brave the walk downtown, all the way to the other end, to Bookish, where I worked with Gramps. It was a gantlet I had to walk every day. The people downtown—I don't mean to snipe but, they're nosy.

Cal just loved them. Every weekend, part of our dates had to include a walk through. He charmed them all. Had Mrs. Simmons eating out of his hand. Told Octavia she was a goddess. (Not that Octavia isn't a goddess, but do you want your boyfriend kissing other women and saying, "My goddess you're a goddess?" Nobody wants that. Except Octavia, apparently.) He even had Officer Palmer smiling and that's something you don't see every day. After he dumped me—I shouldn't say that, it makes him sound too good—after he slithered away like a palmetto bug and left me with seven hundred dollars in credit card debt because he handily forgot his wallet when it came time to pay for his car's AC repair (and from the look of my bill, I also paid for a necklace for Lydia), I couldn't walk the street without everyone asking about him. *Truth*: I ran away crying the first time someone mentioned him. *And* the second time. How long would it take for things to go back to normal? *Normal* being that time before Cal existed. Oh, my, god. I *was* bitter, wasn't I?

I marched along with my copy of *Unraveling Oliver* in front of my face as if I were reading it. Of course I wasn't. It's not possible to walk downtown while reading. If Officer Palmer doesn't tap you on the back with his chalk stick and warn you against the shortsightedness of it, you'll at least find yourself on your butt in a planter. But so far as the downtown population was concerned, I, Sophie Childers, could read and walk the sidewalk at the same time, without hitting any sunburned tourists, without walking into a jutting storefront, and without ever bumping into a fancy light post. Because I was always *faking it*.

I smelled Stogies before I got there and looked up to see Mr. Booker, standing in front of his store, a cigar notched securely between his jaws, looking at his Kindle. If Octavia was a goddess, Leland Booker was a god. Blond wavy hair floated around him like a halo. His face was chiseled out of marble. True, he was old enough to be my father. And sure, he smoked cigars. But he had to. You can't own a cigar store and not smoke the things. He smiled and nodded at me as I approached, holding up his e-reader like it was a prize. He pulled the cigar from his mouth.

"*Love That Dog*," he told me. "Just downloaded it."

"Poetry?"

He laughed. "Have a listen—"

"Wait until Friday."

"Aw," he said.

"And we had a deal," I said as I walked past. "No e-readers."

There were a few people downtown who didn't *tsk* when they saw me. Mr. Booker was one of them. He never liked Cal; I could tell. I think it was because Cal didn't get poetry. No matter how much I told him there was nothing to get—just read it, I'd tell him—he couldn't let a poem run past without snorting and rolling his eyes.

Next up was Sweet Suite. Barb, or Kate, or both never let an acquaintance pass by without calling out to him. "Hoot, Sophie!" I couldn't tell which one it was. They were both plump and brunette, though one was lighter than the other, don't ever remember which. I lifted my eyes from my book, smiled and walked on. I got all the way to Namaste without another encounter but there was Benjamin lighting the day's first stick of incense in their burner out by the always-open door. "Tangerine," he cooed, waving a hand toward me, trying to wash me with odor.

"You know I'm allergic," I said.

"Not to tangerine."

Cute as an inchworm on a daisy, Benjamin was twenty at best. Thin, small, sweet, his hair in one of those tower cuts that lifted itself straight off the top of his head. And he always had a cotton rag or piece of silk as a scarf wrapped loose as a lazy drape around his neck. He smiled as I passed him by. I made it to Burgers before I had to smile again.

Not too bad. But it was Monday, so there you go.

When I finally got to Bookish I was exhausted. It'd been six months since the lagoon incident. *Six months*. I just wanted to get back to being me. Before Cal, most of those downtown people didn't know my name. And I liked it that way. Before Cal, it was all books. Rows and rows of towering bookcases were my lovers. Before Cal, I spent my days and evenings in Bookish with my grandfather, sorting, shelving and re-shelving, dusting, organizing, selling, reading, and smelling books.

And I was finally getting my life back. I was finally going to be happy again and if I never met up with another Cal—another *man*—that was fine with me.

As soon as I pulled open the front door of the little shop and the bell jingled, there was Hugh.

Okay, Hugh doesn't count. He was a man, in the most basic sense; true. But he loved books, too. He was in Bookish nearly as often as I was. I didn't have a problem with a man who had books on his mind.

"Hey, Sophie," he said.

"Hey, Hugh."

And that was that. The hallmark of our relationship. That was how I thought a good man-woman relationship ought to be. If I thought Hugh and I could marry, and spend the rest of our lives together, and the only contact we ever had to have was saying "hey" to each other and swapping books, I'd have done it.

"Gramps," I called out. "I'm in." I took the beeline to the back, dumped my stuff off in the back room, and wandered the maze of shelves to the front again.

When you walked into Bookish, the cashwrap was to your right and to the left, a wonderful bay window, in which we displayed...books. *Duh*. In front of the window, we put a lounge where you could relax and look through a book or out the window at passers-by (or at Gramps who spent most of his time—do not tell him I said this—behind the cashwrap, either staring out the front window or reading). The front half of the left side of Bookish was new books, and our local authors' shelf. The rest housed my paradise. Old books. Used, tattered, read and read again. The shelves there were blissfully stuffed and needed constant attention, a condition I never wanted to change.

Gramps was hiding in the history section, down on one knee, his bouffant of gray hair like a hat on his head. He looked up at me and smiled. We both heard the bell, and Mr. Cornell.

"Childers! She's done it. This time, she's really done it."

"Oh, dear lord," Gramps said and I heard his knees crack as he struggled to stand. "What's she done this time?"

"Trudy painted her window again," I told him. "It says 'Best Antiques in Town.'"

Gramps chuckled.

"Where are you, Walt?" Mr. Cornell called.

Mr. Cornell owned Geezer's Stuff Antiques next door to Bookish. He and Gramps were both gray but two sides of a coin. My grandfather was a distinguished, polished, proper sort of man—the sort you'd think was a college professor, complete with thick, dark-rimmed glasses. Billy Cornell? Wild man of the Andes. Except British...with an American accent. He wore round, wire-rimmed glasses that sat crooked on his face. He had a pale mole, above and to left of his right brow, that was hard not to look at. Gramps' hair always looked as if he'd just come out of Glam it Up!, with a curly whip at the top, and his beard and mustache were neatly trimmed. Mr. Cornell looked like an old hippie, his hair falling like string to his shoulders and his face covered with splotches of beard—as if he often began, but quickly lost interest in, shaving. But they were the best of opposites-attract friends.

I'd become aware of all the other bodies in the store.

You can't see them, the tall shelves traveled the floor in a maze of spines, print paper, and glue, hiding cozy nooks and bins of poetry and science. But you felt the air thicken when the store was full. People other than Mr. Cornell didn't talk loud in bookstores; they're respecters of sacred spaces. But the silence wasn't so loud it roared in your ears, no. It was a peopled silence. Whispers and sniffs and pages turning. I found myself smiling as I pulled a bunch of used hardcovers off our roller cart to shelve, way up top along the wall, as overstock.

Mr. Cornell was complaining about Trudy and her sign. "It's an outrage," he said. "And a lie! A damned falsehood."

Gramps shushed him.

I balanced the stack of books in my right arm and pulled myself up the ladder with my left hand. Loved the ladders on wheels that traveled along the outer walls of our store. Loved stepping onto the first rung with one foot and pushing off with the other, rolling down the aisle when the store was empty. *Don't tell Gramps.* I smiled a hello, without making eye contact, to the bodies eying the biography section as I made my way up, higher and higher—this was why I never wore dresses to work*—until I reached the shelves above the bookcases and as I was about to transfer the stack to the middle shelf, Mr. Cornell let out a roar. Something about that godforsaken woman and her cheap knock-offs. I fell back a bit and let loose the books. They toppled out of my hands onto a body below me and I turned to grab at them. Silly I know. It was a lot like the way I grabbed at Lydia's stuff as I threw it into the lagoon—with a feeling of regret...too late. The books rained down and I fell with them, onto the body. And the two of us staggered into the shelf of memoirs.

"Oh my god!" I was saying. Quite a lot. "I'm so sorry, are you all right, are you hurt, I can't believe I did that, did the books hurt you?" I had my hands on this guy's head, rubbing my fingers all along his scalp, checking for lumps. I'm pretty sure that's what I was doing, because as I was doing it I was saying, "Did you get a bump? Hardbacks have sharp edges." In my mind, though, I was shouting, *shut up, Sophie! Just shut up!*

I didn't notice the eyes at first. No, first it was the hair and how it glanced against my fingers like silk. Then it was the shoulders—something about them made me take in a breath. Strong? Wide? Male? I couldn't say. Then I caught a light, fragrant whiff of, I don't know...manliness. I finally looked up at the guy and he was laughing at me. Not out loud or anything. But there I was leaning against him, both my hands on his head, massaging, looking up into his face, grateful he wasn't shoving me off him in disgust. And I closed my eyes for a moment and opened them again and thought of Sylvia Plath.

"I'm so sorry," I said again, managing to extricate myself from him and start picking up the books.

"What happened?" Gramps said coming down the aisle. "Is everyone all right?"

"I was attacked by your books, sir," Gorgeous Laughing Eyes said. "But my head has been thoroughly inspected and found free of lumps."

I groaned. "I'm so sorry."

*Not true, of course. I simply don't wear dresses. Sue me.

Chapter Two

It's no problem, really," Gorgeous Laughing Eyes told Gramps as he tried to escape him and get out of the store unmolested. Literally. Gramps was trying to feel GLE's head, too. And Mr. Cornell had come down the aisle saying, "What are you doing? Trying to knock my girl off the ladder? Don't pander, Walt. Stop it, don't admit to guilt. Damnit, Walt."

I was on my knees gathering books when I thought I heard the doorbell jingle and Mr. Cornell went back to ranting about Trudy's Treasures and Hugh plopped down on the faded green carpet in front of me, criss crossed his legs, rested his elbows on his thighs and his chin in his hands.

"That was awkward," he said.

Good old Hugh. And it wasn't the dropping books all over the guy, either. That I could live with. I could handle falling into him. No problem. Maybe even rubbing my hands all over his head. But the way I looked up at him— like he was a knight and I was a damsel. *Ugh*. It was horrid. And his eyes! Dear lord. Deep, dark, blue-green pools of laughter.

"Probably the lighting," Hugh said.

"Did I say that out loud?"

"You said, 'beautiful.'"

"Oh. Just the mess I made," I lied. That was it: GLE was the most beautiful person I'd ever seen. I didn't know they came that way, except in the movies, and I never trusted what I saw in the movies.

"You want me to stock them?"

"No. Employees only." *It's written right on the ladder.*

When I stood, my legs were wobbly so I put the books back onto the roller cart and let Hugh follow me back up front where Gramps was still trying to reason with Mr. Cornell.

"Why don't you put up your own sign?" I said.

"What? I should lie, too?"

"It's not a lie to Trudy. She thinks she's got the best antiques. You think you do."

"I can't copy hers."

"Weren't you ever in school?" I said. "Didn't you ever have to write a research paper? You know, you take notes and then you reword them so you're not plagiarizing."

"It really takes more than that," Gramps said.

"I'm not talking about plagiarism. I'm saying, don't say exactly the same thing. Her sign says 'Best Antiques in Town.' Yours can say, 'Best Antiques in Strawbridge.'"

Mr. Cornell stared at me for a few seconds before he bellowed out a laugh. "Brilliant!"

Of course, I'd just started a war.

"Oh, lookie there," Gramps said as he followed Mr. Cornell to the door. "Loverboy is looking in at Café Flamingo."

I blushed. "Isn't it bad enough we molested the poor guy's head? Do we have to give him the name of an Eighties rock band?"

"I could go for a smoothie," Gramps said, raising his brows at me.

"I could call him back over," Mr. Cornell said as he opened the door.

"Don't you dare."

He laughed and winked at me before finally going back to his own store where he belonged.

"Maybe Geezer's Stuff Antiques wouldn't have a problem with Trudy's Treasures if Mr. Cornell spent less time over here," I said.

"That's not very generous, is it?"

I sighed. "I suppose not."

"Why don't you go over and talk to the boy?"

"Gramps!"

"What? I thought it was a new world you were living in. No more boy meets girl...now it's girl meets boy. Girl makes the move. Women's lib and all that."

"I hardly think feminism is about women being able to ask men out."

"Well, maybe it ought to be."

"I'm heading home now, I guess," Hugh said.

I jumped. And before I could stop myself I said, "Hugh! I forgot you were here."

If real lives had soundtracks, we'd have heard a sucking, sighing sort of sound effect there in the silence that followed as Hugh grimaced at Gramps and Gramps gave the poor guy a sympathetic grin.

"I'll see you tomorrow?" I said.

Hugh nodded and left. Even the bell jangled morosely at him.

"You're on a roll," Gramps said.

"He's so quiet. It's easy to overlook him."

When I thought about it, I realized Hugh was simply easy to overlook. Period. He was a bland sort of person. Beige...if you will. There was nothing remarkable about him—his hair, blondish brown, no style to speak of, not usually combed; a round, forgetful face with pale, brown eyes; his clothes: faded pocketless t-shirts, and jeans; sneakers on his feet that made it easy for him to sidle up to people and scare the wits out of them. I liked that about him, to be honest. Hugh was not a guy to get bothered about, and I was past the phase of wanting to be bothered.

"You know the lad's got it in for you."

"Lad? Loverboy? Lookie here? Did you take old people pills this morning?"

"Wilde in the evening, Seuss in the morning. Does weird things to the brain."

"And it's not 'got in in' for me. That makes him sound like a hired gun."

"Anyway, I'm sure I heard you say groovy just the other day."

"I can't help it if old people germs rub off on me.'"

"Sure you can. Go out among the living for a change, soak up the language of the current generation. It'll do you good."

"You didn't sell me your half of Bookish so I could leave you alone to run it all day."

"But I can run it all day. I don't need you here. Go out, Sophie. Have fun."

"This *is* fun."

I let Gramps disappear into the bookcase maze before I peered out the front window. GLE was nowhere in sight. That was a good thing, I told myself, like, twelve times. So many reasons. One. The guy was drop dead gorgeous. Drop Dead Gorgeous types don't date bookish girls who feel up their heads. Two. I felt up the guy's head! Three. I was six months out from Cal. Cal, the pestiferous dolt who taught me that I should never have left the beautiful solace of bookworld and ventured out into the jungle of reality. It wasn't the first time I received that particular lesson. There was Jordan Spilke in my junior year of high school who made out with me under the bleachers at the homecoming game and then went straight back to his girlfriend Gretchen Finkelweiner.* And Peter Crouch in college. Did I have to remind Gramps of that fiasco? You do *not* get over a guy forgetting to pick you up at the airport, after you flew across the country to meet him in Denver for spring break, because he had to take his ex-girlfriend on a microbrewery tour. And, oh, yeah, surprise...ex-girlfriend is going to spend spring break with us at the cabin.

Why was I even going over it in my head? I was done. *Done.* I jumped again when Gramps suddenly appeared beside me.

"Maybe he's out walking downtown. A tourist."

"Why are you still on this?"

"I saw your face, Sophie."

"The red rash, you mean? You know I'm allergic to dust."

"It was the blush of romance."

"Oh, my god. Grandma had a catch in you, didn't she? Please let it go. I'm done with men."

"You don't mean that."

"I do. I really do."

"You can't give up."

"Why not? Look at us, Gramps. We're doing okay. Look at Bookish. Do you have any idea what's going on out there in the world of books? Mr. Booker is reading poetry on a Kindle!"

"People still want real books."

"Paper doesn't make a book real, Gramps. This store is a relic. You're a relic. I'm a relic. We live in a little niche, a snug, warm corner of a mad, mad world. And we're doing just fine. I liked my life before Cal. I miss it. I want it back."

A young couple strolled out from the far aisle, where the fantasy and romance books were shelved, looking at me with something like admiration on their faces...or pity. Hard to tell sometimes. I nodded at them and lowered my voice.

"I don't mind being a relic. An antique."

"You don't get to be," Gramps said. He'd gone around and up the steps into the cashwrap and leaned over the front counter to look into my eyes. "You're too young. And those cats you care for—throwaways. I think you identify with them."

"I never thought about it that way, but, yeah, I do. What's so bad about that?"

"You're not a stray."

"I don't know—" I glanced at an older woman on the sofa, who'd looked up from the paperback she was perusing to smile at me—"I rather like the way that sounds."

"Please, Sophie. Stop the melodrama. It's over and done."

"True."

"Time for you to live again."

"I am living. Why isn't this enough for you? Books, cats, a few friends here and there. What more do you need?"

"Not *me*, Soph. You. A young woman needs love. And eventually a family. Don't you want that?"

I sighed. "Imagine me with a family. Forgetting to cook dinner because I got lost in a book."

Gramps rubbed his hands through his hair and gave me a worried look.

I shook my head. "I like things the way they are," I pleaded. "Love isn't for everybody. And anyway, I'll always have Hugh."

He threw his hands up as if giving in. I turned to try again with the hardbacks and the ladder. But then I remembered that moment in time—when I felt something, before I wanted to *not* feel it.

"Gramps," I said. "What was it Sylvia Plath said? About closing her eyes and the world dying?"

"'I shut my eyes and all the world drops dead; I lift my eyes and all is born again.' Why?"

"No reason," I said. But I was thinking, *huh, how weird is that?*

16

*Not her real name, but the way I like to remember it— with my sincerest apologies to anyone actually named Finkelweiner.

Chapter Three

CrochetMom: *Hey honey. How's the place look?*
ReeseFuller: I like it. It has...
CrochetMom: *It's kitchy*
ReeseFuller: Is that a word?
CrochetMom: *Of course it's a word. Means quaint*
ReeseFuller: Does not
CrochetMom: *Watch this*
CrochetMom: *r u c ing any1*
ReeseFuller: Stop it, Mom
ReeseFuller: And, no. But I did just meet a book assassin
CrochetMom: *Book what?*
ReeseFuller: She got me with some hardcovers
CrochetMom: *Throwing things at you already?*
ReeseFuller: It's love
CrochetMom: *A mother can always hope*
CrochetMom: *:)*
CrochetMom: *Took me a while to figure that smiley face out.*
ReeseFuller: How are you feeling?
CrochetMom: *I'm fine. Don't ask me that every time we talk*
ReeseFuller: Why not?
CrochetMom: *it makes me feel sick*
ReeseFuller: I'm sorry
CrochetMom: *No feeling sorry, either*
ReeseFuller: LOL Okay

CrochetMom: *o i c, u can use abbreviations, but I can't?*
ReeseFuller: That's right
CrochetMom: :)
ReeseFuller: Love you, Mom
CrochetMom: *Love you, too*

Chapter Four

The following comparative exercise was written under duress, but serves as an example of the sort of thing that goes on routinely in Bookish.

A busy day before Cal

1. Wake up to three cats sniffing my face, shower, eat a bagel

2. Walk to abandoned building on Mangrove, feed darlings

3. Cross Mangrove, pass Fiona's clothing store, gaze longingly in window at really cool outfits I wasn't daring enough to wear

4. Enter breezeway, keep head down, no eye contact with people opening up their stores

5. Exit breezeway and head west on Strawbridge Main, avoid early-bird tourists and shoppers

6. Let myself breathe once I reach Geezer's Stuff

7. Get to Bookish, sign in, go to work

8. Say hi to Hugh, discuss books

9. Order lunch in, sometimes cross over to Café Flamingo, but don't make small talk

10. Leave work, head down, do not make eye contact with locals

11. Check in on darlings, feed and water

12. Back home along Manatee Road to Creek Overlook Apartments

13. Chat with Lydia

14. Eat dinner with cats in front of television, go to bed with a great book

A busy day after Cal

1. Wake up to three cats sniffing my face, shower, eat leftover Chinese or a bagel, sometimes brownies

2. Walk to abandoned building on Mangrove through Manatee Park, chat with Alfred, feed darlings

3. Cross Mangrove to Fiona's, gaze longingly in window at really cool clothes, say hi when she comes out to greet me, decide which top to buy next

4. Enter breezeway, hi to everyone: that lady who teaches art upstairs, that couple who own the specialty toy shop, that lady who sells women's clothing and has an accent; promise myself one day I will learn all of their names

5. Exit breezeway and head west on Strawbridge Main, peek in at Brunch to see if they're making the spinach quiche that day and say hi to Melanie, chat with Mr. Booker as I pass Stogies, smile at one of the Rollings sisters at Sweet Suite, resist the brownies, nod at the perky lady who owns Begotten, chat with Benjamin or Suri at Namaste, peek in at

The Fort to see if any drunks are sleeping at the gate, leftover from the night before, smell the wonderful greasy aromas at Burgers as they prepare for the lunch crowd, wave to Mr. Cornell, and finally make it into Bookish

6. Say hi to Hugh, discuss books

7. Order lunch in, sometimes cross over to Café Flamingo, chat with Melissa or one of her employees

8. Walk back east on the north side of Strawbridge Main with a book, wave at Melissa as I pass Café Flamingo, smile at the Bead It! lady, that lady who sells plus sizes and prom dresses, and the man who sells rare coins and oddities, then stop and talk with Mr. or Mrs. Simmons at MacAuley Awley's Irish Pub, peek into the windows at the mysterious old house—every historic downtown should have one—looking for ghosts, smell the pretzels and popcorn at Pops, stop in to see what's new at Kaya Vintage Clothing, maybe buy something, wave at the candle shop lady, smile at the children's shop lady, nod at Mr. Swanson who owns Venerable Trinkets, cross the side street and look in the window at Morgan's Office Supply, watch the ladies having their hair done in the window at Glam it Up!, pass Pub's Sports Bar and enter the mall, sing a few bars of a song with Octavia, usually The Pointer Sisters' "I'm so Excited"—always glad when she gets back onto a Seventies Disco kick—promise Noah I'll be buying more flowers soon, exit back end of mall to find Alfred at the dumpsters. Give him the latest book. Talk about the last one we read. Then walk all the way back to work on one side of the street or other doing it all over again with the, "Hi, how are you," and the, "Love the new window design," and the "Yum, it smells so good," until I flop back into Bookish ready to lose myself in a book.

9. Leave work, doing it all yet again, smiling, smiling,

23

smiling

10. Peek in at the new art in the Strawbridge Art League window, wave at Trudy, and stop off behind the abandoned building to feed the darlings

11. Back home through the park, chat with Alfred

12. Chat with Pari, who took Lydia's apartment after she ran off with my boyfriend

13. Eat dinner in front of the television, go to bed with a great book and three cats

"You see?" Gramps asked me. "Your life is so much better now. Cal did you a favor."

"Are you out of your mind? I'm exhausted. It's like that episode of *Seinfeld* where Kramer puts everybody's picture up in the lobby."

"Peesh."

"Peesh? Really, Gramps?"

"No one's asking for a kiss every time he sees you. You're happier now. Admit it."

"I'm anemic, that's what I am."

"Get a smoothie, then."

"Is there iron in fruit?"

"Just go. Get some fresh air."

So I went.

It was late afternoon, summery hot with warm breezes —that Central Florida suffocation climate unlike any other in the world—and I suppose I *was* a bit hungry. We'd had fancy salads from Pub's for lunch—delicious but not so filling; Mr. Cornell went to get them for us. I grabbed *Unraveling Oliver* from behind the cashwrap and left the store. But as I headed across the street to Café Flamingo, who do you suppose was standing out front looking at Melissa's menu? That's right. Gorgeous Laughing Eyes himself. And some of the Downtown Divas were *all over it*. Three of them today: Melissa, owner of Café Flamingo; Karen, whose family owns Morgan's Office Supply; and Vanessa, who took over Glam it Up! from her aunt last year—sitting at one of the outside tables sipping fancy iced mocha lattes or whatever sort of coffee divas drink. They were eying GLE, smiling, nudging one another. Who could blame them? Well, me. I blamed them. I could have kicked myself for it but I had this unmistakable *mine* episode as they fawned all over him, like he was the shiny new god in the neighborhood. This behavior was unbecoming; we were all—the Downtown Divas and me—mature business owners. Oh, hell, who am I kidding? I was blushing before I stepped onto the sidewalk.

I got to the door just as he'd decided to enter and we reached for it at the same time.

"Excuse me," I said.

"It's you," he said.

I nodded and waited for him to go ahead of me.

"Assassins first," he said.

I thought he'd said something like "asses first" or "I see your purse," but as I pulled the door open it hit me and I burst out laughing...like an ass—ha ha*haa* ha*haa*. Kill me now. Still, the forceful expression of air that occurs with a donkey laugh like that calmed me down, or made me lightheaded—same thing. I got in line, with him behind me, and ordered my strawberry banana smoothie, then moved aside to wait.

He ordered the same and said, "Maybe you could spill your smoothie on me. It would make my day complete."

I turned to look at him, to see if he was joking, because if not, it was a crappy thing to say, don't you think? He was smiling playfully and I took the time to really study him, finally. Hugh was right...about the lighting. In the muted, dusty lamps of Bookish, his eyes looked like mountain lakes—dark and mysterious, algae rich, blueish green or greenish blue. No, definitely blueish green. But in the harsher light of Café Flamingo it was clear they were green, like dark moss drooping in the shadow of an old oak. His square jawline had a hint of dark beard on it, his upper lip trimmed to perfection. His thick, dark brows ran straight across his forehead and his hair danced whimsy atop his head. He was, in short, hot.

"I'm not clumsy, really," I said and blushed again. It needed saying though, I thought.

"That's terrible," he said. "If you aren't planning on regular book drops, I'll have to come up with another name."

"Oh, you named me Clumsy, did you?"

"Nothing so ordinary as that."

"What then?"

"Book Assassin," he said. "BA for short."

Oh, my, god. I laughed. "That's very good."

"So, BA, you come here often?"

My smoothie was ready and I took it and turned to leave. "As a matter of fact, I do."

"Hold on," he said and I think I started to breathe again. "I'll walk you out."

So we waited for his smoothie and I inhaled mine like a starving hyena, thinking about, of all things, what I was wearing. My jeans. Good, good. And that adorable t-shirt tunic, with the frillies sewn into the bottom hem, that I got at Fiona's. Perfect. I did *not* look like a bookstore employee that day.*

"Ow." I put my hand to my forehead. "Brain freeze."

He was kind enough to ignore that and we left Flamingo and stopped on the sidewalk with the three Divas watching, agog.

"You work at the bookstore, then," he said.

"Excellent observation."

We slurped our concoctions and I did it again. "Ow."

26

"Did your mother never tell you not to sip your milk-shakes so fast?"

"I'm a slow learner." So true.

He smiled and everything lit up, literally. Oh my god; in my head I thought 'literally' instead of 'figuratively.' I was *not* going to tell Gramps about that.

"Are you new around here?" I asked him.

"No. I grew up in Strawbridge. Went to Strawbridge High. But I've been over on Cocoa Beach for the last few years."

"So, you're visiting?" There was this disgusting, whiny desperation in my voice and I tried to slurp it away and managed to choke on a thick bit of strawberry that popped through the straw. I could see the Divas out of the corner of my eye, leaning toward us, struggling to hear every word.

"*Unraveling Oliver*," he said.

"What?"

"Your book." He pointed at it and I looked at it, surprised. Yes, there it was. My book.

"Oh, yeah. I finished it yesterday."

He squinched up his face in the cutest way. "So why do you have it?"

"Oh, yeah." I was acutely aware of my inability to form coherent sentences. "I'm taking it to Alfred. That way." I pointed. I'd had about enough of myself and rolled my eyes.

"I'll walk with you," he said, "if you don't mind. You could show me around."

"You grew up here. What don't you know?"

"I left ten years ago for college and didn't come downtown on my visits home; this place has changed a lot."

That much was true. I started walking and he came along. I wasn't going to stop him.

The Historic Downtown Project started long ago, but in the last ten years it morphed the old, decrepit, flea-bitten mood into a new, swanky, antique 'place to be.' There were

27

still bits of hundred-year-old architecture here and there. Shops in what used to be boarding houses. Downtown was somehow fresh and musty at the same time; littered with nooks and crannies, a couple of foot-wide alleys, a few rusty fire escapes, and oddly-angled store fronts, it also boasted its share of stylish modern buildings. And on the north side, between MacAuley Awleys Irish Pub and Glitz Clothing for the bedazzledly disadvantaged, sat a one-hundred-fifty year old house—one of those 'nobody ever goes in and nobody ever comes out' deals.

"So you like it here," he said.

"Love it." Eloquent as ever.

"Lots of business?"

I nodded.

"You don't say much, do you?"

I could feel the heat on my cheeks and chose to continue slurping my smoothie as a response. It wasn't until we were at the mall on the other end of Strawbridge Main that I realized we'd passed Pops, and Across the Pond, and ChocShop, and all the other shops I should have been nodding hellos at, and I hadn't looked at anyone. I wasn't sure what it meant but it felt like something I wanted to run from. It was *him*. Or the ethereal presence of him. As if he exuded a magnetic energy that bound me to him, boggled my mind, froze everything up. *I hated it.*

He followed me into the little mall and I made a point to stop when Octavia waved. She was singing, as usual—that day it was "Happy." I didn't sing along. She noticed.

Octavia was all personality. The woman belted out a tune walking down the street and people danced; she sold clothes and jewelry and handbags out of her little mall booth (complete with a tiny curtained changing space) called Octavia's Closet. She called us all "honey" and "little puss" and "little man" and we loved her for it. She was bulky and curvy and snapped her fingers and made this sound that said "mm hmm" and it could mean good or bad depending on her face when you heard it. You couldn't meet Octavia and not smile.

"Who's delicious?" she said, right in front of him! She had her hand in the crook of his arm before I could stutter.

"Uh," I said a few times and rolled my eyes again. Brain freeze, a stomach full of strawberry banana, my complete lack of personality, never bothering to ask his name (but then he never asked mine, did he?). I was going to vomit, I just knew it.

Shy, scrawny Noah snuck out of his Flower Power booth and joined us.

"Reese Fuller," he said, shaking Octavia's hand.

And Octavia said, "Named for the Terminator or the Witherspoon?"

Laughing, I spit smoothie onto Noah's florist bib. Such a happy day.

*The Bookstore Employee's Uniform consists of baggy, worn jeans or yoga pants, and an oversized, thin, breathable, cotton tee. Sneakers are best. Flats will do, but don't bother griping to Gramps when your toes are pinched. Hair pulled out of the face with a scrunchie, or cut nice and short, as I prefer. Very little makeup—maybe some powder and lip balm. The overarching consideration in the Uniform is comfort. There will be kneeling, crawling, (once I had to lie on the floor to reach what I thought was a piece of wadded paper from under a bottom shelf only to find it was someone's half-sucked, discarded red-and-white peppermint candy), standing, climbing, running (ever had a customer pay and then leave without his book?), and lounging on the sofa in the front of the store once exhausted. You will be dusty, guaranteed. But there is also the chance of becoming sticky, from children's hands mostly, but once I found something sticky on the cashwrap and wiped it off with my shirt), wet (from spilling your drink due to laughter—happens quite a lot in Bookish), and sweat-soaked (sometimes the AC conks).

Chapter Five

When I told Alfred about the entire thing, from Book Assassin to Terminator, he laughed until tears filled his eyes.

"Did you ever tell him your name?"

"I can't remember," I said.

Someone had set up a bench outside the rear mall exit, next to the dumpsters, on a little patch of grass between the paved back end of the shops on Strawbridge Main and the parking lot on the highway. There were lots of parking lots on the highway, a convenience I'd say. All the parking on Strawbridge was of the slanted variety right in front of the sidewalk. Two hour parking only. People fought over those spots. And Officer Palmer walked up and down the street every two hours in his black uniform. He had a stick with a piece of white chalk attached to the end and he marked tires. Up and down, marking tires with chalk. And leering at us... waiting for us to jaywalk.

"You got your poem ready for Friday?" Alfred asked me.

"I'll figure it out," I told him. I thought I had a poem, but I decided, right at that moment, I didn't want to read "I loved you first: but afterwards your love." I'd never hear the end of it. I could practically hear the news of my blushing and feeling up the GLE's head visiting store after store, up and down Strawbridge Main, giggled over and whispered about. Not a love poem that month. No. Uh-uh.

"You like the boy?"

"No," I scolded. "Why would you ask that?"

His smile widened and he made a sound like 'yee-dawg.' "It's all over your face."

I sighed. "I feel like a mouse when I'm with him. And all I can manage is squeaks. Why would I like somebody like that?"

He laughed. "The heart, she wants what she wants."

Alfred was withered with age and too much sun—tanned like leather. His gray hair always looked as if he'd stood in front of a mirror and lopped it off here and there, and he somehow managed a permanent state of merely unshaven. He had a mouthful of big teeth and when he smiled, his whole face beamed, from forehead to chin. His eyes were near black, and sunlight, or moonlight, glinted off them and made them twinkle.

"I know what my heart wants, Alf; she wants to be alone."

"If that ain't the most ridiculous thing I ever heard. Naw, naw—" he held up his hand to stop any protestation from me—"tell me what you brung me."

I gave him my barely worn copy of *Unraveling Oliver*. I read it so fast I didn't have a chance to gentle the spine. "You'll love it," I told him.

Then we talked about *Theory of Remainders* and the way it tore us up and angered us, and that one moment we wanted to smack some sense into Adler—after he hung up the phone with Melanie that time. We didn't always agree on books, but when we did, we could talk for hours. And as I walked back to Bookish, absentmindedly waving hellos, a small rage started to rise within me. At *Cal*.

It was Cal who discovered Alfred. Not that Alfred hadn't always been there, but he was one of those people others pass by without noticing. He wasn't homeless, exactly. He shared a room with three other men in a boarding house a quarter mile from downtown. But he was, well...a bum. He was the guy you didn't make eye contact with as you walked the street. And, because I made it a habit to avoid eye contact with most everyone before Cal, naturally I'd missed Alfred. Until that day Cal and I stopped off at the Pizza Booth and he ordered two slices. I asked him what on earth he thought he was doing—we'd just finished dinner at Pub's. His response was a nod behind me and when I turned, there was Alfred sitting on the sidewalk—next to a bench, mind you—leaning against one of the huge planters that housed various trees and shrubs up and down the street. Cal gave the slices to Alfred; they introduced themselves and talked for a bit and I fell in love with Cal. Right there, I guess.

And now, as I walked alone back to Bookish, and saw Gorgeous Laughing Eyes, a.k.a. "Kyle Reese was not the Terminator but yes, my mom loves that movie," talking with Madaline the Realtor outside her office, I wanted to strangle him. Cal. Not Reese. I couldn't fathom why, exactly, but the memory of falling for Cal made me want to claw at the nearest potted palm. I decided it was somehow Reese Fuller's fault.

I crossed the street so I wouldn't have to walk past him.

"Sophie," GLE called to me.

I scowled. I found the name Reese pretentious. I had never seen *The Terminator*. And I had no intention of liking either one of them. Didn't he know I'd crossed on purpose?

He said goodbye to Madaline and jaywalked—if only Officer Palmer was around when I really needed him—and caught up to me. "How'd it go with Alfred?"

"I don't remember telling you my name," I said. I knew it came out rudely, but at that point, I didn't care.

"Octavia told me. So, how's your friend? She told me about him, too."

"Fine," I fumed. Why was he following me around, anyway? Maybe Alfred and I didn't want everybody to know our names.

"Listen, I just wanted to let you know I'm going to be at The Fort tonight with some of my old friends from school."

"That's nice." *Take the hint Terminator Dude.*

"So, if you go...I hear it's Lipstick Night."

I rolled my eyes and had to apologize to one of the Rollings sisters at the door of Sweet Suite. "Not you, no. No brownie today. No way." Then I turned on him. "Lipstick Night is sexist."

He *smiled* at me! "I'm pretty sure it's the exact opposite of sexist."

"It's nothing more than a parody of ladies night. And its purpose is the same, to get men into the joint by giving girls cheap liquor."

"Not girls. Anyone wearing lipstick."

"You're saying you'll be wearing lipstick?"

"I will if you say you'll be there."

Crap. There's this thing in each of us. This blanket of 'holy cow this person is going to be mine forever.' You know that blanket? It's like an afghan your grandma crochets for you out of the finest, softest yarn. You want to wrap yourself up in it and wear it all day. And that damn blanket fell right over me. Reese was standing there, looking into my eyes, smiling in this crooked sort of way and I told him I'd be there. I'd go. I'd see him at The Fort. I promised. And then, after he looked like that was the best news on the planet (how could this G with the LE be interested in a BA like me?), he was gone and I walked back to Bookish with this awful, horrid smile I couldn't make go away. I supposed it was time to admit to Gramps that he was right.

I mean, let's face it. Pre Cal, I was unanimously voted, by the Downtown Divas, most likely to end up unmarried at forty and living with thirty-five cats.* Post Cal I was unanimously voted most likely to end up unmarried and dead at eighty, my body nibbled on by my seventy kibble starved cats.* And maybe, just maybe, I didn't want to be the Downtown Crazy Cat Lady. Maybe Book Assassin was the way to go.

Here is what I knew about The Downtown Divas, which, admittedly, was very little.

Melissa Stathem owned Café Flamingo. Long blond locks, short and skinny. Several years ago, someone backed his car into a person on a bike in front of her restaurant. Melissa was the first one on the scene and when she screamed at one of her employees to call nine-one-one, you'd have thought she had a bull horn. I've been scared of her ever since.

Pari Logan was what I call...sophisticated. You know that girl who is always put together? Ms. Perfect Eyeliner. One of those women with rich, shiny black hair and yet, pale skin. You wanted to cry when you saw her. That was Pari Logan. She was a counselor over in The Executive Suites building across the tracks. Once I learned that, I tried not to talk to her too much when I saw her at Creek Overlook Apartments. Psychologists are a little bit creepy and I was sure Pari was looking at me sideways whenever she asked me how my day had gone. This is why, I think, the standard issue reply was always: fine.

Kaya Channing owned Kaya Vintage Clothing. She had dimples in her cheeks. Whenever I went into her store, post Cal, she was nice enough. But I got the feeling the Divas were talking about the lagoon incident a lot, so I tried to be just the good side of polite.

Vanessa Torres was much like Kaya. They were both dark complected with short dark hair. Both occupied the 'non-perfect, perfectly normal, beautiful person anyone could be friends with' shelf. She ran Glam it Up! I think it's safe to say I had nothing in common with someone whose life was hair and nails.

And then there was Karen Morgan of Morgan's Office Supply. Family owned. Karen looked like a librarian. Beautiful, yes. But she wore tiny-flower print dresses and flat sandals and pulled both sides of her hair back in tortoiseshell barrettes. Of all the Divas, I thought she'd be the one most likely to want to talk to a bookstore girl. Instead, she was always scribbling in notebooks behind the cashwrap when I went in to buy my Ticonderoga #1s. There isn't another place in town where you can find #1s, much less Ticonderoga #1s.

They were the core of the Divas. I called them Divas because they lounged at the wrought-iron tables outside various restaurants downtown nearly every afternoon, as if they had nothing important to do. And while Cal succeeded in acquainting me with nearly every business owner or employee downtown, he managed, creatively I think, to keep from finding some bond with any of them. I got the feeling, after he left, that Cal was one of those creepy people who knew who he could manipulate and who he couldn't, and I suppose I should see that as a point in favor of the Divas. And the fact that I had yet to find myself asking to join one of their soirées only made me realize how much Cal was responsible for my present state—that of being three-fourths in Social Sophie world and one-fourth still in, and trying to get back to, Old Sophie world. And I vacillated between thanking him—not that I planned to ever speak to him again, mind you —and cursing him, which I did a lot anyway, but for other reasons.

So, it was with some surprise that I found myself hailed by Kaya Channing as I approached Bookish that afternoon.

"Bookish," she called out.

When I turned to see them across the street—Melissa, Kaya, and Vanessa—I saw Vanessa slap at Kaya and she said, "What?" Before calling me again.

"Come sit," she said.

I stood there, my hand on the door handle, wondering what I was supposed to do. Before I could figure it out, I'd crossed Strawbridge Main to the umbrella covered tables out front of Café Flamingo and faced them—the Downtown Divas. Clique Central. Vanessa, her round face beaming, pulled one of the dainty iron chairs away from the table and patted it. So I sat in it.

"Sorry," Kaya said. "We call you Bookish. I hope you're not offended."

Vanessa slapped at her again. "You don't have to tell her."

"It's okay," I said. "I do work at Bookish."

"It's not that; you're just bookish."

"Kaya," Melissa reprimanded.

"Really, it's fine," I said.

"So," Vanessa said, "tell us all about Hombre Caliente."

"You mean Reese?"

"Reese," they all cooed.

"He looks like a Reese," Kaya said.

"What does a Reese look like?" I asked.

"Hot."

They all laughed.

"Go on, scoop," Melissa said.

And so, I sat there with the Divas, had an iced tea with Splenda, and told the story again, almost the same way I told Alfred, but without the bits about how I could barely put two words together and certainly not the afghan-of-love part. And they were shocked when I told them I wasn't going to The Fort for Lipstick Night.

"It's really not my thing," I said, sort of whining. "I'm not the sort of girl who can walk into a place like that alone. Hugh would go with me, I suppose, but I'd never dream of putting him through that."

"Hugh?" Kaya said. "You mean the cutey nerd guy who spends most of his time in the bookstore?"

"You know him?"

"Only that he's a nerd and spends most of his time in the bookstore."

"You *have* to go," Melissa said.

Did I tell you I was scared of Melissa?

"You're going," she said, "and we'll come with you."

"I can't," Vanessa said. "I work tonight."

"I have a date," Kaya said. "Karen might go."

"Really, you don't have to. I don't even want to go."

Melissa's eyes went wide. Scary wide. She plunked her cup of coffee onto the table and glared at me. "The hottest guy to walk downtown in three months invites you out and you're not going to meet him at a bar where there will be drinking and dancing and possible smooching? You're going, Bookish. If I have to dress you myself and drag you there, you're going."

*I totally made that up. But if there ever were a vote on most likely to be eaten by cats, I'm sure I would win.

*ditto

Chapter Six

ReeseFuller: Hey, Mom. You there?
CrochetMom: *here*
ReeseFuller: I sort of have a date tonight
CrochetMom: *So happy*
ReeseFuller: I hope so
CrochetMom: *u r not doing it just for me, r u?*
ReeseFuller: How much longer did it take you to type that?
CrochetMom: *Does it make me look foolish?*
ReeseFuller: No. Well...
CrochetMom: *Once you get to my age, you get to look foolish*
CrochetMom: *What's her name?*
ReeseFuller: Sophie, and you can be as silly as you want
CrochetMom: *Darn. There goes my parental responsibility of embarrassing my children*
CrochetMom: *I really like that name. Is she cute?*
ReeseFuller: Adorable. You'd love her
CrochetMom: *Tell me*
ReeseFuller: Dark short hair. Reminds me of that actress you like...
ReeseFuller: Spock's mom
CrochetMom: *Jane Wyatt?*
ReeseFuller: ?
ReeseFuller: In the new one

CrochetMom: *Winona Ryder?!*

CrochetMom: *Love her*

ReeseFuller: I thought so

CrochetMom: *Where are you taking her?*

ReeseFuller: Just meeting her at a bar

CrochetMom: *That doesn't sound very nice*

ReeseFuller: I said it was only sort of a date

CrochetMom: *Too chicken to ask her out on a real one?*

ReeseFuller: :)

ReeseFuller: Well, she did try to kill me with books this morning

CrochetMom: *You're probably right, then*

CrochetMom: *be safe, keep an eye overhead*

ReeseFuller: LOL

ReeseFuller: Love you, Mom

CrochetMom: *I love you too, sweetie*

Chapter Seven

Melissa did not have to dress me. But Pari did.

First, let me say that I still had no real intention of going to The Fort when I got back to work. Don't get me wrong, I was swoonish over the guy, and it was practically a date. Unfortunately, that was the very thing—the 'practically' part—that was helping me weasel my way out of it. He didn't ask me out, after all. If he'd really wanted me to go, he'd have said we'd go together, right? He'd have said, "I'll pick you up at eight." So, I was thinking, I could show up to Lipstick Night and find myself alone. With Melissa. What would be the point of that? But when I told Gramps about it—you know he needed all the gory details. He'd seen me talking with Reese outside Café Flamingo. He was probably bouncing up and down and saying "Loverboy" and "Golly gee willy" at that. But then he saw me talking to the Divas. He thought I'd joined the human race or something—he was so happy I was going out again that I couldn't manage to tell him I wasn't going to do it. So I told him I would. And as I fed the cats later that evening on my way home, I realized I'd have to go for real. I didn't like imagining how disappointed Gramps would be to find out I hadn't.

"So, in a way," I told Sugar, giving her a pet, "I have to go. For Gramps. Yes. I'll do it for Gramps. I won't like it. But it's my duty to keep him happy in his senility years."

The Downtown Cats

1. Weesie, a black-and-white tuxedo. You know the type, right? Looks like he's ready for a night out with a cute tabby. He was trim, as most strays are, and flopped himself in the dirt to roll over whenever I came by.

2. Sugar, a brown tabby. Prim and proper, always quick to swat at another cat when he stepped out of line.

3. Critter, because the night he showed up, I was short on time and insisted he have a name before I went home. A larger than normal male gray tabby, with a face that'd make you want to run—all scrunched up like. But he was one giant baby. Whined all the time. Feed me. For the love of the cat god, feed me!

4. Roger Dodger, dark gray, who spent most of his time hiding under the picnic table waiting for me to leave.

5. Piddle Paddle. The orange tabby who peed himself. Seriously. I think he just got so happy to see me and Alfred. He ran. He jumped. He skittled. Then he piddled. No one would take him home. Ever. So we loved him a little bit more.

6. Diva. I named the Downtown Divas after her. She was someone's princess way back when. A smoky gray long hair with a wise and arrogant look about her. She lounged with an air of sophistication and superiority. Still wouldn't let me pet her—people germs!

7. And last, but not least, Pooper Scooper did not poop herself. I just liked rhyming things and it popped out. A tortie—splotchedy. And boy, did she have tortitude. By the way the other cats behaved, I got the feeling that Pooper ran the place when I wasn't around, telling them all what was what. And for some reason, they listened.

I'd managed to get all the others homes. I had three of them: Willow (tiny little thing), Midnight (so black he's blue), and Chloe (just a sweet girl I once knew). Mr. And Mrs. Simmons, who owned MacAuley Awley's, had Kamikaze (always pouncing on anything that moved, or didn't move, or wasn't even there). Gramps had Pickles (I had to get him out of a plastic bag once, thus...always in a pickle? Worked for me, anyway). And Cal took Darth Vader, the black monster. As much as I thought Cal was a rotten person, he was at least kind to cats. Lydia took Paris (a snooty chocolate point Siamese, which, I know, isn't French, but...whatever) and so, I guessed Darth Vader and Paris were together again. And my cousin Carrie took Samson (long hair...*duh*) and Waffle (never quite balanced). Sixteen cats down to seven. That wasn't bad. By the time I got to my apartment complex, I was thinking about asking Kaya and Fiona if they considered themselves cat people, and maybe they wanted a particularly loving cat who needed a home.

Pari was getting out of her car when I walked up, ready to go upstairs. When I was finished at Bookish for the day, I tended to be dusty. My hair was generally mussed up and I usually had a stain or two on my shirt. That happens when you eat standing up. But Pari always looked as flawless coming home from work as she did going to. Counseling people, I assumed, was gentle work. She was wearing a mauve pencil skirt and jacket with a silky cream blouse underneath. Her long legs shimmered above her mauve strappy sandals.

She smiled and said, "My sources tell me you've got a big date tonight."

I hit the concrete steps first, with her clicking behind me in her high heels. "Not really. It's more like a 'show up and hope he's really there' night out."

"And what are you wearing?"

"I haven't decided yet." Trying to deflect the conversation away from that awful thought, I said, "Why don't you walk to work? It's only a block."

"Is that a legitimate question, or merely a comment on my ecological footprint?"

"I'd never comment on a person's ecological footprint without knowing her for at least a year."

"Well, then...four reasons," she said. "First, one does not walk a block outdoors in one's Jimmy Choos."

"So, wear sneakers and change once you get there."

"Second, one does not wear sneakers with Dolce & Gabbana. And before you ask: third, if you want to inspire confidence in your clients, you must exude confidence yourself."

"Hence, the Jimmy Choos and Dolce & Gabbana?"

"And fourth, and perhaps most important, this is Florida. You can't open the door to fetch your newspaper without breaking out a layer of sweat."

"That's one thing I like about you, Pari."

"Sweatphobes unite?"

"No. You still get the paper. Me, too."

"Yes, but you use yours to line the litter box."

"I do not. I use clumping litter."

"Then, you actually read the paper?"

"Don't you?"

"Yes, but I'm weird that way."

"Electronic-gadget-phobes unite?"

She laughed in that perfect person way. I pictured Pari as the type of girl who was mature way back in high school. You're still guffawing and awkward, wearing silver braces long past the usual two years—a testament to your crappy genes—and she's class president. You make goofy faces and fart when trying to get a date with the saxophonist in the band and she's dating the quarterback. I always suspected, somewhere in the well of grandfatherly wisdom I keep, that those students grew up to be dorks, in some kind of cosmic turnaround. But no. They're just as cultivated and talented and smart as they were back then. Bothersome.

"I'll be over in a bit," she said before disappearing into her place across the landing on the third floor. And she was. She showed up to inspect my selection and decide on the best dress. And yes, she said, it must be a dress. I only had two. One was a shift—flowery, fluttery pink. I wore it to a cousin's wedding. Pari labeled it too demure. I think what she really meant was: grandmotherly. And the other dress was red. A hand-me-down, low-cut, high-hemmed thing Carrie told me was perfect for a wild kegger.

"But this is what I wore to my brother's graduation party," I said. The Fort was a place of debauchery and sin. And Pari wanted me to embrace it with a little red dress?

"If it was good enough for a graduation party..."

"I learned my lesson. This dress is nothing but trouble. And anyway, I wore this jacket over it."

"Oh, no no no," she said and shook her head, ashamed of me. "You cannot wear a pea coat over a red dress. Why would you even own a wool pea coat in Florida?"

"A pea what?"

"No coat. You should show this god of love some cleavage."

"He's not a love god."

"That's not what I heard."

"What about you?" I said. "You're wearing pants."

"I'm not going. Melissa is your babysitter this evening."

"That's not very nice."

She laughed and waited in my living room with Midnight and Willow for me to change into the dress. I had to admit I liked the way it slipped over my body. The skirt had just enough swing to make me feel like dancing.

"Perfect," she said when I modeled for her.

I'd put on enough makeup to clog my pores and asked her if I'd done a bad thing, but she gave me the hot-mama wink.

"I don't wear makeup often," I told her, "but I do remember how."

"I didn't doubt it."

"Don't you call me Bookish like Kaya and the others?"

She frowned. "Who told you that?"

"She said it to my face."

"We don't mean it in a bad way. We have names for all of us. Melissa is Pink. Because of Flamingos, you know?"

"Pink is nicer than Bookish."

"I suppose."

"I have a confession to make. I call you all the Downtown Divas."

"Well, that's not nice, either."

"Why not? Divas is a compliment."

"It has a negative connotation."

"So does Bookish."

"I see what you mean."

There was a knock at my front door and Willow and Midnight darted into the bedroom to join Chloe.

"That should be Melissa," Pari said. "Listen. If you can embrace the good parts of being Bookish, I think I can find the good in being a Diva. Deal?"

"Deal."

And so I was handed off to Melissa—the perfect phrase, as she was my handler for the evening. She walked me all the way down to The Fort on Strawbridge Main, ignoring my complaints about my heels being too high and my toes being pinched, fake fanning me when I made that remark about being a puddle of sweat by the time we got there, and pep talked me the whole way.

"Don't approach him. He asked *you* to show up so he can come to you. Don't goggle at him like you did in front of the café this morning."

"I didn't!"

"You goggled like a thirteen year old at a Justin Bieber concert."

"No!"

"Look up at him from under your lashes and blush. Be snarky. Men like that love snarky."

"How do I blush on command? And how do you know what sort of guy he is?"

"He's gorgeous, Bookish. That's all I need to know."

Chapter Eight

We stopped short of our destination to don our bright red lipstick—I only had such a garish shade because I was once Wonder Woman to Hugh's Superman on Halloween. Just...don't ask—not that we needed it; I have always suspected girls got their drinks nearly free until eleven o'clock with or without the lip color.

I was certain the The Fort was so named for the high wooden fence all around it, separated in the front by the iron gate. One store west of Namaste, The Fort sat on the corner of Strawbridge Main and a side street called Palmetto Road. There was a patio along Palmetto and, there only, open slats in the fencing allowed for a bit of people watching while you got drunk sitting at the outdoor tables. Inside, the place was a mingling sort of lounge until nine o'clock when the lights dimmed to near pitch and blinking lights flashed colorful bits all around, and the dance floor filled up. It was one of Cal's favorite places. I hadn't set foot in The Fort in six months. It hadn't changed. It was eight-thirty and already there was a crowd.

Melissa pulled me up the steps onto the balcony overlooking the main floor and to a tall table by the railing where we could watch for Reese.

"You want to spot him first," she said. "Never be surprised to see him, unless you're acting."

"You do this a lot, I gather."

She laughed and ordered a margarita from the waitress. "It's called online dating."

"Really?" I asked for a beer.

"I'm afraid so. Did you know there's a site specifically for people in the downtown area? You'd think we could just...I don't know, meet. But no. We need a website to find one another."

"Are you dating someone then?"

"No." She sighed. "I've been on a couple of dates, but no luck yet."

"There he is." I felt a rush of tingles through my arms and legs as I watched Reese at the bar downstairs. He was with two other guys, like he said he would be. They were talking and laughing, ordered beers and as he sipped his, he searched the room. Was he looking for me? "What do I do?"

"Nothing yet," Melissa said. "Be cool. You got here first. That doesn't look good. So, scoot back."

"Scoot back?"

She pulled at my chair until I was sitting beside her instead of across from her and I couldn't see him any longer.

"Let him wait a bit," she said.

Suddenly I was nervous and frightened. "What if he comes upstairs?"

"That's okay. If you got here first, but you're hiding up here, I mean, not down there searching for him, it looks fine."

"Are you sure?"

"I'm never completely sure of anything." She laughed and grabbed the margarita off the waitress' tray and gulped a big sip before the waitress had a chance to lean down a bit. "My only real vice," she said. "What's yours?"

"Do I only get one?"

"Of course not. Most people have dozens."

"I like chocolate."

"Who doesn't?"

"Cal didn't."

She smirked. "Cal. You notice he never comes downtown, anymore."

"Well, I imagine he's being nice."

"Don't count on it. He's ashamed of the way he ran off with your best friend. He ought to be. And everybody liked him so much."

"You don't think they still do?"

"Are you kidding? Look, there's one thing you should know about downtown: we stick by our own. You and your grandfather. And Bookish. You're family."

"Isn't that going a bit far?"

"Not at all."

"But I never even talked to anyone downtown before Cal."

"You don't have to talk to your family."

I chuckled. "I guess not."

When I'd finished my beer and ordered another, Melissa told me it was time to scoot back so I did. But when I looked over the rail, searching for Reese, she scolded me. I had to look around above everyone's heads and smile in a dreamy, non-searching sort of way. I had to rest my chin on my hand in a non-expectant way. And I had to laugh at nothing, in a non-waiting-for-a-guy way. It was really hard stuff. I'd never learned any of that before.

Suddenly, Melissa said, "That's it; he sees you."

I said, "Where?" and looked around below me.

"No!" She swatted at me with her hand. "Don't look. You're still nonchalant, remember?"

I was laughing, which later Melissa said was a really good thing, when Reese showed up at our table with his glass of beer and took a seat.

"You came," he said.

I stared at Melissa. What was I supposed to say? She nodded at me.

"Yes, I did," I said.

Then she rolled her eyes. I was about to try something else, something like, 'oh, I forgot you were going to be here,' thinking that would get Melissa's dating rules approval, but the place went dark for a second before bright lights flickered and danced on the walls and the music started pumping. There was a roar of satisfaction in the crowd and Reese took my hand and held it, leading me down the stairs and onto the dance floor. It was packed full of gyrating bodies and we joined them. Pushed, bumped, pulled, smiling, we held on to each other as we rocked and, as Gramps would say, boogied as all get out.*

Reese was calling something to me between songs and I just nodded and smiled because I couldn't understand a word he was saying. I think he knew that because he laughed. After a song that lasted about forty minutes, I'm guessing, we headed back up to the table to find Melissa nose to nose with a clean-shaven guy in a brick-red fedora. Reese and I finished our beers and he ordered another round for the table.

He leaned in so I could hear him and said, "You drink beer."

"Is that a problem?" I practically screamed.

He shook his head. I stared at him, a bit damsel-ish; Melissa was too occupied to give me a scolding look, but I knew she wouldn't like it. He was looking back at me—we were both searching each other's faces. I don't know what he was up to, but I was trying to get a read on him. Who was he, anyway? It wasn't easy feeling giddy about a guy when you didn't even know him. I didn't get a rush on seeing Cal until...I wasn't sure I ever felt that way with Cal. Reese's eyelids were a bit puffier than I remembered, his eyes a tad bloodshot. Maybe he was high. He *was* smiling a lot. What if he was a drug addict? You never could tell, right? He could be a rapist, or a window peeping perv, or one of those Sasquatch hunters. Was it right to let yourself get involved—in a giddy pre-teen fangirl way—before you even knew if the guy was a regular reader?

The music died down a bit while the Jello shot servers made the rounds.

"What were you doing in Bookish, anyway?" I shouted at him over the din.

"I was checking out all the stores downtown."

"What do you like to read?" *Don't say you don't, don't say you don't, don't say you don't.*

"I'm a thriller kind of guy."

"Well, nobody's perfect."

"I do some fantasy and scifi, too."

"What? No romance?"

"You think I'm sexist, but I'm not. I don't care if our heroine finds love, but I do care if she can slaughter aliens or save Manhattan."

"What about erotica?" Melissa piped in.

I gave her the wide-eyed 'what the hell?' look. It was a little early in this relationship to be asking about the guy's sexual reading habits. And she gave me the 'these are the things prospective dalliances want to know' look.

"I can't say I have," Reese said. He grinned and shook his head, sipping his beer as if to stifle a laugh.

"What did you drop on him?" Melissa asked.

"Some used overstock fiction."

"Hard stuff," he said.

"I like big books," Melissa said. Then she started singing, "I like big books and I cannot lie." The guy she'd been nose to nose with sat back in his chair and sipped his beer. He winked at me.

"If you could throw any book at my head," Reese said,

53

"what would it be?"

"You mean, because it's so good you just *have* to read it? Or because it's so bad I'm throwing it across the room?"

"So good. But you have to use your psychic bookselling skills to throw one I would like to read."

I thought about it for a bit. I'd want a heavy book, for maximum impact. But not a book that would make me look like a snob. "Well," I said, "going for the thickest book I could get my hands on that was something you might like, I'd go with a George R.R. Martin."

"What's the thickest book you know, period?"

"Law books. But novels? The longest I've ever read was probably *A Suitable Boy*."

"So, if you were truly a book assassin, that would be your weapon of choice?"

"If I were a fiction book assassin, yes."

"Well, it's pretty obvious you would be fictional."

"Oh, book assassins are real," I said.

The music cranked up again. We finished our beers and left Melissa with her make-out friend to dance. After a while, he took my hand and led me over to the bar to introduce me to his friends. By that time, I was reeling. The music rang in my ears and the pulsing lights never gave me a solid picture of anyone's face. I was misted in sweat and pretty sure my bra straps were showing. I couldn't hear his friends' names and could only see they were smiling and laughing and drinking.

"We're celebrating," Reese told me and I nodded and smiled.

When there was a lull in the music and suddenly all our voices were a chorus in the abrupt quiet, I snuggled into him and said, "Hey."

"What?"

"Weren't you going to wear lipstick tonight?"

He smiled. His face was so close to mine, his lips nearly

brushing my cheek. "I thought you'd never ask," he said. And then he kissed me.

*Don't tell Gramps I said 'boogie.' Anytime he caught me using ancient words and phrases—like 'hep cat' or 'dig it' or, god forbid, 'sock it to me' (whenever I heard Aretha Franklin's *Respect* on the radio I couldn't help singing sockittomesockittomesockittome as I shelved books for days afterward)—he'd get upset and tell me to get out of Bookish and find members of my own generation.

Chapter Nine

CrochetMom: *How was your date?*
CrochetMom: *Up yet?*
CrochetMom: *Can't wait to hear about it*
CrochetMom: *Any day now*
ReeseFuller: Hi, Mom
ReeseFuller: Had a really great time
CrochetMom: *will you see her again?*
ReeseFuller: Definitely
CrochetMom: *Amy's here*
ReeseFuller: Good. Tell her I said hi
CrochetMom: *she says hi back*
ReeseFuller: I'll call later
CrochetMom: *You don't have to*
CrochetMom: *But I do like hearing your voice*
ReeseFuller: You want me to come back?
ReeseFuller: I can come back
CrochetMom: *You've got a lot going on*
ReeseFuller: I already got the building
ReeseFuller: Can sign the papers long distance
CrochetMom: *No*
ReeseFuller: r u sure?
ReeseFuller: :)
CrochetMom: *Hey! ROFL*
CrochetMom: *truly*

CrochetMom: *Thank you for teasing me, sweetie*

CrochetMom: *Makes everything normal*

ReeseFuller: But you didn't answer the question

CrochetMom: *I'm sure. You were here for six weeks*

ReeseFuller: Doesn't matter

CrochetMom: *How can I feel normal when you're all on death watch?*

ReeseFuller: ...

CrochetMom: *I'm sorry I didn't mean that*

ReeseFuller: It's okay. I understand

CrochetMom: *I would love to see you, when you have another stretch of time*

ReeseFuller: That's a good plan

ReeseFuller: Love you mom

CrochetMom: *I love you*

Chapter Ten

The next morning, I slept in. Willow, Midnight, and Chloe tried sniffing at my face but I turned over and covered my head with a pillow. For a while, they curled up on me or against me, and made funny little half-purr half-mew noises. When that didn't work, Chloe jumped over to the dresser and started knocking stuff off it. I made my 'stop it' noise, but it did no good. Then Midnight was in the bathroom pawing at the tissue roll. I could hear the cardboard tube knocking against the spindle—thump, thump. And somewhere in my room there must have been plastic, because one of the cats was chewing at it.

"All right, all right, I'll get up."

My head ached and my eyes felt dry as sandpaper. I sat up in bed and threw my legs over the edge, remembering the night before. There was a lot of kissing. A very, sort of, exploratory, romantic kissing at the bar. A more lustful, deep kind of passionate kissing upstairs at the table. Oh, dear god, Melissa saw the whole thing. Then outside, the full-bodied, very hot, nearly orgasmic kissing. And then—I jerked around to check the other side of the bed and relief flooded through me. There was no god lying there. Then I remembered him saying goodbye, his hand caressing my jaw line, his last look at me before he took off with his friends. So we didn't manage to defile each other before having a proper date—always a plus. I found the remote, one of my scrunchies, two pens, and a pencil on the floor and playfully admonished Chloe. "Tara's Theme" from *Gone with the Wind* started playing and for a split second I thought my life had a soundtrack, but it was my phone. Gramps calling.

"Hungover?"

"No, no," I said. "I'm good. I'll be in soon."

"Take your time. But, I'll want to hear all about it."

"Nothing to tell, really."

"But you had a good time?"

"I did."

I could hear the relief in the silence before he hung up the phone and I felt bad. Had I really gone so far off the deep end? Sure I talked a bit about living alone for the rest of my life, devoting said life to cats and books. But Gramps wasn't really all that worried, was he? Anyway, I was definitely back on the post-Cal list. Clearly, going back to my days of walking with my head down were over. But I couldn't let that be all about Reese. Reese was just a conduit, shall we say. He was the impetus I needed to see that life as a budding socialite wasn't so bad. And as long as everyone downtown didn't expect kisses a la *Seinfeld*'s "The Kiss Hello," maybe I could handle it.

I was late getting over to the darlings and Alfred was there, keeping them calm.

"I was about to head over to my place and find something to give them," he said when I dropped onto the picnic table bench. "She's here now, darlings," he cooed.

I had to smile. "If I ever don't show up, come looking for me."

"You bet. There's been some activity in the building." He nodded toward it.

"Shoe store; didn't I tell you?"

"They were out here, looking the lot over."

"Madaline said they didn't plan any major renovations."

There was something in Alfred's face that worried me but I was too off to ask about it. I drank two- or three-too-many beers and I was disgusted with myself for not knowing exactly how many. *Not cool, Sophie.* As I walked to work, nodding and smiling hellos, I tried to remember if I said anything particularly stupid the night before. My only hope was that Reese was as tipsy drunk as I was and said equally silly things. Before I could get into the breezeway,* Trudy called out to me from Trudy's Treasures, so I turned and passed the front of the new shoe shop, the art league, and the attorney's office to meet her on the porch of her store.

Trudy's Treasures were stuffed into an 1850-something house, complete with creaking floors that gave way slightly with each step you took. Filled to the brim with antique dolls, jewelry, stoneware, advertising, toy cars, figurines of cats and carriages and dainty women, stepping into Trudy's shop was like walking back in time to when I was five years old visiting my great grandmother in her rickety house in the Smokey Mountains. Complete with wondrous old-people odor.

"I saw his window," she said to me as I climbed the few steps to her porch.

Trudy was a thick woman with a rectangular face and a voice an octave below what you expect when you see her. Her hair was sandy blond with wisps of gray and her face, though wrinkled as Gramps', had patches of shine to it that matched the glistening laughter in her eyes.

"It was my idea."

"I figured as much."

"What are you going to do?" I tried hard to wipe the grin off my face and she knew it.

She smirked. "I got an idea."

"Why don't you just ask him out on a date?"

"Lord a mercy! I wouldn't share a dinner with Old Geezer any more'n I'd share cheese with a rat."

I shook my head and rolled my eyes.

"Anyway, I hear *you* had a wild date last night."

"And where would you hear such a lie?"

"Suri told me."

"Where'd she hear about it?"

"From Benjamin, who had it from Noah, who got it from Kaya, who heard it from you. Least wise, that's how I understand it."

"It wasn't a date. But there was kissing."

"Mm hmmm," she sang.

"He is gorgeous, isn't he?"

"That he is and I'm looking forward to having him around."

"You think he's moving back here?"

"That's what I heard."

I was on air all the way back to Bookish. Smiling like I had a big happy secret. I nearly burst into song, but thankfully did not. A person could only get away with that sort of display with Octavia around—mostly because she could sing and I could not. I told Gramps most of it. The dress and how I'd confessed to Pari that I'd been calling the Divas the Divas, the table and scooching back, and the beers and how I had too many, and the dancing and talking. He had this dreamy gleam in his eyes, nodding, glancing at Hugh every so often.

"I'm glad you had a good time, Soph," he said. "I hope you go out more often now that you got over the hump."

"The hump?"

"Sure," Hugh said. "The break-up hump. You're back in the saddle."

"On a camel?" I said.

I was glad to see that Hugh wasn't too disappointed and I told Gramps so when Hugh left before lunch.

"I told you he wasn't so sweet on me. We enjoy book talk together, that's all."

Gramps said nothing. Later that afternoon, I got a call from Kaya Channing.

"We're at Brunch," she said. "Come join us."

And so I did. Kaya, the vintage dress maven, Melissa, of Flamingos, Karen, my favorite Ticonderoga seller, and Pari were there and we all squeezed in at one of the little tables on the sidewalk and shared thick hunks of strawberry shortcake that Melanie baked fresh. "It's good for you," she said when she set them down at our table. "Make your cheeks pink."

When she'd gone back into her little café, Melissa turned to us and whispered, "I heard her husband left last weekend. She came into the café and baked five pans of brownies. They say she's been sitting in the window eating them all week long."

Karen shook her head and I looked at her for a moment. It felt odd to be sitting there with these women. I knew them. I knew their names. Had for years. But I'd never actually had a conversation with any of them before yesterday; and it felt strange to be included now, as if I'd always been part of their group.

"So," Kaya said, smiling, deepening her dimples. "Tell us everything."

"Oh my god," Melissa said. "What a night." She told them all about it so I didn't have to, as if she'd been watching me the whole time. I didn't know how she managed to do it with her face attached to Mr. Fedora.

"And by the way," I chided, "thanks for introducing us last night."

"I couldn't," she said. "I didn't even learn his name until he left."

"But you were snogging the daylights out of him by eleven."

She shrugged. "He was cute, wasn't he? At least, I think he was. *Ugh.* I need a cleanse."

"So, who was he?" Pari said.

"Name's Kevin. I think he said he was a pit master or a pig master. One of those."

"What's a pig master?" I asked.

She shrugged. "I assume it's someone who orders pigs around."

My phone started playing "Tara's Theme" and I pulled it out of my purse. It was Reese. Hombre Caliente. Love god of downtown. My GLE. I had a vague recollection of scribbling my number on a napkin the night before...in lipstick. *Cheesy, Sophie, very cheesy.*

"What is that music?" Kaya said.

"It's Reese."

"Ooh," they said.

"Well, go on," Melissa said.

I was trembling when I said hello and I wasn't sure if it was because I was falling like a brick or because I was embarrassed to talk to him in front of the Divas.

"I had a good time last night," he said.

"Yeah, me too."

"I particularly enjoyed all the smooching."

"Smooching?"

"The snogging. Lip locking. Kissing. Canoodling."

"Canoodling is the other thing. I think." I glanced up at the Divas; they were fighting their own laughter, hands over their mouths. "I don't think we canoodled." I snuffed out a giggle before it got to my lips.

"I'll look it up later. Listen, I think we should see each other today, before it gets too weird."

"Weird?"

"Yeah, after all that drunken, wild, face sucking and not really knowing each other very well, the longer we let it go, the weirder it's going to get."

"So, you've done this before?"

"Ah, well, I won't...I plead the Fifth."

I agreed to go to dinner with him and couldn't stop smiling through lunch.

"Ah, well," Melissa said. "If I can't find true love, at least my friends can."

*I was never sure why the breezeway was called the breezeway and the mall was called the mall. They were, by all appearances, the same. In the breezeway, on the south side of Strawbridge, there were stores downstairs with offices upstairs. In the mall, on the other side of the street, there were two restaurants, a wine shop, and the two booths—Flower Power and Octavia's Closet. The only difference I could discern was that the doors on either end of the breezeway were always open, and the doors on either end of the mall were not—it was air conditioned. But I did know this: two years ago, the mayor of Strawbridge came downtown and kept calling the breezeway a mall. He said, in an interview, "Historic Downtown Strawbridge has everything you're looking for in shopping and dining. It's even got two malls." Mrs. Lorrington, the lady who ran swank restaurant and sushi bar Raw, took out a full-page ad in the Strawbridge News just to say, "If Mayor Hawn took more time to learn about his constituency, he'd be fully aware that Historic Downtown in fact does not boast two malls and instead has a mall and a breezeway." But she never bothered to tell anyone what difference it made. She ran against Hawn in the next election and lost. I suppose vocabulary, wonderful and important as it is, wasn't enough of a political platform to stand on.

Chapter Eleven

I made my way back to Bookish feeling strange, but glorious. Gloriously strange. I wanted to grab people—the Divas, the Rollings Sisters, Benjamin—and spout this horrid cliché: "I've never felt this way before!" Because I had, literally, never felt that way before. It was unnerving, and a bit frightening. What if, I asked myself, this was what I was supposed to feel for Jordan Spilke in high school, or Peter Crouch in college? What if I was only just now, a young woman in my twenties, feeling that jittery, childish romance I was supposed to have experienced as a teenager? Then it was only infatuation—starry eyed, immature silliness that I'd get over. I was making a fool of myself, wasn't I? I vowed to behave more maturely about the entire thing.

"Sophie," I said to myself quietly, "you will not smile constantly. No moony gazes off into the distance as if thinking about love, and absolutely no singing of *Crazy Little Thing Called Love*. Except, maybe in your apartment."

I got to Old Geezer's and there was Mr. Cornell dabbing at his window with his paints.

"What are you doing?" I asked him.

"Adding pizzazz," he said.

It looked more like stick figures to me.

"She saw it though, didn't she?" he said.

"Yes, she did."

"Ah, hah. And is she going to back down?"

"You mean change her window? I don't think so. Why should she?"

"Because it's a lie. You can't say you've got the best of something without proving it."

"I don't think the world of advertising works quite like that."

"Well, it should. Did you hear the news about Loverboy?"

"I thought we agreed not to call him that. His name is Reese."

"What kind of name is Reese?"

"Didn't you ever see *The Terminator*?"

"What's that got to do with it?"

"How should I know? I've never seen it."

"Well, maybe you should watch it."

"Can't I read the book?"

Mr. Cornell snorted. "Not all films came from books, you know. Some of the greatest films of all time were just films."

"Yeah? Name one."

"*Casablanca, Citizen Kane*."

"Oh, yeah? Well, if there had been books of those, the books would be better."

He made a growling *ach* sort of noise and I laughed and went into work again.

The On Again Off Again Antiques War

It was like this: Mr. Cornell, or as Trudy called him, Billy Bob Jangles—she said it came to her one day while she was slicing a pot roast—was desperately in love with Trudy, or as Mr. Cornell calls her, that godforsaken woman selling cheap knockoffs. I was there the day they met. Mr. Cornell was opening up shop next door to Bookish and Trudy came by to introduce herself and get a look at what sorts of antiques he had to sell. She right off said things that got his back up. Things like, "Well, if you've got to be next door to the bookstore, low stock is probably the way to go." And Mr. Cornell said, "What the hell does that even mean?" And Trudy said, "You don't want a lot of people traipsing through your store bothering the reader types next door, that's what I mean." And he said, "You're saying I won't get much business?" And she said, "Not with that tiny inventory." And Mr. Cornell puffed himself up like a peacock, raised a finger into the air and said, "I sell high-quality, fine antiques, not rubbish." And she said, "Are you calling my goods rubbish?" And he said, "Your store's filled with so many tiny odds and ends it's a wonder anyone can find anything." And Trudy stomped off down Strawbridge Main saying, "I'm doing just fine. At least people feel comfortable in my store." And that was that. It was love at first clash.

Within a week we heard mumbling about Trudy's Treasures being investigated for possible bodies being buried underneath it. Mr. Cornell swore he had nothing to do with such vicious rumors. And he completely underestimated the antiques-browsing public's desire to visit the scene of a possible mass burial. Trudy's business soared. A couple of weeks later, people started asking us at Bookish if everything was okay with Old Geezer's Stuff next door. Come to discover, somebody had painted the word "not" between Geezer's and Stuff on his front window, and changed the *u* in stuff to an *i*. I stood there looking at it— Old Geezer's Not Stiff, it said. Mr. Cornell had apparently not noticed it for days. He naturally accused Trudy, but she denied any knowledge of the escapade. And two weeks later, the word CLOSED was painted, in red, across Trudy's front window. She was livid. There was shouting.

The next thing we knew, they were having dinner together at MacAuley Awley's Irish Pub in a booth in the corner. And there was smooching. Unfortunately, that lasted only until they both bid on a 1750s Queen Ann mahogany drop-front desk at auction. And while they were arguing over it—Mr. Cornell saying she hadn't a spare spot in her store to put it, and Trudy saying he already had one—Mr. Swanson of Venerable Trinkets had won it. No more smooching. They've been at odds ever since.

Reese came by Bookish at six, blushing and smiling, to get me and we walked a few doors down to Burgers and he was right—it was awkward. My giddiness fought with the overwhelming notion I was being foolish and I didn't know what to say to him. We sat across from each other in a booth inside and ordered cheeseburgers and he said, "So..."

I nodded and the first thing that came to mind, and popped out of my mouth, was, "Thrillers."

"Mostly. I guess you get a lot of time to read."

"Why do you say that?" *Seriously, did he just call me homely?*

"You're in a bookstore all day."

"Yeah, I guess so. We do read sometimes, when it's not busy."

"What's your favorite genre?"

I liked that he said genre; it brought a smile to my face and I realized I was staring at his lips. "Oh, genre," I looked away, let my gaze wander around the restaurant. "I'll read almost anything."

"Is that a business requirement, or personal choice?"

"Good question. I suppose I have read some books because I want to be able to discuss them with customers. But mostly...my choice."

"And it's important to get a feel for them...their weight, aerodynamics, flingability."

I laughed and suddenly everything was easy and smooth, like running water in a creek. We ate and talked books, films, high school, college, even exchanged our favorite horrid moments of puberty. When we left, evening was pouring in;

we strolled down Strawbridge, east, toward the lagoon, hand in hand, still talking, as if we'd known each other for years and still wanted to know what went on in each other's heads. At Sweet Suite, we paused and bathed ourselves in the aroma of brownies.

"You like chocolate?" I asked him.

"Is there any better thing on earth? Well, I mean, besides rum. And family, friends, pets, all those things we have to admit to liking more than anything else. And canoodling, of course."

"I don't know," I said. "Chocolate or canoodling. It's a toss-up."

We strolled on, to the point at which Strawbridge Main met Mangrove, across the tracks just beyond Trudy's Treasures, all the way to the highway and across that, to the lagoon and the community center park, along the water's edge, where we sat on a bench and watched the beachside lights twinkle on. Then we both stood up and danced about, slapping at ourselves and each other when the mosquitoes attacked. We walked back to town and into Pub's, air-conditioned and mosquito free. We sat together in a booth and ordered beers. He put his arm around my shoulders and leaning against him, with his chin on my head, I felt like wholeness or perfection and I closed my eyes, hoping I could imprint the sensation on my mind to recall later.

"Do you think everything is chance?" he asked me. "Or do you think some things are meant to be?"

"I'm a firm believer in the randomness of the universe," I said.

"That's not scary to you?"

"No, not scary. Think about it. What are the odds this or that would happen? What are the fantastic, crazy odds that anything happens?"

He nodded, smiling down at me. "What are the odds I would find you?"

"I bet we could calculate them."

"You're not a bit romantic are you?" he said, laughing.

"You'll love it," I said. "Think how easy Valentine's Day will be. No need to hire sky writers—"

"Sky writers?"

"Or manage a proposal on screen at the big game."

"I'm beginning to see your side of things."

"Just dinner, a movie—preferably one based on a really good book—and home for some canoodling."

"Are you going to turn out to be a psycho killer? Or married? Or worse, an outdoor kind of girl?"

I sighed. "You'll have to wait and see."

"Because you are, at this moment, perfect."

The deep green of his eyes lulled me into believing him; his lips parted in a pensive smile, as if he, like me, was working hard to hold on to the moment.

"Nobody's perfect," I said.

When our beers arrived, we were kissing, and we didn't care. We heard the plunk of the glasses on the thick wood table and kept on until I was sure we'd managed somehow to divine the meaning of love, or the universe, or something very profound, because I felt it again—whole.

"Here's to imperfectly perfect people," he said, holding up his glass.

"And the thrill of discovering which one of us is a psycho killer."

He laughed and I was glad.

"That's it," he said. "I claim you in the name of Reese Fuller."

"And the sexist side of you rears its ugly head."

"Lipstick," he called out into the bar. "Anybody got lipstick?" And to me, with a wide grin, "I'll show you who's sexist."

Chapter Twelve

He's perfect," I told Gramps Thursday morning at Bookish. "You wouldn't believe it. It was like being out with my best friend, only well, you know. Perfect. And this morning, as I was getting ready for work, it hit me. He is so different from Cal, it's crazy. I mean, we were downtown, but instead of, like with Cal, stopping and talking to everybody, it was...just us. You know what I mean? Like it was about us, not everybody else."

"I can see you're not going to get any work done today."

"You know what this store needs? Music. We need music." I danced around in the tiny space in front of the cashwrap.

"It's a bookstore, Sophie," Gramps said. "We can't play music."

When Melissa called and told me to come out to lunch with the Divas, Gramps was all too happy to be rid of me. I met her and Karen and Vanessa at Burgers and ordered a salad.

"I was here last night," I told them.

"We know," Vanessa said. "It's all over town."

"Making out at Pub's," Melissa said.

"I'm a classy girl."

"He's worth the reputation, if you ask me," Vanessa said. "But I'm jealous."

"He must have friends," Melissa said. "Ask him to send them over."

"Imagine it," Vanessa said. "A whole gang of Hombres Caliente."

"Well, I have news," Karen said. Her voice was like smooth silk and so quiet people had to shut up to hear her. "I found out why he's in town."

"What do you mean?" Melissa said. "He lives over in Cocoa Beach."

"Trudy told me he's moving back here," I said.

"He's here to stay, all right," Karen said. "Did he tell you about it?"

I shook my head, feeling rather dumb. "I guess it didn't cross my mind to ask him about it."

"What's the big deal?" Vanessa said. "He used to live here, right?"

"He owns a surf and beachwear shop in Cocoa Beach," Karen said. "And he's opening another one over here."

"Surf shop?" I said.

"Summer Sun."

"I've been to Summer Sun," Melissa said.

"He's bought the old building across from Fiona's," Karen said.

"Wait," I said. "You mean the empty storefront on Mangrove? Where I feed the cats?"

"Yep."

"No," I said, shaking my head. "It's going to be a shoe shop."

"I talked to Madaline this morning. The shoe shop deal fell through and your new Caliente Hombre swooped right in and took it."

"Don't look so stricken," Vanessa said. "I'm sure he'll let you keep the cats there. You said the other buyers would."

"Yeah, sure," I mumbled. *Sure.* But there was an empty,

sinking sort of feeling in my stomach.

"You couldn't have planned it better," Melissa said. "You're dating the new owner. Of course he'll let the cats stay."

"Just don't ever break up with him," Karen said.

"You mean I have to marry him, now?"

"It's the only way to keep those cats where they are," Vanessa said.

I looked at each one of them, my unbelieving eyes wide, until they burst out laughing and I tried to smile.

"We're joking," Melissa said.

Vanessa nudged her. "Maybe."

I stumbled back to Bookish after lunch and got to work. There was a cartload of books to be shelved, a mess in the children's section—looked to be some kid's broken crayons and bits of grapefruit—to be cleaned up, and a few endcaps to be changed out. I went through the motions in something of a fog with Gramps casting worried glances my way whenever I came near him.

"Everything's okay, isn't it?" he asked me once.

I nodded.

Reese called later that afternoon.

"I know there's some rule about not saying yes when a guy asks you out at the last minute. But in my defense, I was so taken by your perfection, and maybe a little afraid you'd transform into a psycho killer last night, I forgot. But I meant to ask then. Really I did."

"Rules are for wimps," I told him.

We met at Pub's for dinner, this time sitting across from each other, arguing over whether or not we should have cheeseburgers yet again and how many days in a row we thought we could eat cheeseburgers before becoming sick of them, and once sick of them, how long would it take before we could eat them again. I didn't mind the distractions. I had questions to ask, and I didn't really want the answers.

We ordered the cheeseburgers and talked just as we had the night before, but suddenly it was all silly and meaningless. We kept on when our plates arrived, debating the taste of various types of French fries and as the meal finally began to wind down, I said, "So, you bought the old storefront on Mangrove."

"That's right. Maybe you've heard of us. Summer Sun Surf and Beachwear?"

I shook my head.

"We've had a store on Cocoa Beach for about ten years now. Doing really well."

"Why didn't you tell me?"

He shrugged. "I'm not the kind of guy who introduces himself by handing out his business card. I don't look at every meeting as a business opportunity."

"No, I mean, about the new store."

"I did, didn't I?"

"No."

"Tuesday night, remember? At The Fort. My friends and I were celebrating the deal."

I blushed. "Oh."

"We were lucky to get it. Really like this little area. Quaint, but hip. And busy all the time. Great restaurants. Great people." He winked at me.

"Much renovations to do?"

And he started talking about his store and his plans, his inventory, his floor plan, how they were going to bring in authentic Cocoa Beach sand if they could get some kind of permit—I told him it would never happen, what with beach erosion and all. He asked me plenty of questions about Gramps and Bookish, so he didn't seem to be talking about himself all evening and I could feel myself slipping away, trying to forget about my little cat problem and enjoying his company. And it almost worked. We got all the way to the end of our French fries before I asked him about it.

76

"What sort of changes do you plan out back? The concrete lot, I mean."

"Oh, that's going," he said. "We'll be putting in a new asphalt parking lot, bigger too."

I went numb. "Did you know about the cats?"

"What cats?"

"The stray cats that live out back."

"I don't know anything about cats."

"There are seven of them. They live under the oak and in the shrubs by the picnic table."

"So?"

"What are you going to do about them? I mean, you can't tear up the concrete and pave a lot without disturbing them."

This look came over his face—brows pulled in, confusion at his lips. "They're cats. They'll run off. It's not like they're going to sit around waiting to get splattered with tar."

"But they can't run off. That's their home."

He relaxed and popped a French fry into his mouth. "Not anymore, it's not."

I could feel my heart breaking. "They were there first."

"Are you upset about this?"

"I take care of them."

"Great. You can take them home or something."

"I can't have seven—ten cats, I already have three—in my apartment."

"Well, if you're worried about them, find them homes."

"Why can't they stay where they are?"

"Well, for one thing, as you said, there'll be some major construction going on. They'll run off."

"What's wrong with the lot that's there now?"

"It's cracked. If you're feeding cats there, you've seen it. There are small trees growing up out of it in some spots."

"Most of the stores downtown don't even have their own parking. People park in the street."

"You're saying I should forgo having ample parking for customers because of a few stray cats?"

"At least wait until I can find someplace to keep them, until your construction is finished."

"Whoa, now. They won't be coming back."

"It's their home."

"I just told you it's not, anymore. A parking lot isn't a good place for cats, anyway."

"There are the trees and shrubs. And the table."

"Those won't be there when we've finished."

"But..." I was panicking. "What do you expect me to do about them?"

"Nothing. Like you said, they'll run off when we start work."

My mouth dropped open. "I can't believe you said that."

"What?"

"What kind of monster would say something like that?"

I scooted out of the booth, grabbed my purse and stomped off toward the door.

"Sophie," he said, coming after me. "Sophie, wait."

He grabbed my arm and I turned toward him.

"I still have to pay the bill," he said.

"Oh." I started digging in my purse.

"No, I don't need money. Just wait, okay?"

"I don't think so," I said. "I'm sorry; really I am. But I think I want to go home now."

"I can walk you, if you'll—"

"No thanks." And I left him standing there.

Chapter Thirteen

Well, that was that. So much for Loverboy, for GLE. Hombre Caliente. I should have known it was too good to be true. Thrillers! Really? Gramps would call me a book snob, but I didn't care. Then he'd say something about how a story is a personal thing and would I like it if someone judged me for reading romance novels. I didn't care. And then he'd probably call me a hypocrite for loving every Bourne film ever made and anything with Liam Neeson in it. And I'd have to say, okay, okay, you have a point. There's nothing inherently wrong with a man reading thrillers. I was only thinking how very wonderfully remarkable it would be to hear a gorgeous Hombre Caliente like Reese say he preferred Steinbeck or enjoyed something meaningful like *The Handmaid's Tale*. Okay, so I was a book snob and had no reason to be.

Instead of walking all the way back to Bookish for my cat bag, I went home and got some food and a jug of water and took it out to the darlings. It was dark by then and I sat there on the bench watching them eat. I had to do something. But what? I was going to have to find them all homes. There was nothing else I could do. So, as soon as I got back home, I knocked on Pari's door. She answered, standing there with her head wrapped up in a towel, wearing some little jammy shorts and a tank top.

"Now, what if I'd been Mr. Z?"

She laughed. "I have a peep hole, Sophie, same as you. He'd only see my feet, anyway."

Mr. Zacharias was our landlord. A tiny, bent old man with hairs branching out of his nose.

"I have a favor to ask."

"No," she said. "Would you like to come in and talk about it?"

I shook my head. "How can you say, no? You don't even know what I'm going to ask."

"Yes, I do. I heard your Hombre Caliente is opening up a Summer Sun in the abandoned building on Mangrove."

"So?"

"So, Steve told me he saw you two fighting. One date and already you broke up? It had to be the cats. I can't have a cat."

There were simply no secrets downtown. It's a scary time we live in when the hipster owner of Pub's Sports Bar is so interested in my business he stoops to gossip. Of course, Steve Abbott had the hots for Pari—everybody knew that. But to use me as an excuse to chat her up? Despicable. But that was what I got, I suppose, for learning everyone's names.

"Why not?" I pleaded.

"I'm never home. I leave for work before you wake up. I have classes in the evening, sometimes clients. I can't give a cat the attention it needs."

"They don't need that much."

"Don't be angry with me," she said.

I sighed. "What if you kept it over at my place while you're away?"

"Isn't it bad enough you've got three when you're only allowed one? I'm sorry, I can't help you."

I nodded and told her I understood. And I suppose I did. I'd been through all of that before. But I'd managed to find homes for nine cats; that was something. Okay, so *I* had three of them. Six cats...if I could find homes for six, I could find homes for the last seven. I'd have to work hard at it, that's all.

The next day, I walked Strawbridge Main asking everyone to take one. Just *one* cat. How hard could it be? The Rollings sisters at Sweet Suite laughed at me. They lived at the bakery, they said. Who had time for pets? "We don't even have time for our husbands," Kate...or Barb, said. And they laughed again. "We should have married twins," the other one said. "They'd understand us so much better." I'd lost them at that point as they went on ranting, and laughing, lovingly about their spouses.

Suri, at Namaste, already had two cats. I felt like asking, "How can you have two other cats when there are strays here that need homes?" I realized that was a crazy thing to say before I said it, so that was a relief. But the more people I asked, the crazier I was feeling and it was only a matter of time before I did something stupid. Benjamin had a dog and said there was no way he'd bring a cat into the mix. The dog was nervous enough as it was. Damn *chihuahuas*. Their boss, Pat Willard—the lady you thought was going to look like a flowery hippie sort of person with a long braid of hair, because she owned Namaste with its incense and trinkets and collection of fairies and earthy skirts and sandals, but looked like that lady who played Michael Myers' sister in that really old *Halloween* movie—owned angora rabbits, she said. No cats. I even asked the lady who owned Begotten, even though I was sort of afraid she'd tell me cats were of the devil. Instead she was very kind...and allergic.

Of course, Mr. Booker wouldn't have one. He lived in a big house on the lagoon and had three huge Weimaraners. Hated cats, he said. And though I'm sure he was joking, he was adamant against having any. Said he spent most of his cat time shooting pellets at the neighbors' with his BB gun.

Again, I was sure he was exaggerating, but still. He was a definite *no*. I asked Melanie at Brunch. *No.* Her family had two guinea pigs, a tortoise, three hamsters, and a poodle. I dared to enter ChocShop—I could never get out of there without a pound of Lori's fudge—but no, much as she and her employees loved cats, they couldn't take one. Nobody at Burgers wanted one. Mr. Cornell said he was "dang old" for a cat. Gramps was an "absolutely not another cat." His cat Pickles was, I had to admit, quite a handful. The Simmons already had one of the darlings—Kamikaze—to go with their other cats and didn't want any more.

Octavia said she lived with a ridiculous fear of cats, or as she put it, "Honey, I have a completely rational, entirely logical, horrific fear of the little monsters." When I asked her why, she shuddered, and told me when she was a little girl, one night, in the dark of her bedroom, she heard a terrible, blood-curdling, prayer-invoking, pee-inducing cater-wauling (you see the cat in that?) outside her window and when she dared to pull back her curtains, something wicked lurched at the glass. She fell back onto her bed, rolled over and crashed to the floor, screaming. Her mother told her it was cats. And ever since that time, she has been afraid of them. Noah was there, listening, laughing, and when I turned to him to ask about the possibility of his taking on a cat, just one little cat, he confessed that he lived with five of them. Loved cats. *Well, that was just great.*

"What's another one or two or three?" I said.

He said, "Have you any idea what my house smells like when I get home from work? Why do you think I deal in flowers? Take flowers. They're delicate, fragrant, colorful things that beautify any space."

"He's got it bad, honey," Octavia said with a wink.

"Now take cats," he said. "They're stubborn, aloof. I'll grant you they purr and offer a whiff of companionship at odd moments, like when you're on the toilet—"

"More than enough information," Octavia said.

"But they do two things mostly—they eat and they crap. Their food smells like crap. So their crap smells like double crap."

"Okay, okay," I said. "I get it. Five is a lot of cats."

"It is. Would you like one? I've got a couple I'd be willing to part with."

"You'd give away one of your cats?"

"Of course not."

And that was that. Alfred, naturally, couldn't have a cat. I didn't ask him and he was insulted. So I asked him and he said no. I asked in at the candle shop, the bead and jewelry making shop, the kids' clothing shops, the ladies' clothing shops, and the barber shop. Then I went into Across the Pond, the all-things-British shop, and begged the Trenthams to take a cat. And Mrs. Trentham said, "Harry, Harry, let's." And Mr. Trentham shrugged and said, "I'm not against it." So I danced a bit and told them they should take Sugar, she was the sweetest. And joy of joys, when I brought them over to meet the cats later that day, they also took Critter when they saw him. Critter, bless his cat heart, must have known we were in the middle of a cat tragedy. He purred and rubbed up against Mr. Trentham's legs, getting his multicolored gray tabby hairs all over the man's dark dress pants.

"Well, grab them, Harry," Mrs. Trentham said. "One under each arm."

I laughed. Later, I boxed them up—surprisingly easy— and took them over to Across the Pond and Mrs. Trentham took them home. And I went back to the little spot behind the new, stupid, Summer Sun Surf and Beachwear, sat at the picnic table and cried.

"I'm really sorry," I heard him say.

Looking up, taking a quick wipe at the tears on my cheeks, I saw Reese bent over, scratching behind Roger

Dodger's ears and I gasped. Just a little.

Chapter Fourteen

This is a hard thing to admit, but I was really mad at Roger Dodger. Always hiding under the table, never came out to eat until I left. I knew he did because I walked away plenty of times and turned back to see him sneak out and start nibbling kibble. Never let me pet him—not once in all the time I'd been taking care of him. Bit me, or tried to, when I trapped him to have his Tom taken from him. Well, it wasn't my fault he wouldn't let me put him in a box like most of the others. And there he stood, sniffing the knee of Reese's jeans, letting Reese pet him. *Traitor!*

"Sorry doesn't do me much good," I said. "He likes you."

"I grew up with cats."

"You could take a couple home, then. Couldn't you?"

He straightened and looked at me. "I work too much. Starting up a business takes a lot of time. Having a second store will only mean more work."

I looked away from him, trying hard not to cry again.

"I wish I could get this little guy for my mom." Now he was squatting next to Roger Dodger, petting him snout to tail. "Might cheer her up."

"Why don't you? Living out here is probably hardest on him; he's a scaredy cat."

He chuckled. "No. My mom is sick. I couldn't burden

her."

"I'm sorry." The way I said it, it sounded like I was more sorry about her not being able to take Roger Dodger than about her being sick and I shuddered. "About your mom, I mean. Will she be better soon?"

He shrugged. "She's pretty sick."

"Sorry. When she gets better, if you think she'd really like him..."

"Maybe," he said.

"If it's not too late."

"I guess you're pretty mad at me, then."

I said nothing.

"It's not my fault. It's business."

I rolled my eyes. It was getting dark now. I'd spent an entire day downtown begging people to take cats with very little progress. I'd ditched my shift at Bookish to do it. I was tired, and hurt, and still very clearly attracted to this GLE. It made me angry.

"It's not the business part," I said, startling myself with the coarseness of my voice. "It's the attitude."

"What attitude?"

"The way you carelessly dismissed them, the way you said they could run off. You sounded like some Marie Antoinette character. *Let them eat cake*. Even though she probably didn't say that. I mean, if you ask Gramps; he can tell you. He likes the history section but—that 'who cares' kind of blasé snooty air."

"What are you talking about?"

"I don't understand how you can be so heartless."

He rolled his eyes. "Crazy."

I stood up, grabbed my food bag and water jug and stomped away.

"Sophie," he called after me.

But I kept walking.

"This is a good thing," I told Gramps the next morning

at Bookish. "I found out early what sort of guy he is, right? Better to find out now than later."

Gramps was nodding, which was *not* a good thing. Nodding meant he didn't really agree with you but he didn't want you yelling at him. He'd tell you his ability to nod and stay quiet was the main reason his marriage to my grandmother lasted until her death three years ago. Don't worry; whenever he said it, I was always sure to point out how sexist it was. And he'd say, "Sexist, maybe. But true."

I was reorganizing the romance section—so many of the books somehow found their way onto the wrong shelves, out of the puritanical 'alphabetical by author last name' order I liked to keep them in. I used to imagine that at night, after we turned out the lights and closed the doors, the books had parties. The romance books toddled over to the history section to check out if their authors got their facts right. The fantasy books took up with poetry books, trying to make sense of the world. Law books fraternized with books on muscle cars, tired of being taken so seriously all the time. And they all couldn't find their proper places on their own shelves by the time we turned on the lights the next day. Gramps called this sort of daydreaming "fundoozling."

"You over there fundoozling again?" he'd say with a wink. I think he missed those fundoozling moments. But it was pre-Cal Sophie who fundoozled. Post-Cal Sophie had too much on her mind, what with all the names to remember, and the exhaustion of learning to smile and nod hello and be sociable. If he wanted fundoozling Sophie back, he'd have to stop bugging me about Loverboy.

"He meant no harm," Gramps said.

"He doesn't like cats."

"But you said he managed to get your Roger out from under the picnic table."

I shook my head and offered him a simpering gaze. "If

he liked cats, he'd find a way to help me protect them, to keep them in their home."

Mr. Cornell had come in and stood listening, waiting, I could tell, to start into another rant about Trudy's Treasures. Instead, he said, "Don't make a big deal of this, Sophie. The city's already been eying the cats. Too close to the park."

"I've told them the cats don't go into the park. They're afraid of strangers."

"You don't know for certain," he said. "You're not watching them all day. And they're a threat to the bird population."

"Not that again. Those lazy cats couldn't catch a bird if one keeled over in front of them choking on a worm."

"I'm just saying—" Mr. Cornell held up a hand—"you don't want to call too much attention to them again."

"He's right," Gramps said. "You barely made it through last time."

Last time.

Gramps was talking about the wrangle I had with the city over feeding sixteen cats on an abandoned property near Manatee Park. I fought hard over that. I agreed to have them all spayed and neutered at my own expense—the local feral cat organizations offered to let me include them in a free clinic for ferals, but they'd have their ears tipped (the top of one ear cut off) and I thought it would be easier to find them homes if I didn't have it done that way, and I'd promised to place them all. I supposed Gramps and Mr. Cornell were right. I hadn't found homes for all of them, yet. And if the city wanted to, they could come in and take the rest away and...I didn't want to think about that.

In the silence I'd created by all that thinking, Mr. Cornell cleared his throat.

"Have you seen her window?"

Gramps and I shook our heads. I'd been too worried about the cats that morning to stop by Trudy's Treasures after feeding them.

"What did she do?" Gramps asked him.

He held up his right hand, making a sweeping arc in front of him as he belted out, "Voted Best Antiques Downtown."

Gramps duly gasped—you could always count on him to help a friend. "She didn't," he said.

Mr. Cornell looked at me. "You have to admit *that's* a lie."

He had a point.

"I never voted," Gramps said. "Did you?"

I couldn't help but laugh a little. "No," I admitted. "I don't remember a vote."

"That's it," Mr. Cornell said. "I'm taking this to the Historic Downtown Strawbridge Business Owners Management Board."

Or, as I liked to call it, the HDS BOMB!

"Now Billy," Gramps said, "you don't want to get official with this, do you? It's like Sophie and the cats. You go stirring things up and you could get singed in the end."

We heard Hugh laughing behind one of the bookshelves and turned to see him peeking out at us. "Singed in the end," he said.

"I don't care," Mr. Cornell went on. "She can't get away with this. I'll demand a real vote. We could do one of those 'best of' things. All the best of Historic Downtown. Best bookstore, for instance."

"We're the only bookstore."

"All the better. And Geezer's Stuff Antiques will win in the 'best antiques' category."

"What happens if she wins?" Hugh asked.

I was glad he did, because Gramps and I wouldn't dare.

"She won't," Mr. Cornell said. "Of course she won't."

"But she might," Hugh said.

Mr. Cornell was giddy with his new plan and as the door

dinged when he left, my phone rang out "Tara's Theme." I found it at the cashwrap. Reese was calling. I stood there looking down at the phone and Gramps said, "Well, answer it. Make it stop that racket."

So I did.

"Hey," Reese said.

"Hey," I said.

"Are we going to go out again? Or is this cat thing in the way?"

Wow, I thought. Just, wow. He had to be the most thoughtless, self-centered, ailurophobic—that's the fear of cats, mind you, which I knew was not true about him, but still wanted to think it—man I knew, other than Cal, and that wasn't saying much.

"This cat thing," I said, "is very important to me, yes."

"So..."

"So, I imagine I'm going to be very, very busy with it for the foreseeable future."

"I see."

"Okay, then."

"Okay."

"Goodbye then," I said.

"Right," he said. And then he hung up.

I felt like screaming, but Gramps and Hugh were staring at me—Gramps with his brow crinkled up with worry and Hugh looking at me as if I'd just done the most amazing thing ever. And I guess I did. I stood up to Reese, stood up for the cats. I should have felt brave and proud and energized. But instead, I felt like crying. Was this what Social Sophie had to look forward to? Crying all the time? Old Sophie was looking better and better. I told Gramps I needed to take my lunch early and he waved me out the door. I walked toward home, my head down, avoiding all the smiles and nods and hellos, until I heard Melissa.

"Bookish!" she was calling. "Bookish."

They were gathered out in front of Brunch again—Melissa, Kaya, and Vanessa—and grabbed a chair from another table for me. Brunch had adorable, round wrought-iron tables with dainty wrought-iron chairs. They reminded me of French pencil drawings where obscenely skinny French women sat in front of French cafés with French poodles on leashes. I sat. And tried to feel French.

"What's wrong?" Melissa said. "Where are you going?"

"Home for lunch, I guess."

"Eat with us; I'll tell Melanie to add a sandwich. What do you want?"

I asked for a tuna salad sandwich with chips and she went inside to tell Melanie. I felt awkward, yet again. It would take some getting used to, this friendly thing. But the truth of it was the more I talked with these women, the less I thought of them as divas, in the strictest sense of the word.

"We heard about the fight with Reese," Vanessa said. "Perhaps he's not so *caliente*, after all."

"He's not," I said.

"Yes he is," Kaya said.

We looked at her, our mouths open.

"Well, I'm sorry, but he is hot."

Melissa came back to the table and agreed with Kaya. "Pari told us about Downtown Divas," she said.

I blushed.

"We like it," Vanessa said. "It's our new thing. We are now the Downtown Divas."

I tried to smile.

"Aw, cheer up," Melissa said.

"Yeah," Kaya said. "There are plenty other *hombres caliente* in town."

"It's not that," I said, even though I was pretty sure I was lying. "It's the cats. I have to find homes for them all and soon." I was pleading with my eyes and they looked away. "None of you can take one?"

91

"Oh, look," Melissa said. "Here comes Noah. You should ask *him*; he's really lonely."

"You think so?"

"Heck, yes. He's been on that Strawbridge dating site I told you about with no luck at all. It's sad, really."

We quieted as he approached. He nodded as he went into Brunch and stood in line inside the café.

"He's really a sweet sort of guy," Vanessa said. "But so shy. And he could use a good haircut."

"*You* would think so," Kaya said. "It must be torture for you, walking around, forced to look at all the people with bad haircuts."

"You don't think he could use a wardrobe makeover?"

"Touché," Kaya said.

"You two should get together then," Melissa said. "Vanessa, do his hair and give him some pointers on skin care. And Kaya, set him up with some clothes."

"I don't know if vintage is right for Noah," she said.

I peered through the window at him. He was a scrawny, mousy sort. Carried reading glasses in his front shirt pocket. But I thought his thick, wavy brown locks were fine; and his scraggy jeans, with the ragged knees, and his collared, un-tucked shirt were as fashionable as a girl could want. The more I looked at him, the more I thought my problem with men might stem from this fascination women have with the beautiful, hot bodies. What if I was going after a type, and missing something good, albeit boring in appearance?

"We should fix him up," Melissa said.

"You know who would be perfect for him?" Kaya said.

I turned back to the table to find her looking at me.

"Who?" My heart skipped the tiniest beat and I blushed, thinking Kaya had read my mind and was going to propose me as a likely candidate. I was ready with a few reasons why I would have to decline.

"That cousin of yours," she said. "What was her name?"

"Yes," Vanessa said. "Such a cute thing, but nerdy."

"Carrie?"

"She's perfect," Kaya said.

"Well..."

Noah came out of Brunch with a white lunch bag and stopped at our table.

"Noah," Kaya said, a huge fake sort of smile on her face. "Sophie has something to talk to you about."

"I do?"

"You do?" he said.

I looked at him—I never realized until that moment how depressed he always appeared. "They think you should adopt a few more cats," I said.

Chapter Fifteen

ReeseFuller: Hey, Mom

ReeseFuller: Just checking in

CrochetMom: *Hi, sweetie, what's up?*

ReeseFuller: Not much. Making plans for the new location

CrochetMom: *We're so proud of you*

ReeseFuller: I know

CrochetMom: *Send some pictures, will you?*

CrochetMom: *Your father says you can send them in this message thing*

ReeseFuller: I'll do that

CrochetMom: *You could take a picture of the house, too*

CrochetMom: *I'd like to see it again*

ReeseFuller: You'll see it again this winter

CrochetMom: *And maybe the beach*

CrochetMom: *I miss the beach*

CrochetMom: *The lagoon*

ReeseFuller: You'll see it all again, soon

CrochetMom: *But I'd really like some pictures just in case*

ReeseFuller: Don't think like that

CrochetMom: *Just in case*

ReeseFuller: ...

ReeseFuller: I'll send them in email, they'll be bigger

CrochetMom: *How's your new girl? Seen her again?*

ReeseFuller: Went to dinner

CrochetMom: *Maybe you could send me a picture of her, too*
ReeseFuller: Maybe
CrochetMom: *Is she shy?*
ReeseFuller: She and her grandfather run the bookstore
CrochetMom: *You told me in email*
CrochetMom: *What does that have to do with being shy?*
ReeseFuller: I don't know :)
ReeseFuller: No. I wouldn't say she's shy
ReeseFuller: I think she's an introvert
CrochetMom: *I can relate*
CrochetMom: *Don't much care for crowds, people*
ReeseFuller: <nodding>
CrochetMom: *Your father dragged me to every party in town*
ReeseFuller: You were a trouper
CrochetMom: *He made it easy, he was the outgoing one. I got to hide in his shadow*
ReeseFuller: You were never in anyone's shadow, Mom
CrochetMom: *Amy's got my lunch ready*
ReeseFuller: I'll let you go, then
CrochetMom: *I love you, sweetie*
ReeseFuller: Love you, Mom

Chapter Sixteen

There was a brief, joking kind of argument, as I insisted I only wanted Noah to take a cat, despite his earlier refusal, and Kaya insisted there was more, until she finally told him outright.

"Sophie has the perfect girl for you."

"You do?" He looked at me, surprised, interested, cautious.

"Well..."

"Absolutely," Kaya said. "What do you say? Would you go out on a blind date?"

"Sure," he said. "I'm not risk averse."

"Don't you want to know all about her?" Melissa said.

He shrugged. "If you know her—" he turned to me— "and you think she'd be interested in me, then she must be nice."

I melted. I expected him to ask me if she was hot, or easy, a term I detested and did not approve of at all, or had big breasts—all of those things that are important to the Cals of the world.

"She is nice," I said. "But Kaya shouldn't have told you. I haven't even asked her about it yet."

"Oh, I see," he said. "Well, let me know if she's interested."

"I will."

We watched him cross the street and head toward the mall and his flower shop; I think we were all a tad saddened by the whole thing.

"Kaya, you really shouldn't have done that," I said. "What if Carrie says no? He'll be so disappointed."

"I'm sorry." She winced. "I didn't think of that."

"That's our Kaya," Vanessa said. "We should call you Mouth."

"Pari told me you all had names for one another," I said.

"Girl, we have names for everybody," Kaya said. "Melissa's Pink. Not just because of the Flamingo thing, but she also looks like a little girl who would wear pink."

"I'm not against the color," Melissa said.

"They call me Glam Ham," Vanessa said.

"Your shop is Glam it Up!" Melissa said. "And you're a ham."

Vanessa rolled her eyes. "I don't see it."

"Please," Kaya said. "You'd you put yourself in every picture taken on Triple F if you could."

Vanessa turned to me, leaned in a bit and said, "I can't help it if people want to take my picture."

"You've seen her," Melissa said.

It was true enough. I attended Triple F almost every month—that's Family Fun Fest—a once-a-month, evening street party held on Strawbridge Main. I was pretty sure people took pictures of Vanessa because of her hair. While she had short, dark hair, every month, she did it up in some wild way or wore a wig. Often, she wore a kimono and put a geisha bun on her head with baby's breath bouquets all around it and some drooping tendrils of wisteria dangling from one side. Another time she wore what could only be described as a rag doll outfit and had her hair twisted into dozens of tiny spikes with tufted ends.

"So I dress up," she said.

"And what do they call you?" I asked Kaya.

She blushed and shook her head.

"Poodles," Vanessa said.

"Poodles?"

"I was wearing a poodle skirt when they first met me. My store's opening day."

"It literally had a poodle on it," Melissa said.

I couldn't help laughing.

"I will never live it down," Kaya said.

"What's Pari called?"

"Fashionista, of course," Melissa said.

"Fashionazi when she refuses to come to lunch because of her Jimmy Choos," Vanessa said.

"I love the way you say Jimmy Choos," Kaya said.

"Karen was harder," Melissa said.

I thought of Karen over at Morgan's Office Supply. She was quiet, kept to herself, always scribbling in a notebook. "Why didn't you call her Bookish?"

"Because you were Bookish first. Nope. We tried all sorts of names and none of them stuck."

"You mean she demanded we stop calling her Mouse or Flats or Sticky Note," Kaya said.

"I admit," Melissa said, "they weren't very flattering. Then we tried Cross and Grumpy."

I must have made a face.

"Because they sell Cross pens and Grumpy Cat merchandise. But she wouldn't go for those."

"At all," Kaya said.

"And you ended up with...?"

"Bella Brella."

"Bella Brella," I said, as if committing it to memory.

"She had this Belle umbrella...from the movie *Beauty and the Beast*."

"I like it."

"She hates it," Vanessa said. "But she's stuck with it, like I'm stuck with Glam Ham."

"Not anymore," Melissa said. "Now, we're Divas. I'll be Pink Diva. You can be Glam Diva. You, Kaya, are Vintage Diva. Pari will be Fashion Diva. Karen can be Bella Diva. And you—" she pointed at me—"are Bookish Diva."

"Well," I said, pushing my wrought-iron chair back into the sidewalk to get up, "Bookish Diva has to get back to work. Are any of you going to Poetry Night on Friday?"

I knew better, of course. I hadn't seen a Diva there yet. Not even Karen, aka Bella Brella. They all shook their heads.

"Isn't that for geeks?" Melissa said.

"Snobs more like it," I said and gasped. "Did I say that out loud?"

They laughed.

"Girl, you did," Kaya said.

"Well, I didn't mean it. I'm...I think I'm angry."

"About Reese?" Melissa said.

"Why don't you put the *gato* thing aside and go out with him?" Vanessa said.

I knew they wouldn't understand; and normally, I wouldn't even try to explain it. I don't know why I said anything. It wasn't like me at all. But there I stood, with my mouth running. "It's like this," I told them. "There are two types of people in the world: those who get cats and those who don't. Reese Fuller doesn't get cats. And that makes him not suitable for me. That's just the way it is."

My plan was to avoid the GLE—to act as if I'd never tried to assassinate him with hardcover overstock, never felt up his head or looked longingly into his Loverboy green eyes. I was certainly going to forget I made out with Hombre Caliente all over The Fort. I decided that, in time, I would forgive Roger Dodger for liking him. But it was a sad fact of life that Reese was the wrong sort of person.

His plan, apparently, was to pester the hell out of me until I relented. Not going to happen, I told myself when he had the gall to show up at Stogies for Poetry Night.

Chapter Seventeen

Mr. Booker liked to call Gramps Mr. Cigaro. He thought it was just so funny that *his* name was related to books and Gramps ran a bookstore. He thought it would be the wildest thing if Gramps' name was related to cigars. Mr. Booker was odd like that. You know what I'm talking about, right?—odd in that 'non-thinking, irrational, let's make everything fun' way. All the older women in town loved him; he told me that was why he liked cigars. I mean, he did actually like cigars, but he said they were the equivalent of bug spray to women...if women were bugs. Then he told me this story about a woman who acted like she didn't mind the cigars and they went out a few times until she started asking him to stop smoking them after lunch, and then to stop smoking them after dinner, and then to stop smoking indoors at all.

"Nowadays," he told me, "on the first few dates with a new girl, I lodge a cigar in my mouth and don't take it out until I'm sure she's good with it."

"And how is that working out for you?"

"So far, I haven't had a second date."

"I know what your problem is."

"Is that so?"

"First of all," I said. "*Gross*. Second, they're not girls; they're women. And third, Mr. Booker, if you're looking for a woman who doesn't mind a man who smokes cigars, you're going about it all wrong." I told him sorting women by how tolerant they were to a fat greenish brown phallic symbol stuck in his mouth every minute of the day was only going to lead him into a life of lonely bachelorhood. Because no woman wants to see that. Okay, I didn't say the phallic symbol part—saying phallic to Mr. Booker would be like saying it to my father; I said elongated wad of tobacco, but judging by the way he flinched, I think he got my point. I told him he ought to ease a potential partner into cigars, rather than bashing her over the head with them. And the visual of that, along with the phallus part, made us both blush and laugh. I think, in the end, Mr. Booker decided to let it go and be himself. I'd ask him how that was going for him, but judging by his continued bachelor status, I'd say it wasn't going well.

Stogies was more than a cigar shop to Mr. Booker; it was a cigar aficionado's paradise. If it was related to cigars, he had it—including a picture of a scene from Michelangelo's Sistine Chapel ceiling. You know the one where God is reaching out to touch Adam? Only, on Mr. Booker's wall, it was an up-close shot of their hands, and God and Adam were holding cigars. While he had a counter behind which he did sell cigars, most of the place was a lounge with soft, brown leather chairs on which he and his pals sat and smoked the things. There was a poster on the wall outlining all the shapes they come in: parejo, pyramid, torpedo, perfecto, and presidente. I had it memorized, mostly because every Poetry Night I stood in the back of the room, in the corner, leaning my head against it. Another poster showed all the different colors of cigars: double claro, claro, Colorado claro, Colorado, etc. And still another poster had all the different types of cigars and their lengths and circumferences. Cigars are very serious business.

Strangely enough, on Poetry Night, there was no smoking.

Mr. Booker said that was because the place was so packed, it would be best if they refrained until after the proceedings. And Poetry Night was generally a packed affair. I didn't know why. And I didn't know why I always went. Gramps talked me into it, initially, probably hoping I would meet someone nice. I didn't meet Cal at Poetry Night.

We were an odd group of people, to be honest. There were young kids who attended, the girls dressed in plaid skirts and black, hip-length boots—the boys wearing ripped jeans and dirty t-shirts with their hair spiked. A few of the local nerds, like Hugh and Noah, were there scouting for intellectual, assertive women. Alfred, of course. There were always a few women who showed up and hung on every word Mr. Booker said, especially when he read a poem— they always acted like they understood it, but you could tell they didn't really. They were usually the types who wore a lot of bangles and made tinkling noises as they moved. It was very annoying to hear, when someone was reading a particularly heavy verse. I could tell those weren't Mr. Booker's type of women. Mr. Booker thought women who wore leather and rode Harleys were his type. I thought his type would wear mom jeans with blousy blouses, sport unbound, windblown, blond hair and sun-kissed skin, and like to ride horses. I didn't think Mr. Booker realized that was his type. But he would. In time.

I walked into Poetry Night that Friday, and made my way through the crowd of bodies to my usual corner, my little notebook cradled in my arm, and looked up to find Reese Fuller standing in my spot. I turned and weaved my head around looking for Mr. Booker. I was sure he'd told Reese where to stand. He had to have done it. It was no coincidence. But I couldn't find him. I could hear him, somewhere near his counter, laughing, probably talking cigars, but I couldn't see him.

"What are you doing here?" I said.

"I was invited."

"Who invited you?"

The next thing I knew, Karen was standing there smiling at me. Well, if it wasn't Bella Brella. AKA Bella Diva. AKA sneaky quiet girl who...*what*? What was I going to do about it, anyway? Reese Fuller hated cats. I, therefore, hated Reese Fuller. If Ms. 'Look at me scribbling in my book like I'm all deep and intense' wanted him, she could have him.

"Hi, Sophie," she said. She was smiling. Open like. Not mousy and quiet at all. Well, sure, I supposed being with GLE made a girl happy. Just not *this* girl.

Oh, for crying out loud, I thought. Get over it, will you?

"You like poetry, do you?" I said to both of them, and cringed. I didn't mean to be a snob, but there were times when those things fell out of my mouth. That was one of those times.

Reese smirked.

"I don't know if I do or not," Karen said. "But Reese was in the store earlier and he asked me about the flyer in the window, so I thought, why not?"

Sure, I thought. Why not? But at least I had my answer. She and Reese were gawkers. We got them on occasion. They'd show up and listen, and when they realized we were actually going to read poetry, they tended to slip out quietly, or at the very least, never show up again. So, I stood aside and waited. I figured Karen and Reese would last a good twenty minutes, tops, and then I could reclaim my spot under the poster.

Mr. Booker started us out, as always, but instead of reading a selection from *Love That Dog*, like I thought he would, he read Byron:

"Though the night was made for loving,
And the day return too soon,
Yet we'll go no more a-roving

By the light of the moon."

My eyes fluttered a bit, because, well, I was expecting to hear about a dog. I didn't pay much attention to the other selections, dazing out a bit, until he called me up to read. I put on my best cloy smile and pushed my way through the group. I saw the fear in Mr. Booker's face. He knew I had a dark side. He'd opened with Byron. Then came the rash of the usual: a Shakespeare sonnet or two, always a Maya Angelou, usually the one about the bird, Frost, always someone had to read Frost. Well, I read Billy Collins' "Flames."

"Smokey the Bear heads
into the autumn woods
with a red can of gasoline
and a box of wooden matches."

You know how it goes, right? Anyway, I got the laughter I was looking for. I was so glad I didn't read Rossetti's "I loved you first: but afterwards your love." Can you imagine the look on Reese's face if I had? I was glad he was laughing with everyone else as he passed me on my way to the back of the room, until I realized he'd passed me. He was going to the counter. He was going to read a poem! I looked at Karen and she was beaming; she gave me one of those 'isn't this exciting' shrugs and I nodded, thinking he'd better read Frost. But he didn't.

"You did not come," he began. I craned my neck to catch a glimpse of him. He was reciting, not reading. And looking at Karen with a smile. "And marching time drew on, and wore me numb."

I admit, the tiniest gasp left me when I recognized it was Hardy's "A Broken Appointment." My gaze was riveted on his face. From memory! I have to tell you I hated him so much more that night than I thought I ever would. *The nerve of him!*

And then his eyes met mine as he read, "Once you, a

woman, came, to soothe a time-torn man; even though it be, you love not me?"

I could have spit.

And the crowd went wild.

Seriously. They went crazy. And I...I slipped quietly out the door like a gawker.

Chapter Eighteen

CrochetMom: *Yoohoo, Reese*

ReeseFuller: LOL

CrochetMom: *Amy tells me you recited a poem? Explain*

ReeseFuller: There's this cigar store here, very quaint, and the owner hosts a poetry night once a month

CrochetMom: *Wonderful. Did you recite one of your own?*

ReeseFuller: Hardy

CrochetMom: *A Broken Appointment?*

ReeseFuller: How did you know?

CrochetMom: *Moms know these things. Why not one of your own?*

ReeseFuller: ...

CrochetMom: *?*

ReeseFuller: Poetry is personal

CrochetMom: *You think Hardy didn't feel that way?*

ReeseFuller: So, somebody else can read one of mine

CrochetMom: *Maybe one day someone will. Was your girl there?*

ReeseFuller: She's not my girl

CrochetMom: *Yet*

ReeseFuller: Yet

CrochetMom: *If you read "Eclipse" to her, she would be*

ReeseFuller: Not every girl swoons over a poet

CrochetMom: *Your girl would.*

ReeseFuller: :)

ReeseFuller: Mom

CrochetMom: *Yes*

ReeseFuller: There are these stray cats at this new building

CrochetMom: *Oh, that's too bad. Poor dears*

ReeseFuller: Once we start tearing up the parking lot, they'll run away

CrochetMom: *And you want me to tell you it's okay?*

ReeseFuller: ...

ReeseFuller: Yes

CrochetMom: *It's okay, sweetie*

ReeseFuller: ...

CrochetMom: *You can't save everything*

CrochetMom: *That's just life, right?*

CrochetMom: *Reese, honey*

CrochetMom: *Life is beautiful*

CrochetMom: *And life is hard. And there is pain. And there is sorrow*

CrochetMom: ...

ReeseFuller: Grab the happy. Embrace the good. Feel the joy

CrochetMom: *Weep for what you cannot hold...*

ReeseFuller: Know you are not boundless

CrochetMom: *And what is lost, forgives*

ReeseFuller: And what is saved, is lost

CrochetMom: *For life, beautiful...*

ReeseFuller: ...

CrochetMom: ...

ReeseFuller: is finite

CrochetMom: *You were only sixteen when you wrote that*

ReeseFuller: And you still know it by heart

CrochetMom: *I love you, sweetie.*

ReeseFuller: I love you, Mom.

Chapter Nineteen

The next morning, I was on my hands and knees in the romance section, dusting the bottom shelf, when a pair of worn ballerina slippers, tiny bows of dyed string at the toes—peach to match the shoes and tipped with textured gold beads—appeared in my periphery. I looked up to see Karen grinning at me; she was wearing a peach and white wrap-around of indistinct print—one of those you wanted to look hard at, to determine if it was dogs, cats, or the Eiffel Tower, but knew better, because staring like that is rude. I climbed to my feet and brushed the dust out of my hair.

"What happened to you last night?" she said.

"What do you mean what happened?"

"Where did you go?"

"Home." I rested against the bookshelf and nearly winced as my shoulder pushed some of the spines deeper toward the back. I blushed, realizing I was trying very hard to look carefree. "Did you two stay until the end? Did anyone read a nasty limerick? Someone always reads one; it's like a tradition."

"There once was a man from Bonaire—"

"Nope, nope—" I held up my hand to stop her—"I've heard it, thanks."

She laughed. "I don't remember the rest anyway. So,

why did you leave? I think Reese was disappointed."

"Why should he be?"

"I don't know. I got the feeling he wanted to impress you with his poem. He did a great job, don't you think?"

"Yes." I had to admit it. He recited beautifully. It was *awful*.

"Answer me something, honestly."

I pushed off the book case and nodded.

"Do I look like I work at an office supply store?"

My brows went up and my head popped back. "Why would you ask that?" It was Reese, I thought. She wondered how she looked to him.

"I don't know. I get the feeling some of the others...you know how they are. I think maybe I'm dumpy."

I gave her a once over. The wrap-around was sort of motherish. Her hair was, as usual, pulled back at the top and sides and fastened within a, no doubt, tortoiseshell barrette in the back. No makeup to speak of, except for some pale, peachy lip gloss.

"You're not dumpy," I said. "But you do look like a librarian."

She gasped. "And that's not dumpy?"

"Not to me, it isn't. I mean, you also look like an artist."

"I do?"

"Sure. And a writer. You look...natural."

She nodded. "Natural. Yeah, I like that."

"What about me? Do I look like I work in a bookstore?"

"Absolutely."

"Is that a bad thing?"

"How should I know? I look like a librarian. Well, come on. I was sent over to get you, take you across the street for lunch."

"A Diva lunch?"

"That's right."

I followed her to the front, willingly, I admit. "Did they

tell you you're Bella Diva now?"

"I heard. I guess I'm glad of it. Could be worse."

At the door, I nodded a goodbye to Gramps who smiled and nodded back, like I was his champion off to do him proud. It's the little things that make grandparents happy: that first smile, that first hug, that first attempt at making friends. I flashed back to when I had my first sleepover and how proud all the family was—you'd think I'd gone off to war.

"Why were you sent?" I said as we took the crosswalk. I could see Melissa aka Pink Diva already lounging in the sunshine, her chair pulled far away from the wrought-iron table in an attempt to avoid the shade of the umbrella. She was sipping something, probably one of her specialty smoothies. Vanessa had just left the café with a tall cup, taking a seat. "I mean, why 'sent?' It sounds...forceful."

"You *are* bookish, aren't you?"

"If you mean I over think everything, guilty."

"Well, the truth is..."

"Once again, my conspiracy senses pay off."

She laughed. "Vanessa thought you might be mad at me."

"For what?" Of course, I knew what.

"For asking Reese to go to Poetry Night with me. But I didn't mean anything by it. He's your...Caliente Hombre, or whatever."

"Hombre Caliente," I said. "And he's not."

"Does it matter?"

"Sure it does. I can't claim him if we're not dating."

"No, I mean which comes first, the *hombre* or the *caliente*?"

"Oh. Yes, I think it does. It's backwards in Spanish."

"What's backwards?"

"The adjectives and the nouns."

"Hmm," she said. "I'll have to remember that. Anyway,

111

you saw him first."

Vanessa, I mean, Glam Diva smiled as we got to the table and Melissa pulled her chair back under the umbrella.

"It's not like calling dibs on the front seat of your dad's car," I said. "Anyway, he's not my anything."

"But you like him, don't you?" Vanessa said.

It was only the four of us at lunch at Café Flamingo that day. Pari and Kaya, they told me, both had to eat in—Pari in her office at the Executive Suites building, and Kaya at Kaya Vintage Clothing. We all agreed they ought to be brought dessert and Karen volunteered to run a slice of cheesecake over to Pari if I'd take one to Kaya.

"Of course I like him," I said after I'd got myself a salad and rejoined them. "But I'm not seeing him."

"I can't honestly believe," Melissa said, "you'd ditch him just because of the cats."

I shoved a mouthful of romaine in and nearly choked. "You didn't hear him." I covered my mouth to keep from spitting ranch all over her. "He didn't think it was a big deal to start construction and let them run off."

"Well—" Vanessa winced—"they're strays. Now, I know you love them and you take care of them. But it's the truth."

"Could you date someone who didn't think what you cared about was important?"

She sighed. "I suppose not."

"So that's that. Can we drop it now? It's no big deal. If any of you want to ask him out, go ahead."

"Tell us about this poetry thing," Melissa said. She spit the word poetry out like a bug had flown into her mouth.

"I thought that was for snooty, literary types." Vanessa turned to me, blushing and said, "No offense."

"It's an eclectic crowd, really."

"What the hell does that mean?" Melissa laughed.

"Varied," Karen said. "Diverse."

112

"Oh, look who else is snooty," Vanessa said.

"Did you read a poem there?" Melissa asked Karen.

Karen shook her head. "I didn't even know Reese was going to."

"What did he read? Dr. Seuss?"

"I don't know who wrote it?"

"'A Broken Appointment' by Thomas Hardy," I said.

"It was beautiful," Karen said. "I thought he'd written it himself, the way he spoke it...like from memory."

"What sort of poem is it?" Vanessa said.

"A love poem," I said.

They all gave one another smirking smiles and giggled, then turned to me. I shook my head.

"Sophie read a poem about Smokey the Bear lighting a fire," Karen said. "It was funny and all, but..."

"But what?" I said.

She shrugged. "Reese called it a diversionary tactic."

They all laughed and applauded.

"It's not funny," I said. But they didn't care. "He can say what he wants. I'm not going out with him again."

"I forgot," Karen said. "I wanted to give you this." She dug a torn piece of notebook paper out of her purse and handed it to me.

It had a name and phone number scribbled on it.

"Duke Wells?"

"He helped my uncle with some stray cats last year. It's what he does."

"Stray cat whisperer?" Melissa said.

Staring at the name, I started to melt. I was finally able to admit to myself that I'd been angry with Karen—a little bit. It was stupid, of course. But I was finding that nothing was making sense anymore, least of all my emotions. What was the big deal? That's what I wanted to know. So what if I thought Reese Fuller was adorable? And funny. And was a poet. I didn't like him. Did I? I mean...I *liked* him liked him.

But I didn't *like* him like him. I rolled my eyes.

"Are you okay?" Karen asked me.

"Just worried about the cats."

"Well, call that guy."

"What does he do with them?"

"He finds them homes."

Relief started to seep in, from the toes up. *Help.* Someone was going to help me with the cats. "Thanks. I mean, really. I don't know what to say?"

"You just said it."

I managed to keep up with the banter for the next several minutes. It's amazing how much three women can talk and eat at the same time. At least, I thought I'd been keeping up, until Melissa gave me the tiniest shove and I realized I'd been daydreaming.

"Hello," she said. "Did you hear me?"

"What?"

"Have you called your cousin...about Noah?"

"Oh, yeah. No." Somehow I'd let myself drift from helping the cats find homes with the Stray Cat Whisperer to kissing Reese in Manatee Park. How had that happened? I mean, what connective train of thoughts could possibly have led me to that?

"So, when are you going to do it?"

"As soon as I get back to the store," I said. "Promise."

I carried a little box with a slice of cheesecake in it over to Kaya Vintage Clothing and was glad to get out of the summer heat and into her store. Kaya was behind her cashwrap, sitting on a high stool. A pencil was stuck behind one ear. She wore a white peasant blouse with tiny milk-chocolate brown lace trim, a bit lighter than her smooth skin. She danced in her seat and reached out for the dessert box, all smiles.

"So," she said, as she opened the box and breathed in the cheesy goodness. "I hear our Hombre Caliente read a love poem last night."

"Can't a man recite poetry without everyone psycho-analyzing it?"

"*Unrequited* love."

"So?"

"What do you suppose he meant by it?"

"I think he meant he likes Thomas Hardy?"

"Thomas who?"

"And anyway, how did you hear about it already? What is it with this town?"

"Karen told me."

"Oh."

"Don't worry; I don't think she likes him. I mean, sure, she likes him. But she doesn't *like* him like him."

"I think we've all lost our minds."

"Speaking of jalapeños..."

I turned at the sound of the bell over her door to see Reese Fuller walking in.

Chapter Twenty

Reese entered Kaya Vintage Clothing, nodded a hello to Kaya, smiled at me, and turned to walk through the store, looking at the clothes and jewelry. I must have stood there at the cashwrap with my mouth open for a full thirty seconds, before Kaya caught my attention by calling out to him, "Looking for something special?"

He approached us and I could feel my face burning hot. I kept my eyes turned to Kaya, trying to act like he wasn't there.

"I was thinking of a locket—an old fashioned one. The Old Geezer told me I might find something here. He's got a couple—antiques, very expensive."

"Mr. Collins does tend toward the finer stuff," Kaya told him. She led him down to the other end of the counter to show him her lockets and I stood there, feeling awkward —okay, more awkward than usual. I should have left, just walked out the door, but I was afraid that would be rude. I had to say goodbye at least. And to do that, I'd have to say something and my mouth wasn't working at that particular moment.

"What do you think?" I heard him say.

I turned my head and they were both looking at me. So, what else was I supposed to do? I went over and looked at the locket...and gasped. It was...well, it was amazing. Heart-shaped, of course—all the best lockets are—the golden color of fallen leaves in autumn, with a twisted vine carved into it. At the top, where it looped onto the gold chain, there was a key, and two cream-colored stone flowers dangling from it. Reese held it up and it tinkled.

"It's beautiful," I said.

"I'll take it."

There was a split second, only a tiny, *tiny* fraction of a split, in which I thought it might be for me. I can't say if that wish was born of envy—I had to have that locket—or lust—*Reese* was buying that locket! But it vanished as quickly as it had come.

"Who's the lucky lady?" Kaya said with a wink.

"My mother," he said.

Together, Kaya and I sang out, "Oh!" I touched my chest at my heart; Kaya's arms crossed at her waist. We were...sappy. Sappy women.

"Well," I said, "I have to get back to the store and call Carrie."

"Ah, yes, the big fix up."

"Playing matchmaker are you?" Reese said, pulling cash from his wallet for Kaya.

Who says that? *Who?* And there was disdain in his voice. As if he was saying I had no right, no right at all, to fix two people up—two perfectly good nerds, who would be perfectly nerdy together.

"Why not?" I said.

"If you ask me—"

"Oh, did I ask?"

"Yes, you did."

"You did, Sophie," Kaya said, frowning, sifting dollar-bill change onto Reese's palm.

Oh, right. I did. My face burned even hotter and I hated him for what he did to me whenever he was near. Seething, raw, lava, no...magma. That's right...*magma hate.*

"Fixing up your friends," he said, "is like meddling in

118

their relationships—wait, not like it, it *is* meddling. It can only turn out bad."

"Well, Carrie's my cousin, not my friend—"

"Even worse—"

"—I mean, she's my friend, too. Never mind. It's none of your business, anyway."

He took the bag from Kaya, in which she'd put a soft brown velvet box holding his new purchase, and smirked at me. "You're exactly right. None of my business. Thank you," he said to Kaya. Then he brushed past me without so much as 'a fine how do you do' (Don't tell Gramps I said that) and I kicked the base of Kaya's counter out of frustration, mostly from thinking the old-people phrase 'a fine how do you do.'

Kaya eyed me with this simpering sort of 'I know you better than yourself' look.

"How much was it?" I asked her. "It's not what you think." She was looking at me as if I'd asked about his bank account. "I want one."

"The one he bought was three-fifty."

"Three-fifty!"

"Still want one?"

"Well, yes. But three-fifty? And he paid with cash?"

"You want to look at them now?"

"I'll have to save up for that, I'm afraid."

I said my goodbye and mumbled as I left, "Three hundred fifty dollars?" Think about it. How many cats could I feed with three hundred fifty dollars? My heart sank. I wouldn't have them much longer. I had to find them homes; I just had to. As soon as I got back to Bookish, I called Mr. Wells. He answered the phone with a sing-song "hello" and listened while I explained my predicament. Then he said, "I can help." But there was a silence after—in that space where I was supposed to say thank you, or I was supposed to be happy. Instead of saying something, any-thing, I got stuck on the idea that I would never see my darlings again. They'd go to strangers, people I didn't know, people Mr. Wells might not even know. He told me he worked with a variety of rescue groups.

"But they're all full up right now."

"Oh," I said. *A ray of hope?* Why would that make me happy? *You can't keep them, Sophie!*

"If I can't get them into a group, I'll take them myself."

"You will?"

I imagined I could get behind that. I mean, I had his number. I could meet him. Then I'd know him. Maybe he'd let me visit. I was busy telling myself how silly that was, while at the same time, my mouth was saying to Mr. Wells, "Can I come and meet you? Maybe see where they'd be? I guess I'm worried."

"Sure, come by the house."

He gave me his address and it was right in town. This could work, I told myself. Up front, at the cashwrap, I told Gramps I was going to meet Mr. Wells, the Stray Cat Whisperer.

He said, "Huh?"

"This man, Mr. Wells, he'll take the cats in. He'll keep them until he can find them good homes."

"Wait," Hugh said, coming out from the maze of book shelves. "What?"

"He said I could come to his house and check it out—check him out. I mean, meet him."

"You're going to meet some strange man we don't know?" Gramps said.

"He's a cat lover," I said. Like...*duh*.

"I'll go with you," Hugh said.

Gramps was relieved, so I was okay with it. And anyway, he had a point.

Because I was bouncing around like a woman high on knowing her troubles were over (and maybe thinking she could get past the idea that Gorgeous Laughing Eyes wasn't as nice to felines as he ought to be), Hugh said he would drive us across town. As I sat in the front seat of his little blue stick shift, I couldn't help scolding myself. This wasn't about Reese. This was about the cats. And why would I want to be with someone who would make me hand them off to a stranger? I wanted to forget him—forget the whole thing.

The entire episode reminded me of my addiction to Harry Potter. It might be better described as a phase, but I suppose that would depend on whom you asked. If you asked Gramps, it was a phase, one he also enjoyed. But Cal said it was an addiction. I was all Harry Potter all the time. I had figures, books, ornaments, jewelry, my own wand (naturally), pajamas, scarves. Anyway, I knew at some point I had to get myself off Harry Potter. There was more to life, I kept telling myself, than the world of Harry Potter. There were other books that begged to be read. I mean, why read the Harry Potter series of books yet *again*, when there were stacks and stacks filled with Hugh Howey, Gillian Flynn, Craig Lancaster, and Patrick Rothfuss waiting for attention. Not to mention all the classics I'd yet to read.

All it took was a catalyst—one big thing—through which I managed to carve some space between myself and Harry Potter. I can now stand proudly and say, out loud if necessary, 'my name is Sophie Childers and I am no longer a Potterhead.' Sure I still like Harry Potter. But I only like it, see? I don't *like* it like it. And what was that catalyst? It was, I'm not ashamed to say, vampires. Not real ones, of course, but the fictional kind. I read a few vampire books and *boom*, off to the races with the stack of authors who deserved just as much of my attention as J.K. Rowling (though I still cringe with guilt).

That was all I needed with the GLE, the Loverboy. Hombre Caliente. Just one thing to put it all in perspective. And then I could move on.

"This is it," Hugh said.

Chapter Twenty-one

CrochetMom: *Reese? Are you there?*
ReeseFuller: Here, what's up?
CrochetMom: *Just want to let you know all is good*
ReeseFuller: ?
CrochetMom: *If you hear anything*
ReeseFuller: What's going on?
CrochetMom: *It's a hiccup, that's all*
CrochetMom: *There will be hiccups*
ReeseFuller: I'm coming up
CrochetMom: *No*
CrochetMom: *That's the whole reason I'm texting*
CrochetMom: *Your father is overreacting*
ReeseFuller: You're sick, he's worried
CrochetMom: *I'm not sick, Reese*
CrochetMom: *We all know I'm not sick*
ReeseFuller: What are you talking about?
CrochetMom: *This isn't sick, Reese, honey*
CrochetMom: *I wish everyone would stop acting like I just need a rest*
ReeseFuller: ...
ReeseFuller: I understand
CrochetMom: *Do you?*
ReeseFuller: I do. I'll call you, we can talk
CrochetMom: *I'd like that*

CrochetMom: *But not on the cell phone, anymore. Have you tried talking on one of those?*

ReeseFuller: I do it all the time

CrochetMom: *Give me a handset to prop between my shoulder and my ear, please*

ReeseFuller: House phone it is

ReeseFuller: I love you, mom

CrochetMom: *I love you too, sweetie*

Chapter Twenty-two

Hugh pulled up to the curb in the little Pelican Bay neighborhood just off the lagoon south of town. The houses were old; some residents had remade their carports into garages, but not all. Some still had jalousie windows, those slatted glass panes you crank open. Mr. Wells had new windows put in and on the sill by the front door, I could see three cats. I knew right then he was my savior. His house was beige with an aged oak out front, droopy with Spanish moss, and a paint-chipped wood fence in the back. As Hugh and I walked up the driveway the Stray Cat Whisperer came out onto his porch to greet us. He was not much taller than I was and sported a fat belly in front threatening to pop a button from his pinstriped shirt. He shook our hands and warned us to enter carefully. I had no idea what he was talking about. Until I slipped inside his hazy front room.

Cats everywhere. Cats at our feet, dozens of them. Cats covering the ragged sofa and the battered recliner—six cuddled up on the seat, two on each armrest, and two atop it. Cats on the counter over by the kitchen. Cats on the table and chairs. Cats on the bookcases—bookcases empty of anything but cats. The house was literally filled with cats. Now I suppose Gramps could argue with my use of 'literally' there, because the cats were not, in fact, filling the house like ice fills a glass...but the house was littered with cats, I'm telling you. Speaking of litter, it stank to high heaven. Hugh's hand went straight to his nose and he tried to hide it by turning away from Mr. Wells. I winced; tears filled my eyes.

"It's pungent," Mr. Wells said. "I'll give you that. We scoop almost constantly."

I was thinking he should get rid of the 'almost.'

"It's very colorful," I nearly sobbed. It was the nicest thing I could think of. Calicos, brown tabbies, gray tabbies, orange tabbies, black cats, black-and-white tuxedos, torties, white cats, yellow cats. It was *Go Dog. Go!* but with cats. A Dr. Seuss nightmare.

The Stray Cat Whisperer showed us around and we waded through the cats to see the bedrooms, the bathrooms, the closets, the screened back porch. He even had air-conditioned sheds in his backyard. All full of cats. The yard itself was home to several as well.

"The neighbors won't allow too many in the yard, so we rotate them," he said.

I did a lot of nodding but my mind was racing, my heart thumping in my chest. On the one hand—the horror of so many cats! On the other—a wonderful haven of cats! I could see my future there. I could *be* the Stray Cat Whisperer, standing in a puddle of cats, my belly bulging out the bottom of my ratty tee shirt because I had no life beyond scooping cat poop all day and all night. Was that heaven or hell? I couldn't decide; I was too scared. Scared of stepping on a cat tail, scared the Stray Cat Whisperer would mumble the killing command and Hugh and I would never be heard from again, scared that this really was my future.

Mr. Wells told us to have a seat on the sofa in the front room—"just chase the cats off"—and as soon as we did, cats appeared on our laps and at our feet. There was a tabby behind me so I couldn't lean back, but that was for the best;

there would, no doubt, have been a cat on my head if I'd dared to put it near the head rest. Wells shooed the cats off the recliner and sat in it, not minding at all when they jumped back up onto his lap. One climbed to his shoulder and perched there.

"You got five, you say?" he asked me.

I nodded, not wanting to open my mouth after realizing the dusty, fuzzy atmosphere was a result of cat hair floating about in the air.

"Are they fixed?"

I nodded again. It was awkward; I knew I was going to have to speak. "So, you'd keep them here, until you find them homes?"

"That's right."

"Why don't you find homes for all of these?" Hugh asked him.

Mr. Wells shrugged. "It's not as easy as it sounds. Sometimes, there are too many cats."

That was, to me, profound. A metaphor, really, for life. Sometimes, there are just too many cats.

"How many do you have?" I said.

"Last time I counted, I was at seventy-two."

"Seventy? Two?"

"So, you probably won't be able to find homes for Sophie's strays?" Hugh said.

"Honestly, probably not."

"But you'd keep them here?" I asked.

Mr. Wells nodded. "It's better than the alternative."

"What's that?"

"Euthanasia, of course. If I can save them from that, I will."

"Of course," I said somewhat blankly.

We thanked him and I told him I'd be in touch. When Hugh started the engine of his little car and I pulled the seatbelt across my body I turned to him.

"Seventy-two cats?" I said.

Hugh shook his head. "I counted fifty in the front room alone. He's got hundreds."

"He's a hoarder," I said. "A cat hoarder."

"Still, you need someplace for the cats. It's better than having them run away."

"Is it? Were they healthy? I mean, is that a good life for a cat?"

"But like he said, 'it's better than the alternative.'" He pulled away from the curb and at the stop sign, turned to catch sight of my face. "Are those tears from the stench of the house, or are you crying?"

I was crying. This was the choice I was down to, I realized. Sending the darlings off to live in a stifled, cramped, cat hell or having them euthanized.

And just like that, I was back to hating Reese Fuller.

Chapter Twenty-three

T hose aren't the only options," Gramps told me when we got back to Bookish.

"What's another?"

He shrugged and looked guilty. "Listen, if they run away once the renovations start, chances are they'll find their way back sooner or later."

"But think of all the things that could happen," I said. "They could be hit by cars, or mistreated by some mean person, or lost, or starve."

"Or taken in by a caring person," Gramps said.

I sighed and shook my head. "Reese said they couldn't stay on his property."

"Are you sure you don't want to keep them for yourself?"

"I wouldn't be handing them over to the hoarder if that was true."

"Wouldn't you? If they were at this man's house, you could go visit them, help him take care of them. I'll wager you'll find a way to get them back into the park as soon as the new store is up."

My eyes lit up and I gasped. Why hadn't I thought of that before?

"Now, now," Gramps said. "You can't keep them on the man's property without his permission."

"But the park..."

Gramps frowned. He was right. I couldn't get away with keeping them in the park for long. As it was, I had a hard time keeping them confined to the back parking lot of the old building. The only thing separating their space and the park was a road and a bit of parking in front of the playground.

"You know it's only a matter of time anyway, Sophie," he said.

"This is all Reese's fault. The shoe store was going to let me keep them."

"You don't know for sure. Once they got moved in and started making upgrades...at some point, the cats would have to go. You said you'd find homes for them all, but you've been mighty slow going at it."

I didn't want to talk about it anymore and was glad when Gramps went off to shelve some new books he'd picked up at an estate sale. I remembered then that I promised I'd call Carrie, so I got my phone out and touched on her name. She answered in her usual way, breathless, as if I'd interrupted her...but she was always only watching television or eating lunch.

"Enjoying summer?" I said. Carrie taught fourth grade at a little charter school a few miles south.

"I miss children," she said, then snorted out a laugh. "What do you think? What's up? Going to do the Mouse House with me this year?"

"Maybe. Actually, I have something to ask you. I sort of got talked into this; I want you to know it wasn't my idea...I don't think. I can't even remember now how it all got started."

"You're scaring me. Spit it out."

"Do you remember—did you ever meet—have you gone into the mall here...downtown. The flower shop. Flower Power, it's called."

"Sophie you're talking gibberish, just say it."

"Can I set you up on a blind date?"

Silence.

"His name is Noah...Holland, I think. He runs this little flower shop...booth...thing. In the mall. Not the *mall* mall, the one here in downtown. I don't know much else about him aside from that. Well, and he's sort of..."

"Is he cute?"

"Well, sort of. I guess. I mean, in a sad kind of way."

"Dear god, Sophie."

"He's sweet, though. I think he is cute. Really. I guess I hadn't noticed."

"Would you go out with him?"

"Oh, sure, I would. Maybe."

"You wouldn't, would you?"

"He's not my type."

"What makes him *my* type?"

"He's...quiet. Shy. Kind of..."

"He's a nerd. You think I'm a nerd and you want to fix me up with another nerd. Like we're separated from our pod people and need to get together to await the mother ship."

"No, I don't think that. I'm sorry, really. It was a bad idea. Forget I mentioned it."

"I didn't say I wouldn't do it."

"Really?"

"Tell me more about him."

"Well." I winced and searched my brain for any information at all that I could use to paint Noah in a good light. "He dresses down. Casual, I mean. He's got really dark hair and a beard and mustache."

"Facial hair, huh? What's he covering up?"

"Uh. I don't know. He's, well, he's okay looking."

"Just give it to me straight."

"I think he looks kind of like a horse and his lips are too red."

She laughed and snorted again.

"And he looks like a bachelor. Always wrinkled and mussed. But he smells nice."

"He smells nice?"

"I guess that could be the flowers."

"And he works in a flower booth." She sighed. "Ah, what the hell. He sounds malleable."

"Malleable," I echoed. "Sure."

As I walked home from work that evening, I hesitated out front of Fiona's shop, pretending to look at the dresses in the window, checking to be sure no one was at the abandoned building...or, the new location for Summer Sun, as I supposed I ought to start thinking of it. It looked deserted, so I headed over with my big bag of food and water. Alfred was there already, petting Weesie, with Piddle Paddle rubbing at his leg. I wiped out their bowls with the paper towels and poured food and water, then sat down on the picnic table bench and sighed.

"I finished *Unraveling Oliver*," he said. "What did you think of the end?"

"Which part?"

"Should he have told her the truth or not?"

"Yes."

He nodded and stood, stretched and picked up his backpack.

"I'll bring you another one, then," I said.

"Make it a happy one this time."

"Is everything all right?"

"Everything is as it's supposed to be," he said. "Sometimes we need a little reminder of the happiness that comes and goes."

I watched him walk back toward town, thinking he was a pretty amazing old man. When I got upstairs and was unlocking my apartment, I heard Pari's car so I went to the railing and watched her walk up. She was, as usual, perfect. She looked as if she'd just stepped out of her room, ready for the day.

"Don't you ever look tired?" I said.

"Never in public."

"Got plans for tonight?"

"I have a date."

"Anyone I know?"

"Eric Lawson. I've been seeing him off and on."

I nodded, feeling silly.

"Call Melissa," she said. "See what's up."

"That's okay. It was just a thought."

We said goodbye and I went inside, flopped down onto my sofa and let Willow and Midnight climb all over me.

"Where's Chloe?" I whispered. I could see her peering from the bedroom. I meowed at her. My phone played out "Tara's Theme" and I saw it was Melissa calling. I had to laugh.

"Pari says you're ready for a night out. Let's hit it. Where to?"

"Anywhere Reese Fuller isn't."

Chapter Twenty-four

ReeseFuller: Mom...
CrochetMom: *I'm here*
ReeseFuller: I got a call from Amy
CrochetMom: *Oh, Reese. I warned you*
ReeseFuller: She's just worried
CrochetMom: *I told you on the phone*
CrochetMom: *I'll let you know. Don't worry*
ReeseFuller: You have to know we're all worried
CrochetMom: *There's nothing left to worry about*
ReeseFuller: ...
CrochetMom: *I'm sorry*
ReeseFuller: No. It's okay. I'm sorry. I can't keep unloading on you whenever they call me
CrochetMom: *True enough. It's not like I don't already know what they're saying*
ReeseFuller: Okay. Truce. You'll tell me when you want me to come back up to see you
CrochetMom: *I will. I promise*
CrochetMom: *It's Saturday. Going out with your girl?*
ReeseFuller: I hear she'll be out tonight, so yes
CrochetMom: *Recite something lovely and she'll be yours forever*
ReeseFuller: If the mood's right, I will
CrochetMom: :)

CrochetMom: *I hope it's not too weird to say, but...*

ReeseFuller: ?

CrochetMom: *I like to imagine you getting married*

ReeseFuller: Not weird. Seems normal to me

CrochetMom: *Good. No rush, of course. In your own time*

CrochetMom: *You remember you asked me about those cats?*

CrochetMom: *Amy says she might be able to help*

ReeseFuller: Thanks, Mom. But I'm not sure we'll have time to arrange anything

CrochetMom: *We'll talk later*

ReeseFuller: I'll call you again tomorrow. I love you, Mom

CrochetMom: *I love you, too*

Chapter Twenty-five

I'm just saying—" Melissa took a guzzle of her beer and put it back on the little table on the back porch of MacAuley Awley's—"if you didn't like him, you wouldn't care about running into him."

"Leave the psychoanalyzing to Pari," I told her. "I don't like him. He's the reason I'm losing the cats. Seeing him would just upset me."

"You keep telling yourself that. Anyway, what are you going to try next?"

"I have no idea. Karen's Stray Cat Whisperer will take them; but his house is filled to the brim with cats. They're everywhere."

"Sounds like a cat paradise to me."

"It's not. Cats need space and solitude. I'm pushing it with three in my little apartment."

"And you can't take them home?"

I shook my head. "Mr. Z would flip. He doesn't even know I have three. You sure you can't take any?"

"Oh, no. No cats."

"What's your excuse?"

She looked at me, closed up her eyes and titled her head.

"I'm sorry," I said. "I didn't mean it to come out that way."

"Damn straight. Remember, Bookish Diva, nobody has

to have an excuse. If we don't want a cat, we don't have to have one."

I nodded. "Sorry."

"Anyway, I have three dogs."

"Really?"

"What?"

"You don't look like a dog person."

"What does a dog person look like?"

I opened my mouth and when nothing popped into my head, I closed it again.

"Well, hello ladies," Reese said.

I turned and he was standing at the back door, giant mug of beer in hand, grinning at me. "Oh, pardon me," he said with a bow. "I mean Book Assassin and friend."

"Ignore him," I muttered to Melissa.

"Mind if we join you?"

He'd brought along one of his friends from the night I danced with him at The Fort. Jim, Jeremy, Jason... something with a J. He was a half head taller than Reese, with short brown hedgehog spiked hair. His collared shirt clung to his chest so tight I could see his nipples and abs—a sight so unnerving it struck me as fake. And he had the goofiest— okay, okay, sweet—smile, crooked and playful; it made you want to talk to him like he was ten.

"This is Jake," Reese said. "You met him last weekend, remember?"

Jake nodded at me and winked at Melissa. "Sure," I said. I barely remembered him.

They took seats at our table before I could say 'go away' and Jake was leaning in to Melissa like he'd already had a few pints. He said something that made her laugh and slap at him. I stared at her, my mouth open. Traitor, I thought. Back stabber. Diva. *Traitorous backstabbing Diva.*

"How are your renovations going?" I asked Reese. I thought the question would sting him, but I forgot he was a cold hearted cat hater.

"We haven't signed on the property yet, so we're still in the planning stage. But we expect to be done and moved in within a couple of months. Nothing major."

I rolled my eyes. "How nice for you."

"We're setting up a booth at Family Fun Fest next week."

"Oh," Melissa said. "Triple F. Have you been before?"

"I have," Jake said. "I told him about it."

"It sounds like a lot of fun."

"What kind of booth will you have?" Curiosity got the better of me, clearly. I could have kicked myself for talking to him like he was a normal human being.

"We'll be announcing our new location, selling and giving away tees."

"And accepting applications for Summer Babes."

"Summer Babes?"

Reese looked at me and smirked. "He's joking."

"They get to work in bikinis."

"That's not entirely true," Reese said.

"That is so sexist," I said to him. Then I blushed, because immediately I was reminded of Lipstick Night at The Fort which reminded me of kissing him. A lot. On the dance floor, at the table upstairs, at the bar, at the door, out by the front gate. I suddenly found myself staring at his lips and shuddered. I looked away.

"They wear beachwear," Reese said. "Not bikinis."

"Bikinis," Jake sang.

"What are you?" I said. "Fourteen?"

"Leave him alone," Melissa scolded.

Traitorous Diva.

Reese pulled his phone from his pocket and glared at it. He scooted his chair from the table. "I have to take this. I'll be back."

"Never mind her," Melissa was saying to Jake. "She's just upset about the cats."

"What cats?"

"Your friend is opening up a store where her strays live. He wants them gone and she's got nowhere to put them."

Jake frowned and nodded. "Yeah, man. That does suck."

"I don't suppose you want a cat or two?" she asked him.

Suddenly Melissa was my Hero Diva. Such a sweet girl. And so cute, too. No wonder Jake couldn't take his eyes off her.

"Me with a cat? Are you off your meds or something?"

"What does that mean?" I said.

He chuckled. "Men who own cats are losers."

Melissa laughed. And she was back to Backstabbing Diva.

"I know a lot of guys who like cats," I said.

"Name one who ain't a friggin' loser, man."

"My grandfather is not a loser."

"An old fart," Jake said. "Same thing. When your *man* days are done, sure, have a cat."

"I bet you drive a truck," I said.

"So what if I do?"

"I'd take a man with a cat over a man who loves his truck any day."

"I bet you would—"

"Sorry about that," Reese said as he sat back at the table. He was pale and looking at his beer as if it had done something awful to him.

"Everything okay, man?" Jake said, his voice light and kind.

"Sure, go on," Reese said. "What were guys yelling about."

"This chick wants me to get a cat."

"Right. The cat thing."

"Your friend thinks cats aren't manly. Is that your problem?"

"What?"

"Is that why you won't let the cats stay at your building? They aren't manly enough for you?"

He shook his head and sighed, like I was an idiot, which, yeah, okay...I was acting like an idiot.

"I told you," he said. "It's nothing personal. My customers are more important than a bunch of cats."

"Not just your customers, man," Jake chimed in. "You. Your livelihood."

"You think people are more important than cats?" I said, glaring at Reese.

His face went dark. "You think they aren't? You think a bunch of stupid stray cats are more important than people?"

I glanced at Melissa for some support, but her eyes were on Jake as she sipped her beer. *Fine.* I could handle this. I turned back to Reese and raised my chin. "Yes. I happen to like cats a lot more than people. You put a cat and person side by side. Who's more important? The cat."

I cringed as I said it. It was, partly, the look of disgust that came over his face, but mostly it was the ridiculousness of my words. Not only could I not manage to speak properly or coherently around Reese Fuller, but the things I said made no sense at all. I knew it was stupid. I mean, I do love cats. And some of them are very important to me. But I suppose I would have to admit, if pressed, that if it came to saving the life of a person, say a child, or Alfred, and a cat...I'd go with the person. But I didn't have to admit that to Reese Fuller and I didn't care how disgusted he was, which was pretty disgusted, judging by the way he took his beer and left the table.

I left too, but not to follow Reese. Jake glared at me. Melissa frowned. And then he whispered something to her and they both giggled. I couldn't stay. As I made my way back through MacAuley Awley's to the front door, I caught sight of Reese at the bar, his hands on the sides of his head as if trying to hold his ears on. It was as if the funny, light-hearted guy I met before was gone—and in his place was a troubled, overworked businessman. I'd have been fine with all that, if I didn't have to suffer through the god-awful urge to wrap my arms around him and tell him everything would be all right.

How had this happened? How had I gone from bookish, to Cal's girl, to clawing my way back into my comfort zone—and quite pleased to be doing it—to falling for the exact opposite of 'let's stay home and read' and managing to screw it all up within two days? It ought to have been little wonder to me that I was confused.

"Get back on track," I mumbled to myself as I crossed Strawbridge Main toward home. That was more like it—walking alone on a dark but busy street talking to myself. Very Old Sophie.

Chapter Twenty-six

Octavia was singing "Party Rock Anthem" out in front of her booth in the mall and I tried to sing along, but my heart wasn't in it. It was Monday afternoon. I'd spent all day Sunday hiding, first at Bookish and then at home. Reese Fuller was everywhere and I wished he would just go away. I'd heard rumors that once his new store opened, he'd be leaving its management to someone else, maybe Jake, and going back to Cocoa Beach where he belonged. I could only hope. I had a copy of *The Hitchhiker's Guide to the Galaxy*, the funniest book I knew of, for Alfred and was making my way toward Noah's Flower Power shop when Octavia started belting out her song.

"Dance with me, honey," she said.

It's so hard to dance when your feet are sad, but I gave it my best shot.

"Hey, Noah," I said when he came out to dance with us. "I talked to my cousin, Carrie."

"Praise Jesus," Octavia said, freezing mid-twerk. "You got a date?"

Noah blushed and we all stopped flapping around for some serious discussion.

"She said I could give you her number." I handed him a sticky note with her number on it.

"She's nice," he said. "Right?"

"She is. She's...well, she's quiet. Shy, sort of. Not very talkative with people she doesn't know very well." I knew this whole set up was a bad idea. I didn't know how I'd let myself get talked into it.

"Is something wrong with her?"

"Oh, no. Nothing like that. She just doesn't go out much."

"Is she one of those people with that disorder?" Octavia said. "What's it called where you can't go out of the house?"

"Is she agoraphobic?" Noah said.

"She's not afraid to go out. She just doesn't. She likes to be at home. A homebody."

"Isn't she pretty?" Octavia said.

"Well, she has a certain charm about her."

"So, she's not attractive," Noah said. "That's all right."

"No, she is attractive. She just...well, she doesn't wear makeup. She's not fancy, you know? She doesn't care about clothes and all that."

"Heavens a mercy, Noah," Octavia said. "She sounds awful."

"She's not," I said. "I swear."

"Then, girl, why are you saying otherwise?"

Noah's eyebrows hit his hairline and they both waited for an explanation.

"I guess I just don't want you to get your hopes up."

"I'm fine," he said. "This wasn't even my idea, remember? I didn't go begging someone to find me Miss Perfect."

I felt better. I supposed. The truth was, I had to admit, I didn't see them together. Noah was, well, dweebish. And Carrie—talk about bookish. I cringed, thinking about the two of them sitting across from each other at Pub's Sports Bar, a plate of cheesy nachos between them, in silence. Noah would be looking around the place, doing his best to avoid her eyes and she'd be staring at his hands, probably wondering if he had his nails done professionally. She's particular like that. It had catastrophe written all over it. My cousin crushed on gods like Gerard Butler and Mark Ruffalo (who wouldn't?). She'd never shown any interest in nerds. She didn't even watch *The Big Bang Theory*. And Noah... Well, I'd seen him in his little flower booth watching *America's Next Top Model* reruns on his little television. And Carrie, bless her, was no top model.

I laid it all out for Alfred behind the mall as he turned *The Hitchhiker's Guide to the Galaxy* over in his hands.

"This science fiction?"

"You've never heard of it?"

He made a humming noise and shook his head, his lips twisted up in something of a smirk. "You say it's funny?"

"Hilarious," I said. "It'll change your whole outlook on life. Now, about Noah and Carrie. Do you think I should tell Noah not to call her?"

"Nope."

"Really?"

He looked up at me, smiling. "Really, really."

"But—"

"Sophie, it ain't your concern. They're two people who have no problem going on a blind date."

"But I'm responsible."

"For what? For adventure. That's all a blind date is. If it works out, you get all the credit. And if it doesn't, they say, 'oh, well, we tried.' No harm, no foul."

"You think?"

"I know."

I didn't believe him. On my way back through the mall I stopped off at Noah's flower booth and told him, one more time, that he didn't have to call her if he didn't want to. Nobody would mind. He seemed to take it as an insult, so I ended up begging him to do it.

"I mean it," I said, whining. "I want you to call her. You have to call her."

"I will. If for no other reason than to gall you."

But he smiled when he said it.

I reported my successful negative interference into the lives of two decent people to the Divas that afternoon when I found Pari, Vanessa, Karen, and Melissa—I mean...Fashion Diva, Glam Diva, Bella Diva, and Pink Diva—sipping iced coffees in front of Brunch on my way back to Bookish. "Diva!" they all called out when they saw me. I laughed, but still felt a tad out of place as I joined them. This clique thing was not part of my repertoire.

Think about it: People like me, and Carrie, and Noah — we like to be alone. It's quiet. And there's a lot going on inside our heads. We can talk to ourselves—and believe me, we do. I know for a fact Carrie can carry on an entire conversation between herselves before answering a simple question like, "Do you want to go to the movies?" And I've seen Noah over there in Flower Power mumbling to himself. We're used to there being one to three people, at most, in a discussion: ourselves, another part of ourselves, and one other person. But with the Divas, sometimes there were, like that day, four of them talking and laughing and tossing off witticisms, quoting popular films, offering tidbits and private jokes—I couldn't keep up. At that point, I could only imagine sitting with all five of them. But it was, in a word, exhilarating.

"You're the contact," Vanessa said. "Carrie will tell you all about it and then you have to get us together for lunch and give us the juicy details."

"I'm not sure Carrie will give me juicy details. She's like me—quiet."

"Right," Melissa said. "And it's those quiet ones you have to watch out for."

My mouth fell open, but I blushed. What could I say? Melissa knew I'd locked lips with Loverboy all over The Fort and in a booth at Pub's.

"What's next for you, then?" Pari asked me.

"What do you mean?"

She shrugged and the other girls were smirking.

"If it's a no-go with Reese..."

I shook my head. "I'm not dating. I mean, I wasn't looking for a man."

"It's been six months," Karen said.

"What?" I was shocked. "Have you guys been...?"

"Been what?"

"Paying attention?"

They laughed.

"Girl," Vanessa said, "we know all the goings on of every girl and guy in lovely Historic Downtown Strawbridge."

"Speaking of," Pari said, digging a few flyers out of her purse. "These showed up in the lobby of the Executive Suites this morning." She set them on the table and I took one.

"Oh, no," I said when I realized what it was.

'Vote Now for the Your Favorite Shops in Downtown Strawbridge!' the flyer read. 'Ballot Boxes available at MacAuley Awley's, Pub's Sports Bar, and The Executive Suites lobby or visit the new Summer Sun Surf and Beachwear Booth at Triple F this Friday!' And, of course the choices for 'Best Antiques Shop' were: Old Geezer's Stuff Antiques, Trudy's Treasures, and—I suppose to make it seem official—Venerable Trinkets.

"I heard it was all Old Geezer's idea," Pari said. "He's fighting Trudy over window messages."

"Did he get the board to okay this?" Karen asked me.

While it bothered me a little that they all looked at me for answers, there was nothing I could do about it. Everyone knew Mr. Cornell was my grandfather's friend and he spent a lot of time in Bookish. If anyone knew about this, it would be me...unfortunately.

"He said he was going to take the matter to them, but I

didn't know what became of it."

"Looks like this did," Melissa said.

"He's got votes for jewelry shops, clothes shops, restaurants, bars..." Karen said.

"Is Café Flamingo there?" Melissa grabbed a flyer and scanned it. "Yep."

"Looks to be only downtown proper," Pari said. "Some of the outliers won't be happy."

"It's really all about him and Trudy," I said. "Everybody probably knows that."

"So, who are we voting for?" Melissa said.

"Are you actually going to do it?"

"Why not? He wants to know our favorite antique shop, I don't see why we shouldn't tell him."

"The real question is," Pari said to me, "who are *you* going to vote for?"

"I'll never tell."

Melissa winked at me. "You've got Bookish locked in."

"It's silly to include favorite bookshop when there's only one."

"If this Carrie Noah thing is a success," Vanessa said, "we should see if we can't get Mr. Cornell and Trudy back together. They went out once or twice, didn't they?"

"They let antiques come between them," I said.

"Which makes no sense at all," Pari said. "Antiques should bring them together, not tear them apart."

"It's business," Melissa said. "Trudy needs a man outside antiques."

"Mr. Booker, maybe," Vanessa said.

I laughed. "I don't think so. Cigars are a hard sell to a non-smoker."

"Your grandfather, then," Pari said. "Is he looking?"

"He couldn't," I said. "Mr. Cornell wouldn't be able to forgive him."

"Well, then," Melissa said, "we're going to have to focus

on the Cornell Trudy angle."

"And after that, we'll work on the Reese Sophie problem."

"No, no, no. I'm Bookish Diva, remember? You all said so. Bookish Diva spends most of her time in the bookstore and the rest with her nose in a book. It's my thing. You can't change it."

"So, you'll have to be fixed up with another bookish sort."

"Yes, absolutely," I said. "And preferably one who loves cats."

"Must read," Pari said, "with cats."

"No," Melissa said. "Crazy cat lady seeks bookish man—"

"Not afraid to scoop!" Vanessa said.

I laughed so hard I had a cramp for three hours. But don't think I didn't seriously consider that ad.

Chapter Twenty-seven

CrochetMom: *Reese! Thank you so much*

CrochetMom: *Reese, sweetie, are you there?*

ReeseFuller: Here. What's up?

CrochetMom: *Amy brought the mail in. I got the photos*

CrochetMom: *They're beautiful! Amy says she'll go out today and get frames*

ReeseFuller: I had Jake take them for me. He's really good, isn't he? You remember him?

CrochetMom: *I do. They're just perfect. The beach at dawn! And then at dusk*

CrochetMom: *And the lagoon! I don't remember it being so beautiful*

ReeseFuller: It's hard to appreciate the sights when you're here every day

CrochetMom: *Please thank Jake!*

ReeseFuller: I will

CrochetMom: *Our house looks lonely*

ReeseFuller: I have to agree

CrochetMom: *Why don't you take it?*

ReeseFuller: I might

CrochetMom: *Really?*

ReeseFuller: I might hand the Cocoa Beach store over to Jake and stay here in Strawbridge

CrochetMom: *Ah. Sophie?*

ReeseFuller: No. It's just...

CrochetMom: *?*

ReeseFuller: It's like you said. The house is lonely

CrochetMom: *I think it's Sophie*

ReeseFuller: To be honest, Mom

CrochetMom: *Uh oh*

ReeseFuller: I'm not sure Sophie likes me all that much

CrochetMom: *Nonsense. I thought you said she was smart*

ReeseFuller: :)

CrochetMom: *If you really like her...*

ReeseFuller: I do

CrochetMom: *Then don't give up. Just pester her until she realizes how much she loves you*

CrochetMom: *I mean "likes" you. Sorry. No pressure*

ReeseFuller: Really, Mom. We haven't known each other that long :)

CrochetMom: *Anyway, it worked for your father*

ReeseFuller: LOL

ReeseFuller: Did you tell dad about our conversation yesterday?

CrochetMom: *Did you change your mind? Do you want me to talk to him?*

ReeseFuller: No. I'm wondering if I should have even told you he called me

CrochetMom: *Reese...you are my son and when you are upset, I will be here for you*

ReeseFuller: But I don't want to make things worse for you so if you want to tell him you know about him calling me, you can tell him

CrochetMom: *You think it will help? You think he'll stop doing it? Stop obsessing? Stop bothering you?*

ReeseFuller: No

CrochetMom: *You have a lot to deal with because of me. You and Amy both. All of us*

ReeseFuller: ...

CrochetMom: *We're not the only family in the world going through tough times*

ReeseFuller: Did you know you're amazing? I love you, Mom.

CrochetMom: *Love you too, sweetie*

Chapter Twenty-eight

I got three calls from The Stray Cat Whisperer that week. The first time, he was checking to see if I was still thinking of bringing the cats to his house and I said I was. The second time he told me he might have another place to put them and it turned out it was a feral colony way down south. *No way.* My darlings aren't feral, I told him. The third time he told me he'd just acquired four kittens and at some point, he would be too full to take mine in, so I'd better decide. I didn't laugh out loud so he didn't hear me, but it was pretty funny. I had the feeling Mr. Wells never turned a cat away.

"You think we should call that show?" Hugh said after I ended the last call that Friday afternoon.

It had been several days since I'd seen Reese and I felt things were getting back to normal, except for the cat issue. But I reminded myself many times that my original intent had been to find them homes. Nothing had changed, I'd gotten lazy, that was all. And now I was simply refocused on the problem, thanks to Reese. The 'thanks to Reese' always came out as something of a growl.

"The animal hoarding show?"

"That's the one. He's a great candidate."

"That would be cruel." But I was smiling.

"Are you sitting at the Bookish booth tonight?"

"Yep. You want to join me again?"

"I'll come to give you a break," he said.

Triple F, or Family Fun Fest, was put on every fourth Friday evening downtown. The main street was blocked off from Morgan's Office Supply to the railroad tracks. Booths were set up by both locals and shop owners, selling merchandise, artwork, jewelry, or providing services like face painting and henna. Live music from local bands or djs filled the air. Food booths offered fair foods like cotton candy, corn dogs, and waffle cones. Kids had bounce houses and sometimes a family from Grant would bring ponies and lay down a thick layer of hay for them to walk on as they gave rides. Often ramps were set up in one corner and skateboarders showed off their talents. It was, for me, the time I sort of absorbed that downtown community feeling, a feeling of belonging, being a part of something bigger than Bookish and my apartment. And I liked that I could soak up that feeling while tucked away behind a table filled with books.

Gramps was a big fan of the event. "People should remember to read," he liked to say. So we always had a booth offering our cheapest books. This Friday, I'd decided to put up a poster with pictures of my darlings on it. 'Free To Good Home' it read at the top. Gramps said I ought to offer twenty bucks to anyone who would take a cat. Don't think I didn't consider it. Naturally, when I pulled our wheeled cart full of books down the street to our booth at five o'clock Friday, I discovered the Summer Sun Surf and Beachwear booth was next to the Bookish booth. My face froze and my teeth clenched, as I shook my head. I just knew Reese Fuller did it on purpose. He'd gone to the board to sign up for a booth and asked if he couldn't have the spot next to Bookish so he could remind that girl who tried to kill him with hardcovers that her cats were meaningless compared to his customers' parking needs. He was tormenting me and that only made me dislike him all the more. What sort of person does that? First he threatens my cats, laughs about it, calls me crazy, and now follows me around poking fun at me about it. The man was deranged, clearly. I was determined to not let him get the best of me (and to stop sucking in a breath whenever I caught sight of him).

(And maybe also to stop wanting to touch his hair again.)

(And there was that hugging thing, needed to stop wanting to comfort him.)

He showed up a few minutes after I did with a rolling cart piled with tees, flops, and shades. He was wearing colorful bathing shorts and a Summer Sun tee; I could smell his coconut suntan lotion from ten feet away. I got woozy over it, mostly because it reminded me of the chocolate coconut fudge at ChocShop and I'd struggled those past few days to keep myself from binging. Our booths faced south, located across from Sweet Suite, and I noticed one of the Rollings sisters standing inside peering out the front window at him. That's right, I wanted to shout, he's gorgeous. But he's an animal abuser!

"You should put out some beach reads," he said.

I blushed. I was acting like I was in seventh grade. I sucked in a grown-up breath and turned to him. His green eyes were laughing at me, as usual. His hair, wild on his head, made him look like he'd come from the beach. He probably styled it that way on purpose—part of the job. As much as I tried to frown, I smiled instead.

"We could work together," he said.

I nodded. "I usually bring that sort of book. We don't get many poetry or history readers on Triple F."

"It's my first time—I guess you know that. I don't really know what to expect."

"Well—" I walked to the edge of my booth, to where he was standing—"there will be drinking. It's the only time public drinking is allowed downtown."

"So...revelry. Ever get out of hand?"

"Sometimes. But Officer Palmer has backup."

He flashed another smile and leaned in a bit. "I'm glad you're talking to me."

"Why wouldn't I?"

"I guess I thought you were mad at me."

"I am."

He nodded, large. "But you're the polite sort."

"That's right."

"Well, I appreciate it." He softened and it surprised me.

A band started up, rock from the sound of it. Drums and cymbals and electric guitar. The event had begun. I spent most of the night trying to avoid Reese, an impossibility.

An introvert's guide to Triple F

1. Get your booth set up early so you can hide behind the table

2. Smile. Smile. Smile until your mouth hurts.

3. Call out to customers—*right*. No. That's not going to happen. Just keep smiling and nodding and keep the tears at bay. It only lasts a few hours and you have to do it because Gramps is getting too old to stay out past sundown and you can't rope Hugh into doing it; he's got a life outside his Bookish habit, you know.

4. When customers ask you if you'll take less for that book, say yes. It's always easier to make up the difference than say no. Gramps can't tell.

5. When a kid takes a book and walks off with it, say nothing. It's okay. He's reading.

6. When the unicyclist rolls around, clap with everyone

else and smile.

7. When the clown dances by, hide.

8. When the magician walks to your booth, hide.

9. Start packing up early

10. Cry when you get home. It's the exhaustion of being in a crowd for so long, that's all. Not that the absorption of community spirit is poison or anything...well, maybe a little.

You might wonder how a bookish girl like me manages Disney World. Not very well, to be honest. It's better than Triple F, in that I'm not on display. No one's asking me questions and looking at stuff I'm responsible for. But the crowd is tough and I make it about five hours before I have to head home. Coincidentally, Triple F lasts about five hours and the only difference is the crying.

Reese Fuller's guide to Triple F

1. Set up whenever you please, because talking to people while you lay out your shirts and stuff is fun. "Oh, wait, hang on, I got just the thing for you...just...let...me...find—here, what did I tell ya? You'll look fabulous in it." *Sheesh.* He's like a male Diva. What is that? A Divo?

2. Laugh, yell out to people, talk, talk, talk, make faces at kids, smile. I was exhausted watching him...I mean, *ignoring* him.

3. Call out to customers. "You look like you could use a Summer Sun tee!" "Shades, shades, get your shades here!" Seriously. Is this what they teach at Cocoa Beach Business School?

4. When customers try to bargain you down on price, smile your dazzling smile and tell them about all the fab qualities they're overlooking. "I couldn't. Check out that supreme printing technique, the lettering, the style. This is superb merchandise, if I do say so myself." And they buy it!

5. When a kid takes some flops off the table and tries them on, lean way over, admire them on her feet and tell her she really must have her mom buy those for her. Only twenty bucks!

6. When the unicyclist rolls around, beg to have a turn. Take a turn. Fall a lot. Get applause.

7. When the clown dances by, make fun of the bookish girl in the booth next to you by cowering with her and shrieking, "Clown! My god, the horror!"

8. When the magician walks up to your booth, pull a quarter of *his* ear.

9. Stay to the bitter end—we assume.

10. Probably spend the rest of the night at The Fort entertaining all the pretty girls who filled out applications for employment at your new surf shop.

Honestly, looking at it all laid out like that makes me think Reese was the reason I went home that night and cried in the shower. When he called the next morning, I almost cried before answering the phone.

Chapter Twenty-nine

I was in bed when my phone started playing out "Tara's Theme." I rolled over and grabbed it.

"Hey," he said. "Did I wake you?"

"No." That was all I could say. I *wanted* to say, why are you calling? Did you have a good time last night? You seemed like you had a great time. I think you're going to fit in really well, here in Historic Downtown Strawbridge. In fact, I think you livened up the place. I think you could become a fixture here and make everyone like you, maybe love you. Which reminds me of another guy who took downtown by storm, so to speak. Things didn't work out so well with that guy. But I was dating him and I'm not dating you, so I guess I shouldn't care.

"I found a book in my stuff," he said.

So that was why he called. I felt a little bit let down and I hated myself for it. But at times like that, I'd decided I would just say over and over again to myself: he's a cat hater, a cat hater, a damnable cat hater.

"You want me to bring it to the store?"

"Sure, that would be okay."

"When are you going in?"

"I usually get in around ten. Gramps opens all the time." Why was I talking to him like that? I slapped myself on the head and sat up in bed.

"Okay, I'll be there before lunch."

"Thanks?" I was confused. But he hung up before I could ask him anything else.

My campaign to save the cats at Triple F was unsuccessful, to say the least. Not one person took any interest in my poster. And, being the bookish type, I didn't hawk cats to them like a carnival barker. I should have asked Reese to do it, seeing as he's so good at it. The irony would have been poignant. Speaking of Hombre Caliente, he gave out so many applications for employment I got the feeling most of the women taking them just wanted an excuse to see him again. He also did a brisk business in taking ballots for the best shops downtown.

When I got into Bookish later that morning, Mr. Cornell was inside the door, a bunch of ballots in his hand.

"Did you vote, yet?" he asked me.

I mumbled an excuse.

"Well, go on." He handed me a ballot. "You too," he told Hugh who'd come out of hiding from the science fiction section.

"Later," I said, making my way to the back room where I could deposit my purse and cat supplies.

"Why wait?" he called after me.

"I'm not doing it with you around," I said.

I heard him talking the whole time I was gone. Why would I need privacy? I was going to vote for Geezer's, right? Of course I was. There was no point in hiding it from him. Oh, sure, there was the integrity of the blind voting process. But the ballots weren't going to him; they were going to the Historic Downtown Business Owners Management Board.

"It doesn't matter," I said, once back up front with him and Gramps. "I wouldn't feel right marking a ballot in front of you."

"No problem. Just promise me you'll do it before the

deadline."

"Mr. Cornell," I said with a sigh, "why are you doing this?"

His face pinched up and he shook his head. "You know why. We can't let that woman get away with false advertising. There are principles to abide by. What kind of world do you want to live in? To do business in?"

"I'm not sure everyone is as passionate about this as you are."

"Well, they should be."

Mr. Cornell spent the morning coming and going, from his store to ours, following Gramps around discussing the antiques business, truth in advertising, and *Pinot noir* for some reason. When the bell over our door jangled at eleven-thirty, I expected to hear his voice calling out, "...and one other thing." Instead, there was silence—the peopled silence of customers in the store.

I made my way up to the cashwrap to make sure no one needed any help, only to find Reese Fuller standing there, spinning the rack of bookmarks. He was clean-shaven, his dark brows furrowed as he stopped the rack, pulled off a tasseled bookmark and read the quote; his face broke into a smile.

"Hey," he said when he saw me. He handed me a worn, fat, glossy mass market by Sidney Sheldon—the ultimate beach read. "I don't know how it got in my stuff."

It was probably one of the people looking at the books in my booth, suddenly enthralled by what was going on next door. They carried the book over to see what Reese was up to and just...left it there—reading completely forgotten in favor of a little attention from GLE.

"These things happen," I said.

The doorbell jingled.

"And another thing," Mr. Cornell said. "Walt, where are you?"

"Hey, Mr. Cornell," Reese said. They shook hands. "I turned in the ballots this morning."

"How'd we do?"

"I didn't look at them."

"Of course not. I meant how many."

"A lot."

Mr. Cornell slapped Reese on the back as a thank you and disappeared into the store in search of Gramps.

"I, uh," Reese said, turning to me. "I guess I'll see you around."

"Sure," I said.

After Reese left the store, Hugh sidled up to me. "So, that's it?" he said. "You're really not going to go out with him again?"

"I'm really not."

"So, we're still on for Nerd Fest?"

"Are you kidding? I wouldn't miss it."

"Okay. So, next Saturday morning. I'll meet you here?"

I nodded. I got the feeling he wanted to say something else, so I gave him an encouraging smile.

"It's okay with your grandfather, right? If you take the day off?"

"Of course."

He took in a breath and pulled his lips in, nodded. "Okay then." And he turned and left the store. It was odd, if you asked me.

That evening, before I left work, I found Gramps at the cashwrap, sitting in a metal folding chair, reading from *The Complete Works of Oscar Wilde*. He put the book down and looked at me over his reading glasses. "It's not a good idea, Sophie, my dear."

"What isn't?"

"Going out with Hugh."

"It's not a date. It's a nerd festival."

"You'll only break his heart."

"How do you—I will not."

He shook his head again and went back to reading.

On my way home, I got a call from Carrie and I have to say, I welcomed it. There was too much speculation all over downtown about Reese and me. I could see it behind everyone's smiles, underneath all the hellos and how are yous. I needed time for it all to die down. What had I been thinking, anyway, making out with him in public like that? I should have known it would set the whole street ablaze. It's the Historic Downtown Strawbridge motto: We're In Your Business! Carrie allowed me to ignore them all.

"Well," she said, "he called me and asked me out. We're set for Friday night."

"I hope this wasn't a bad idea."

"It's too late for you to say stuff like that. You fixed us up, it's all on you. For better or worse."

"Well, did he at least sound...confident, over the phone?"

"He sounded squeaky."

"That's just great."

"It's not like I've never gone out with a dweeb before. Anyway, it sounded more like he was afraid."

"Afraid of what?"

"Of this whole thing. I get the feeling neither one of us was keen on being fixed up."

"That's true enough, I suppose. It was the Divas' idea, really."

"Divas? You mean the girls who always lunch downtown?"

"Mm hmm."

"I thought you didn't like them. You said they were stuck up."

"Did I? Well, I've been...sort of hanging out with them. And they're nicer than I expected."

"Funny how people work, isn't it? Maybe this Noah guy will be better than I expect."

165

"Don't get your hopes up."

She sighed. "I can't believe you fixed me up with a guy you can't even be excited about."

"I told you, it wasn't my idea."

"Sure it wasn't."

"I'm sorry. It's the worst thing I've ever done to you. I'll make it up to you, I promise."

"I'll make sure you do."

When the call ended, I was behind the abandoned building—the soon to be Summer Sun Surf and Beachwear. The cats meowed and Weesie rubbed up against my legs. I think they all missed Sugar and Critter. I certainly did. But the Trenthams would take good care of them.

"It's for the best," I told Weesie. "Everything will work out. I promise." Even I could tell I didn't believe it.

Chapter Thirty

ReeseFuller: Mom, you there?

CrochetMom: *Yep*

ReeseFuller: You sounded good on the phone earlier

CrochetMom: *I feel good*

ReeseFuller: I just found out. They have a swing night here at a dance club called Tracks

CrochetMom: *No! Are you going?*

ReeseFuller: Jake wants to. So, yeah

CrochetMom: *Jake? What about Sophie?*

ReeseFuller: I'm working on it

CrochetMom: *Hmm. Wouldn't working on it mean asking her to go to the swing dance?*

ReeseFuller: Trust me. She'd say no at this point

CrochetMom: *What's wrong with her?*

ReeseFuller: Nothing is wrong with her

CrochetMom: *Did you...*

ReeseFuller: I didn't do anything

CrochetMom: *Well, you must have done something*

ReeseFuller: I'd really rather not talk about it

CrochetMom: *Of course. I didn't mean to pry. But you'll have to tell me all about the swing dance tomorrow*

ReeseFuller: I will. You remember the mother son dance?

CrochetMom: *How could I forget? You were the best dancer in the entire sixth grade*

ReeseFuller: And I got beat up the next Monday at school for showing up all the other guys in front of their moms

CrochetMom: *You never told me that. I thought it was just that one time in high school*

ReeseFuller: I was joking. Okay, poor taste. But that was when I started getting picked on

CrochetMom: *Is that why you never asked me on another date?*

ReeseFuller: Heck no. I wouldn't let any dumb kids keep me from my best girl

ReeseFuller: It was that other guy you're in love with

CrochetMom: *Ah, yes. I have to admit, he is more my type*

ReeseFuller: More your age

CrochetMom: :)

CrochetMom: *But wouldn't it be lovely if Sophie was there and you danced her off her feet?*

ReeseFuller: Mom... <said with that little kid whine>

CrochetMom: *LOL Backing off*

ReeseFuller: I'll call you and tell you all about it

CrochetMom: *Or text me. I like this texting. Nobody's listening*

ReeseFuller: I love you, Mom

CrochetMom: *I love you, too*

ReeseFuller: I'm coming up to see you again soon

CrochetMom: *I know*

Chapter Thirty-one

"Come on, come on," Melissa begged me. She was standing in the small living room of my apartment, nestling Chloe—much to my surprise—in her arms. She'd shown up ten minutes before, and only an hour after calling, to drag me out for more Historic Downtown nightlife.

"I'm hurrying." I was on the sofa, bent over, buckling my black-and-white Mary Janes.

"Wait, what?" she said. "You're not wearing those, are you?"

I should back up and give you the gist: I'd finished feeding the darlings and was nearly to Creek Overlook Apartments when Melissa called, frantic. "You have to come with me to Tracks. You have to." And I said, "Why?" And she rattled off this frenzied story about Jake and how she'd fallen madly in love with him—to which, I assure you, I interjected with, "You've only just met the man!"

"It's crazy, I admit," she said. "But I'm telling you he's all I can think about. And he's going to be at Tracks tonight. I can't go by myself."

I asked her how she knew he'd be there and she claimed Steve, the owner of Pub's Sports Bar, overheard him talking about Saturday Night Swing, saying he was going. And I said, "Seriously? I can't see Jake doing the Lindy Hop." She said, "What's that?" And I told her it was dancing from, like, the 1940s and she said, "Wha?" So I asked her if she hadn't seen that movie, years ago, with Brendan Fraser and Alicia Silverstone. I had to explain the plot of the film to her and she finally said, "Oh, yeah, and he does that dance and waves his finger in the air." Then we were off on a bit of a tangent about the right sort of physical composition a guy who does the Lindy ought to have, and did Jack have it.

Anyway, Steve told Madaline, the realtor, for some reason, maybe because he too didn't think Jake was the swing type. And Madaline told Officer Palmer, because he always goes. Talk about a man with the wrong physique for swing—and yet, he was a regular. Officer Palmer then told Karen, because he tells Karen everything and she mentioned it to Melissa.

"Why would anyone gossip about Jake?" I asked her. "Nobody even knows who Jake is. Do they?"

"I don't know and I don't care," she said. "All I know is no one will go with me and I can't go by myself. It'll look bad."

"I wasn't your first choice, then."

"Of course not. He's Reese's friend—"

"Reese is going?"

"No. I just didn't think you'd want to be reminded."

"But I don't have anything to wear."

"Of course you do. You must."

"I must not. Really, Melissa. I've got nothing. I don't go out. I don't have going-out clothes. I could wear jeans and a tee, I suppose."

"Absolutely not. You have to wear a dress. A dancing dress."

"I only have the one I wore to The Fort."

And she said, "Oh, please, please, please."

So, I turned around, walked back to Fiona's, and bought a gorgeous Forties-style, white dress with black polka dots, perfect for swing, with little puff sleeves and a sweetheart

170

neckline. It even had a thin black belt at the waist with a bow. I splurged. Royally. I still had some old-fashioned white socks with lace at the hem from my days of lessons with Gramps. I put a black barrette, with a bow on it, in my hair and thought I looked fabulous, if I didn't say so myself.

"They're dancing shoes," I told Melissa.

"Could you be any slower?"

"You don't want to rush in there and make it look like you're after him. Remember your rules?"

"I remember, I remember, but..."

"But what?"

"What if some other girl gets to him first?"

I laughed; I couldn't help it. We walked to Mangrove, past the park and the cats, and along the storefronts—the art league and Trudy's—until it met Strawbridge Main, and headed for the tracks.

"So, you swing, then?" I said.

"What? No. I'm strictly a *mano y mano* kind of girl. One man one woman. I mean, I'm not homophobic, so one man one man and vice versa is fine, too."

I shook my head with my mouth open trying to figure that out. "I mean, do you Lindy Hop?"

"Is that what they're calling it these days?" She stopped walking and glared at me. "Where are you going with all this, anyway?"

"Melissa," I said. "I don't know what you're talking about."

"Yeah, well, pot kettle and all that."

"I'm asking if you're going to dance tonight."

Her face pinched itself up for a second and then opened into a smile. "Oh, dance. Swing, Lindy Hop. Right, you mentioned that before. Heavens, no." She started walking again and we crossed the tracks and turned toward Tracks Night Life—the swankiest restaurant, bar, and dance club in town.

"What if he asks you?" I said.

"You said he didn't have the body for it."

"I was just saying... Anyway, he might ask you."

"Well...what do I do if he does? Do you...swing?"

"It's not that hard. Here—"

We stopped again and I did a little basic Lindy circle with a swivel step on the out-swing. "Step, step, triple step, walk, walk, triple step," I said and she started trying to follow.

"Slow down."

"And here's the swivel: point ball change, point ball change, point ball change, point ball change."

We danced for a while in the parking lot until we were breathless and sweaty.

"How did you learn that?"

"Gramps took me to lessons. You're going to see a lot of the older set tonight, I bet."

"So you're going to dance?"

"Well, I'm prepared anyway. How do you know Jake won't be there with a date?"

"I just know."

"How?"

"Steve said so."

"How would Steve know?"

"Why are you asking so many questions?"

When we reached the door of the bar, it hit me. She was pulling it open and I said, "He's here, isn't he?"

And she had the gall to wink at me, shove me inside and say, "Yep."

I'd been to Tracks before, long before, with Gramps, but it looked different somehow. It might have been the dress I was wearing, and the way a few heads turned when Melissa and I walked in. I blushed and part of me wanted to turn around and go back home.

"Why didn't you just tell me," I whined.

I followed her through the throng of people, my ears

172

adjusting to the noise and the dark and the chill of air conditioning. Big Band music already played somewhere in the back, in another room. Live music, from what I could tell.

"I knew you wouldn't come if I did," she said.

We took a small table near the bar and a waiter was at our side instantly reading off a list of 1940s drinks on special. Melissa ordered a Manhattan and I went for a daiquiri.

"You're right," I said. "I wouldn't have come. I don't particularly want to see him."

"He's opening up a store on the path you walk to and from work every day. Face it: you're going to be seeing a lot of Reese Fuller. You might as well get used to it."

I sighed and looked around at all the beautifully dressed people. I had this strange thought—that this was going on once a month for years. It was the same with Poetry Night at Stogies and Lipstick Night at The Fort. Every night, especially every weekend, I was at my apartment, watching television, eating macaroni and cheese, or pizza, watching a movie with the cats. And all the while, these people were out—dressed up, made up, having a wonderful time. I had it for a while, with Cal. Maybe I thought all the fun resided in the 'with Cal' part and that's why I didn't want to do it anymore. But, Melissa was right, of course. There was life outside of my apartment, and there was life after Cal; I couldn't stop living because I might run into Reese Fuller. Who was Reese Fuller anyway? I'd known him, what, two weeks, if that. The real question was...was I going to start living again at all? Or was I going to go back to pre-Cal days, back to the comfort of my own company? Old Sophie. The truth was—I liked my own company and I wasn't sure I wanted to be part of the 'out' crowd.

Melissa leaned over and grabbed my arm. "There he is."

I turned to look for Jake, but met the green, laughing eyes of Reese Fuller instead.

Chapter Thirty-two

When Reese saw me sitting at the table with Melissa, he smiled, offered a bit of a wave, and turned away. Melissa made a sad gasping sort of sound.

"I told you," I said. "It's done. Now, where's Jake? He's why we're here, right?" I fought to conceal the bit of hurt that came with Reese's snub and I think I managed it with a healthy dose of anger. Anger is glorious at making hurts go away...temporarily, at least.

Melissa was giddy and not following the rules at all; she twisted this way and that in her seat, looking for Jake. It made sense; Melissa was what I liked to call a teacher. She could tell *me* how to behave to lure a man, but those who can't do, teach.

"What happened to being aloof and all that?" I said, teasing her. "About looking up at him through your eyelashes and blushing on command?"

"This is completely different."

"How so?"

"I told you, I'm in love."

Even she laughed at that. I told her we should check out the dance room and she said if Jake was in there dancing she didn't know what she would do; she'd have to reevaluate their entire relationship. And I said, "What relationship?" So we gave up our table and took our drinks with us.

The back of the house was consumed by an enormous, rectangular dance floor with some seating on either side and a standing room only bar, along the walls all the way around, where we could set our drinks. The band was staged at the back, playing "String of Pearls." There were a dozen couples on the floor warming up and I watched, smiling. Mostly gray heads. I wasn't sure when Jake had shown up but he and Melissa disappeared soon after. When "Sing, Sing, Sing" started, none other than Officer Palmer—out of uniform and decked out in polished black trousers and jacket, a white shirt and white spats on his shoes—took my hand and led me out onto the floor. I tried to beg off, but he said, "No, no. I saw you and your grandfather a few years ago at the dance off. I know you can swing."

Sure, I can dance a little. But Officer Palmer was a pro—I saw *him* at the dance off, too. I did my best to slow him down. Some side-by-side Charleston into the Lindy Circle, a little swivel stepping on the out-swing; he even managed a few simple spins. I was holding my own up until the fighting started. It was a dance fight, so it's not like anyone drew blood. I first noticed it when the song ended and the band went into a little ditty I didn't recognize. Officer Palmer kept looking at one of the couples in the crowd and it seemed that with every glance, he got more elaborate with the spins. At one point, he got me into a pretzel spin. Luckily, some of my lessons were coming back to me. After that, the band went straight to "In the Mood" and the dance floor thinned out noticeably. I figured a couple was really good and everybody was stopping to watch. It was known to happen. I was slowing down to follow everyone else off the floor, when Officer Palmer pulled me into a lift and swung me around. So much for quitting.

Gramps wanted me to take lessons with him about six weeks after Grandma died a few years ago. Most of the family was against it; they thought he was in denial or something—thought he'd lost his marbles and refused to grieve properly. As it turned out, he told me, he and Grandma had promised each other they'd take the lessons, but before they could sign up, she was hit by a car as they both crossed U.S. 1 to see dolphins in the lagoon. Her scarf, he said, had blown off and she turned to catch it.

"Her hand left mine and that was the last touch...I can still feel her fingertips," he said.

And so, I agreed to take the lessons and we danced at The Track, on three Saturday Swing Nights, and then did the Strawbridge Dance Off at the mall. It was supposed to be Grandma; but Gramps said I was the next best thing and she'd be proud.

As good as those lessons were, and as much as I enjoyed the style, I didn't think I was good enough for a dance off. But there I was, one of two couples duking it out for applause. I didn't have time to blush, or to tell Officer Palmer I wasn't up to it. We were just *doing it*. Okay, I thought, go for it. I followed him the best I could, let him spin me, throw me back and twirl me and then we settled into a bit of basic triple step while the other couple did whatever they had in mind.

That's when I realized it was Reese Fuller, lifting Pat Willard—owner of Namaste and none other—off the ground and swinging her across his body to the left and then to the right and then slinging her—like a four year old with a bowling ball—onto the floor between his legs. She slid behind him, turning over onto her belly; he reached down, pulled her up by the armpits, and they hopped right back into the Lindy.

"West Coast!" Officer Palmer yelled and started throwing me around.

That's when it got really weird. The crowd was crazy wild, mostly for Pat Willard I'm sure. The woman, her pixie cut of salt-and-pepper hair stiff and spiked, spurred them with flips of her head and the most excellent pecking I've ever seen. She and Reese bobbled their heads on their necks to the left and right of each other and then bucked their butts out and back into a, to be honest, rather inappropriate bump and grind. With each silly move Reese and Pat Willard pulled off, Officer Palmer's lips thinned more and he gathered me into spins I didn't even know I could do. "Frog jumps" he yelled and on every out-swing we were up in the air. I was thinking the whole time *please don't make me Shake the Change. Please, please, anything but that.* Suddenly it was "Zoot Suit Riot" and somehow, we'd switched partners. Officer Palmer was doing the Lindy with Pat Willard and Reese had hold of me. It was all so fast, I didn't even know how it happened. But I should have seen it coming.

The Greatest Love Story Ever Told in Downtown Strawbridge

The fact was, Officer Palmer was in love with Pat Willard. Everybody knew it, except for Pat Willard. Pat owned Namaste and Namaste was, well, the one store in Historic Downtown Strawbridge that actually drew controversy when it opened. There were accusations running about in the rumor mill that Pat was a gypsy, or a witch, or an atheist. Because, nobody normal would own a store like *that.* I suppose the fine folk of Strawbridge in the late Eighties didn't yet realize there was a thriving community of spiritualists, liberals—*egad!*—and Universalists in their midst ...until Pat Willard dared to open a shop and sell funky trinkets, like crystals dangling from chains, incense burners, hippie skirts, and bundles of sage for burning to ward off evil spirits.

And when they saw her, well, let's just say their mouths

opened and from what I hear, didn't close for weeks. Pat Willard looked nothing like a witch.* She was petite, trim, with a shock of dark hair and dark, but bright, eyes. She smiled all the time and laughed like a lady, not a witch—however witches laugh, don't ask me. She dressed conservatively, in suits and closed-toed shoes. She drank wine, for heaven's sake. Over time, the curmudgeons had to admit she was not a witch and her store would not turn Historic Downtown Strawbridge into a den of licentiousness. And, over time, Pat Willard let her inner hippie out more and more.

I'm told she was twenty-two when she opened her shop. Officer Palmer came along seven years ago and from the start, spent a lot of time hovering around Namaste. Suffice it to say, if you parked in front of Namaste, you got extra attention and had better not be a minute over your two-hour allotment. Need to cross the street near Namaste? Get thee to a crosswalk or suffer the wrath of the anti-jaywalker! Officer Palmer had what many called an unhealthy interest in incense—there were rumors he was somehow using it to entrap drug dealers. But it became clear early on that he was just mooning. That's what the Old Geezer and Gramps called it, anyway. This, in itself, caused quite a little stir. Officer Palmer was clearly a good ten years Pat's junior. That's why, most of us surmised, she didn't have a clue the man was puddles in her presence. It was probably inconceivable to her.

So, I suppose when Officer Palmer saw Pat Willard doing the Lindy Hop with someone very much younger than herself, he got worked up into a snit of dancing jealousy. Result: dance off. Officer Palmer had finally made a move.

"Are you wearing underwear?" Reese said as he pulled me into the turn.

My response was little more than a horrified cheer.

"Let's do this!"

He started with spins, then said, "flail" and tossed me up, turned me out, letting me fall backward against his hip, up again, turning me to face him, me straddling his leg on my fall, and up once more—way up into the first flail, my feet reaching for the ceiling. Back down, straddling his leg. "Again," he said and I was flying. Absorbing another fall, he said, "One more."

The house roared with cheers and suddenly we were back to the Lindy Circle. "Sailor kicks," he said and I let him lead me into the duck and we kicked out around the circle and back into the Lindy. "Rag doll," he said and swung me out and back to his chest, and all the way across the floor we did the rag, and the crowd applauded. He called the moves and I did my best to remember them. I messed up a few times, but he went with it.

When the music stopped, the band applauded the four of us and announced a break. I was breathing heavy and wet with sweat—exhilarated.

"Thank you," Reese said.

I nodded. "It was a pleasure." That was what Gramps always said.

Pat Willard put an arm around me and I tried to listen to her as I watched Reese disappear into the crowd that had invaded the dance floor, all working on their steps for the next set. She was laughing and telling me she'd never danced so hard in all her life.

"If I'd known Buddy Palmer could twist a foot like that I'd have dragged myself here long ago."

Officer Palmer winked at me. "It's hard to stay angry when you're dancing, isn't it?"

And I thought, what is that supposed to mean?

*What does a witch look like, anyway? I once made the mistake of telling Mrs. Albertson, the barber's wife, that witches, or Wiccans to be more modern, looked like everybody else. She didn't come out of the barbershop for weeks because I'd scared her silly. She'd begun to suspect everyone of being a witch! It took Mr. Booker to get her out. He told her that I didn't know what I was talking about. Everybody knows, he said, all witches have one big, hairy wart on the very tips of their noses. This worked...until the day poor Rita Faulk went to the barbershop with her five boys for their 'return to school' haircuts. Let's just say...the lawsuit is ongoing.

Chapter Thirty-three

ReeseFuller: Well, she can dance

CrochetMom: *Hey, sweetie. You mean, your girl?*

ReeseFuller: She's not my girl. But yes

CrochetMom: *Did you dance with her?*

ReeseFuller: I did. But only one set

CrochetMom: *So you had a good night?*

ReeseFuller: Not with Sophie

CrochetMom: *Why not?*

ReeseFuller: I was there with Jake

CrochetMom: *Jake? He was your date for the evening?*

ReeseFuller: LOL. No, but...

CrochetMom: *So you could dance with whoever you wanted*

ReeseFuller: Yes

CrochetMom: *It says something when a boy dances with only one girl the whole night through*

ReeseFuller: And it says something when said girl leaves the venue right after you dance with her

CrochetMom: ...

CrochetMom: *That Sophie is a tough nut to crack*

ReeseFuller: You're probably right about that

CrochetMom: *So crack her*

ReeseFuller: I'm not liking the direction this conversation is taking

CrochetMom: *ROFLMAO*

ReeseFuller: Who taught you that one?

CrochetMom: *Amy. She's laughing now*

ReeseFuller: Me too. Tell her I said hi

CrochetMom: *She says hi back. Wants to know when you're coming back to visit*

ReeseFuller: When you tell me I can

CrochetMom: *You know you can anytime you want*

CrochetMom: *I just...*

CrochetMom: *Treatment starts soon and I don't want you*

CrochetMom: *I don't think anyone should see me*

ReeseFuller: I understand

CrochetMom: *Are you sure?*

ReeseFuller: I'm sure. You and me, we got that connection, right?

ReeseFuller: Amy and Dad were always jealous of us

CrochetMom: *We understood each other*

CrochetMom: *Stand. We understand*

ReeseFuller: Peas in a pod, isn't that what they called us?

CrochetMom: *Peas in a pod. Amy says to tell you: Mama's boy*

ReeseFuller: Like that's not a compliment

CrochetMom: *...*

ReeseFuller: You still there?

ReeseFuller: Mom?

ReeseFuller: Are you all right?

ReeseFuller: I'm calling

CrochetMom: *I'm here. Just...a twinge*

ReeseFuller: A twinge...

CrochetMom: *I'm good now. But, could you call me?*

Chapter Thirty-four

A week later, late Friday morning, I sat on the ground, on a patch of dirt surrounded by the cracked and broken concrete that was once a parking lot for the abandoned store where my darlings lived. I'd fed the cats, then wiped out their water bowls and filled them with fresh water, and was watching them eat. Roger Dodger, deep blue like a storm cloud, peered at me from under the picnic table—glaring more like it—waiting for me to leave so he could get some food before the others ate it all. He broke my heart.

"All right, all right," I said. I got up and poured more food in his bowl—Diva had eaten half of it, the beautiful fatty—and scooted it under the table before leaving.

It turned out Melissa and Jake had left Tracks before the dancing debacle, so at least the stories surrounding my turn with Reese were mundane, and most likely spread by Pat Willard to Suri and Benjamin. Pat meant well, of course, and I could tell by the snippets that got back to me: thrilling sight, wonderful dancing, what a pair. No one was saying anything about the kissing all over The Fort or at Pub's anymore and that was a good thing. All in all, things had got back to normal, so far as I could tell. Unfortunately, *normal* was that I had five cats in danger of losing their home and no idea how to help them. That week, I'd put up a few flyers where I could find bulletin boards—at the community college, at the local veterinarians offices, that sort of thing. I knew if nothing came of it, my only alternative would be to sneak them into my apartment. I planned for it by purchasing three more litter boxes and three extra tubs of litter. Pari saw me struggling to carry them up the stairs and raised her brows with an 'I know exactly what you're doing' look. Still, she helped.

I was scheduled for the 'noon-thirty to closing' shift — my way of avoiding going out with one of the Divas yet again and running into Reese. On my way to Bookish, though, I noticed the front door of his new store was propped open. I thought I could get a look at the interior, so I peeked in and found him and Jake standing just inside, with Madaline, the realtor. Before I could sneak away, Reese saw me; he smiled and came out to talk to me.

"I haven't seen you since Saturday Night Swing," he said.

I nodded. I'd seen him a time or two and ducked into the nearest store to hide. I ended up buying a brownie at Sweet Suite, a tin of John West kippers, in oil, at Across the Pond, and a four-inch fake bronze Egyptian cat statue at Namaste—all trying to keep from having to speak to Reese Fuller. And there I'd been stupid enough to walk up and look in the door of his new storefront. I banged my right foot against my left ankle as punishment. "Ow," I said and seethed.

"You okay?"

I smiled weakly.

"We should do it again next month. It's hard to find an equal partner, sometimes."

I nodded again.

"You going to say anything?"

"Yes," I said. "I, actually...I need to know...when I have to have the cats off the property."

The light went out of his eyes and he looked sad. I guess

I appreciated that.

"As soon as we sign. We've got a crew on hold."

I could feel my brow pinching in as I realized he was serious. I must have been expecting him to change his mind. I can't imagine why I would hope for that, but I must have, because at that point, I became nauseated. I could feel the slight tinge of a headache coming on.

"Okay," I said. "If you could give me a heads up. I don't want to get them too soon; it's going to be hard to hide them from my landlord."

I turned and walked across Mangrove; I passed Fiona's without looking at anything in the window and didn't feel as if I could breathe again until I entered the breezeway to Strawbridge Main and knew he wouldn't be watching me anymore. On my way to Bookish, I could hear "Tara's Theme" playing in my purse. I shuffled my cat supply bag around so I could get at it, but when I looked at it, I froze. I stood still, right there on the sidewalk in front of Stogies, staring at Cal's number on the screen, letting the *Gone With the Wind* music play on.

"Well?" Mr. Booker said. He was leaning against the door jamb of his store, the door wide open and the fragrance of sweet cigars hovering in the air around him. "You going to answer that?"

I put my phone back into my purse and shifted my big bag to both arms. "No."

"Loverboy?"

"Cal."

His eyes widened. "First time since...?"

I nodded. "What do you suppose he wants?"

"I think that's obvious."

"Not to me."

"Be careful. No sense in going back to something un-pleasant just because you're not happy with the present."

"Who says I'm not happy?"

"You don't look happy."

I mumbled about the cats as I walked on. I had good reason to be sad, didn't I? Why would I take Cal back just because I was worried about the darlings? And why would Cal even think it would be possible after what he did? Cal was a dog, sure, but not a Rottweiler. No offense to Rottweilers. And by that I mean, he wasn't stupid. Again, no offense to Rottweilers, but I hear they're not the brightest of the breeds.

He called me three more times while I was at Bookish and each time I ran to the phone at the cashwrap, each time my heart sank and I realized I'd been hoping Reese was going to feel bad and let me keep the cats, each time I kicked myself for thinking that, and each time I saw it was Cal, my mood grew darker.

When "Tara's Theme" played in the store the fourth time that afternoon, Gramps called out, "Why won't you answer that?"

I said, "Fine!" and did so.

"Hey," he said.

I could picture Cal in my mind at that moment. He'd be sitting in his recliner, one leg hitched over the armrest, his head lying back, eyes focused on the ceiling. One hand would be playing at his long, blond hair and the other would hold the phone away from his face at an angle, his wrist lazily bent. And he'd be smiling.

"What do you want?" I said.

"Harsh."

We were both silent for a few moments. Normally I would have broken and apologized, but I didn't and as the seconds ticked by I started to feel uncomfortable and the more agitated I got the more determined I was not to say anything.

Finally, he said, "I'd like to see you."

"What for?"

"Cut me a little slack, will you?"

I chuckled—a snorting, derisive laugh. "Really?"

"Tonight," he said.

Melissa popped into my head...and rules. Not necessarily her rules, but rules. "How do you know I don't have a date?" It was Friday, after all.

"Do you have a date?"

Great. Now I had to admit I didn't have a date...or lie about it. I thought the rule was you had to say no whether you had a date or not, because, how dare this guy expect you to be free on a Friday night when he called you at four-fifteen Friday afternoon? But this wasn't a date. It couldn't be. Cal was my ex, not a date.

"No," I said. "No date."

"So, let's get together."

"Why?"

"I'd just like to talk. Things didn't end well."

"That was six months ago."

"So, it's about time, right?"

"I don't think so, sorry."

"Aw, come on."

"I have to go."

"Don't go, Sophie. We can be friends, can't we?"

"Really, I have to go. Bye."

I was trembling when I put the phone down and looked at Gramps. My face was hot.

"I'm sorry," Gramps said. "I thought it was Reese."

"It's okay."

I tried to work the rest of my shift but couldn't concentrate. Hugh came in at six-thirty to remind me for the fiftieth time about Nerd Fest the next morning and I was so abrupt with him he skulked over to the cashwrap to get an explanation from Gramps. I heard them mumbling and called out, "Go home, Gramps. Why are you even still here?" More mumbling. I knew exactly why he was there. He couldn't very well leave the store to me when I was going around grouching at everyone. He wouldn't say that. He'd say it was a Friday night; it was busy—all those people out and about at the shops and restaurants. But I knew it was me. After a few minutes of sulking and feeling lousy for treating everyone so cruelly, I made my way to the front to apologize and try to make things right. There was only a half-hour left before closing; maybe I could get Gramps to go home. Hugh would hang around with me to the end of the night.

As I got there, the bell above the door jangled and I put a big, fake smile on my face to greet the next customer only to see Cal walk in.

Chapter Thirty-five

I'd forgotten the charm of Cal's good looks—that sweetness of his face and eyes that belied the fact that he was a pernicious twit. He'd been to the beach; I could tell. His hair was shocking blond against his skin and he reached up and put his hands over his head, smoothing the thin, straight strands against his skull; it's what he always did when he was nervous. It was the only sign—Cal Saunderson never appeared unsettled in any manner. He was all ease and calm and confidence all the time.

"Hey," he said.

Gramps looked defeated when I turned to him. But what could I do? I didn't want Cal hanging around the store waiting for me to go home so he could follow me—and that's just what he'd do. Gramps knew it as well as I did. There was nothing for it but to give in and have dinner with him. It wasn't the end of the world, certainly not bad enough to warrant that look of despair Gramps gave me. And Hugh! His face was stoic but his eyes wide, as if he was in shock. He said nothing as I got my purse and turned to offer a smile before I was out the door.

We walked over to MacAuley Awley's, but I made sure we crossed Strawbridge Main farther down the street from Bookish so I didn't have to run into Melissa at Café Flamingo. Still, I felt like all of Downtown Strawbridge was watching us and when we walked into Awley's and paused to let our eyes adjust to the dim light inside the pub, I could have sworn everything went quiet and all eyes turned to us. I might be exaggerating...or paranoid.

We took a booth along the left side of the wall and Katie Simmons, plump as her mother and with the same cantaloupe colored hair, came over to get our drink order.

"Long time no see," she said to Cal.

He smiled broadly and stood to hug her.

"Lovely as ever," he said to her and she blushed.

"Do you two need a minute?"

Cal looked at me, his hand on the closed menu in front of him. "The usual?" he said.

I sat there staring at him, wondering if he actually remembered our usual. I nodded.

"Two burgers, medium well, with fries."

He remembered. I was torn between melting and freezing. How dare he remember our usual? And anyway, what stupid sort of 'usual' was a burger and fries in MacAuley Awley's Irish Pub? Shouldn't we have tried the corned beef? Or the shepherd's pie? At least once? I couldn't blame Cal—it wasn't his fault he was boring. And it wasn't his fault I didn't order for myself when he was around. Katie winked at me as she gathered up our menus and turned toward the kitchen; my turn to blush. I wasn't sure if it was from shame over being with Cal, or shame over ordering the burger, yet again, at the best Irish pub and restaurant this side of Ireland.

Cal rested against the back of his seat and said, "So, I guess you're pretty mad at me."

"Really? That's how you want to start?"

He scooted forward and rested his arms on the table, more attentive. "You're right," he said. "I owe you an apology."

"After six months you're going to apologize?"

"So, I can't do anything right, is that it?"

"Pretty much."

"I'm sorry, okay? I did a stupid thing. I shouldn't have done it that way."

I nodded. "Apology accepted."

"Does that mean we can be friends?"

"Why? Are you in need of friends these days?"

"It's not that. I just..."

"Did she dump you?"

He pulled his hands over his head and wilted against the back of the booth. "She moved out a few days ago."

"You didn't cheat on her, too?"

"No. And I didn't cheat on you."

"You told me you were in love with her. How'd that happen without cheating?"

"We didn't have sex until after I broke up with you."

"So, going out with her behind my back wasn't cheating."

"Not technically, no."

"Yes, Cal. Technically, it's cheating."

"Okay, fine. Still, no, I didn't cheat on her."

I chuckled a bit, realizing what a lost puppy he was— always had been. Watching him try to avoid looking at me, I began to wonder if I'd imagined the whole thing. Was it really two years with him? Did I really spend two years thinking I was in love with Cal, thinking we'd get married and have three kids and buy a house and a minivan? How could I have not seen beneath his totally successful, oozing of confidence demeanor? All he really was, I saw finally, was a guy. An ordinary guy who cheated on me. An ordinary guy who rarely actually looked at me, as he was *not* doing now.

"You always did that," he said. Eyes on the front door.

"What?"

He shrugged. "Talked to me like I'm stupid." Eyes across the room.

"I did not."

"You did." Eyes on the table.

"Cal, I did not."

"You corrected my pronunciation of some words. You were always bringing me books and asking me to read them." A glance behind him at the bar.

"What words?"

"Esssss..." he hissed, "spresso. Remember that?" His hands...what was that on his hands? *It's nothing Cal. There is nothing on your hands. Stop examining your hands and look at me.*

"You were calling it expresso.'"

He laughed. "I know. And to be honest, I'm glad you corrected me. I don't like looking stupid in front of agents and clients."

"So there," I said.

"F. Scott Fitzgerald, remember that?" Picking at a tiny knot of thread at the hem of his sleeve.

"I'll still never understand how you couldn't at least finish reading it."

"Uh, hello: boring. You were trying to get me to be bookish, like you." Brushing the fabric, now smoothing it down.

Finally he looked at me. I thought he might be blushing. Was it...really? He was! He shook his head and looked away quickly.

"We used to get along," he said.

"To hear you talk, we didn't."

"I liked that about you—that you read and worked with books. I didn't think we had to be the same."

"I went fishing with you; I watched football. I did your things."

"I thought you liked those things."

"I didn't hate them; but I don't do them anymore now that we're..." I didn't know why I left that hanging in the air. When I caught his eye, he smiled.

"We got along a lot better when we were together."

Katie brought us our iced teas and Cal asked her what

she'd been up to lately. She said she was engaged and he winked at her, took her hand, and confessed his heart was broken. He was looking at her the whole time. When she left, he turned to me with that usual fabulous smile and proposed a truce between us; we clinked our glasses together. And he started finding other things to look at again, mostly his glass, his hands, and the table.

"So what happened?" I said.

"I don't know. I thought I loved her."

"What did that feel like?"

"Huh?"

"What did it feel like? Being in love with her?"

"I don't know, Sophie. Geez. It felt like—I just wanted her. You know? I really, really wanted her."

I laughed. "You mean, sexually?"

"Yeah, hell yeah."

"Who wouldn't, right?"

He opened his mouth and then shut it. Then opened it again. "She's not as pretty as you."

"I didn't ask for any consolation."

"But it wasn't like that. I mean...Lydia has this way."

"Oh, I know."

"You do?"

"Sure. She's very sexual. With other girls' boyfriends."

"You're saying she went after me, to steal me away."

"You say that as if it compliments you."

"Doesn't it?"

"I suppose it might."

"I didn't feel like she was flirting with me. I saw her and I wanted her. All I could think about was being with her. Touching her." He looked up at me and winced. "Sorry."

I sucked in a big breath. "It's okay. Anyway, that doesn't sound like love to me."

"No?"

I shook my head. "Lust isn't love."

"It's not?"

"I'm pretty sure it's not."

"So what's it supposed to feel like?"

"Love is when you—" I got stuck for a moment, realizing I didn't know anything about love myself. But maybe, like Melissa, I thought, those who can't do...teach. "It's looking at that person, looking in his eyes, and feeling light. Expectation, not of touch. Touch, sure, but no, it's the expectation of what he's going to say. Because he makes you laugh, and he makes you think, and he makes you feel like you could say anything—anything at all—and he'll hear you. He'll understand. Love is when you worry about him, is he happy? Is he hurting? Love is when you wish you were a better person, knowing he deserves the best you can give him."

Cal was staring at me with his face squished up, like he was in pain. We sat silent for a bit, me trying not to look at him again and he...probably thinking I'd lost my mind.

"So," I said, searching for something bland to make me forget I'd just said all that stuff to Cal. "How's the agency?"

"Booming. We've moved to a larger space beachside. I've got three more agents working for me."

"The market's good then?" I knew nothing about real estate, but I was pretty good at faking it for the two years I dated him.

I let him ramble on a bit about properties and taxes and whatnot while I sipped my iced tea.

After a few minutes, he said, "So, what do you say? You want to go out again?"

Behind me, the front door opened and Cal's face darkened. "Oh, man, I hate that guy."

I turned to look behind me and Reese Fuller had walked into MacAuley Awley's.

Chapter Thirty-six

CrochetMom: *Reese, you there?*
ReeseFuller: Here
CrochetMom: *I got the photos of your new store. Looks real nice*
CrochetMom: *You there?*
ReeseFuller: Yes. Sorry. Just got seated for dinner
ReeseFuller: The site's good, yes. We sign next week
CrochetMom: *Dinner, eh. Is Sophie with you?*
ReeseFuller: She's here
CrochetMom: *Wonderful. Tell her I said Hi. Wait. Don't*
ReeseFuller: Yeah, I don't think that's a good idea
CrochetMom: *It's weird, isn't it?*
ReeseFuller: A little
CrochetMom: *So, where did you take her?*
ReeseFuller: To tell you the truth, she's here with someone else
CrochetMom: *Oh...hold on...let me figure this out.*
CrochetMom: :(
ReeseFuller: You had to figure that out?
CrochetMom: *I was only taught to smile. Frowning wasn't supposed to happen*
ReeseFuller: Very profound
CrochetMom: *Write me a poem about it*
ReeseFuller: It will have to be in the voice of a child

CrochetMom: *You're my child; it works. So, who is she there with? Wait...*

CrochetMom: *If you're with a date, too, you shouldn't talk about Sophie*

ReeseFuller: I'm here with Jake. We've been at the site all day. Lots of plans

CrochetMom: *Tell him I said hi*

ReeseFuller: He says hi back (Literally)

CrochetMom: *Question stands*

ReeseFuller: She's here with Cal Saunderson

CrochetMom: ...

CrochetMom: *I have no words*

Chapter Thirty-seven

Katie sat Reese and Jake in a booth on the other side of the restaurant, directly in my line of sight, if I turned my head a bit. He saw me when he came in, nodded, and looked at Cal. His jaw set into a sneer and when he looked at me again it was...well, let's just say I could feel the daggers.

"You know Reese?" I asked him.

"Can't stand the guy."

"Why?"

"I've known him since fifth grade when he was just an annoying little prat. He only got worse with age. It wasn't enough for him to be better than everybody else; he did everything he could to ruin my life and nearly succeeded."

"Like what?" I was stunned by his vitriol; could he really be talking about Reese? The GLE? It didn't fit, like a piece from the wrong puzzle.

"I really don't want to get into it."

"Well, you're not alone." I had to confess. "I don't like him much, either."

"What did he do to *you*?" There was a protective tone to his voice and it almost brought me back to the time I loved him—er, I mean, when I thought I loved him.

"He's buying that old building, where I feed the cats. Opening up a surf shop."

Cal turned to look behind him at Reese and Jake and

then back to me. *Sure, now he can't stop looking at me.*

"He's going to dig up the parking lot and he doesn't care what happens to the cats."

"Oh yeah, those cats."

"I don't know what to do. I've asked everybody to take one, but no one can. I don't suppose you could have one or two more?"

He shook his head. "Sorry, Sophie. Lydia left her cat at my place, so now I have two."

"How could she do that?"

He shrugged. "They get along really well—the cats, I mean. She said they should stay together."

"Maybe she's hoping they'll be a catalyst for you trying to get her back."

"Catalyst?"

"Sure. A reason to call, to stop by." I laughed. "*Cat*alyst. Get it?"

He didn't laugh. "I don't like games."

"Mine or hers?"

His head twitched, tiny little jerks left and right, and he looked at me as if I were crazy. I couldn't remember if talking with Cal had always been so difficult. It was as if we kept missing each other and fought for understanding.

He said, "Hers."

"I can't blame you for that. But...if you really love her..."

"Ah, who knows?"

"Shouldn't you know?"

"I thought I loved you."

My mouth fell open at that. "You did not."

"I did."

"Then why would you run off with Lydia?"

He leaned forward and took my hand in his. "You know what I think, Sophie? I think I felt like you were too good for me. Like I didn't deserve you."

"Cal."

200

"Listen. It makes sense. I didn't think I was good enough, so unconsciously or whatever, I went after Lydia. She's the type of girl everybody would expect a guy like me to be with."

"What does that mean?"

"Come on, you know. She's like me. A loud, outdoor king of guy. And she's...you know, social."

That much was true. Lydia was all over the place—at the beach, boating on the lagoon, at major league football games, rock concerts. She used to say I was her only quiet friend and what would she do without me to come home to, to sit down with, be calm with. I thought it was a compliment, but now that I looked back on it, I wasn't so sure.

"It's true," I told Cal. "We were—are—really different. Before we started dating, my life was subdued. It was a good life though."

"Aw, come on. You didn't know what you were missing until you met me."

"No, I think I knew. Look, it was easy to be social with you. You did all the talking to everybody else and I only had to talk to you. In a way, I guess I have to admit, you taught me a lot."

"So, I was good for you."

"Gramps says you were."

"I find that hard to believe."

"It's true. He says you brought me out into the world and now I can't go back into hiding."

"I made you come alive." He smiled and winked. "I like that."

"I thought I was plenty alive before you came along."

"But you're happier now...with the result, right?"

I shrugged. "I guess. Sometimes I want to go back to the time before. It was easier to stay focused on books and Gramps, Hugh."

"That nerdy guy?"

"He's my friend. A good friend."

"So, what about it, Sophie? You and me again."

"I don't know."

"You'll think about it, though, won't you?" He gave me that smile of his that always charmed us all into doing what he wanted us to do.

I always thought what Cal had was confidence, but just then, him looking at me like that, I realized he was spoiled. And selfish—a guy used to getting his way. I wondered what it was Reese had done to him—was it something that spurred Cal into learning how to get what he wanted from people? Did Reese take something of his?

"What about the shelters?" he said.

I was taken aback a bit, wondering how we'd gone from getting back together to the cats so quickly.

"The shelters are full of cats and kittens. I've called a few and they told me they have no openings. Even the people who foster them in their homes are full. There was one guy who would take them, but he lives with about a hundred cats already. That's no way for them to live. Come to think of it, a cage at a shelter isn't a way to live either. And they're not feral, so I wouldn't want to relocate them into a colony."

"You'll have to take them home with you, then."

"I'll be evicted if Mr. Z finds out. But you're right. It's my only option."

Our burgers arrived and we ate for a while. Katie Simmons took every opportunity to visit Reese's table and laugh at something he said. One time, she put her hand on his shoulder and leaned in. I caught Cal looking at me and realized I was scowling.

"You know what you need?" he said, dragging a crinkle-cut fry through a pool of ketchup on his plate. "A campaign."

"What sort of campaign?"

"To save the cats. You could picket his new store

location, write letters to the editor, maybe go before the business owners' board and plead your case."

"I can't. Remember the city told me a few years ago I had to find homes for them all. If they find out the cats are still there and I'm trying to keep them there, I'll lose them for sure."

Cal glanced over his shoulder again at Reese and Jake. Katie was still there. When he turned back, he kept his eyes on his plate. I remembered then, all the times we ate at MacAuley Awley's when we were dating. It was our table Katie visited a little too often. I'd be scowling after some meals and he'd tease me and tell me she was just being a good waitress. "She knows I'll tip her more if she flirts a little," he'd said. It's funny how you forget a lot of the bad things people do to you, especially when there was one, last, really awful thing overshadowing them.

"Maybe a different kind of campaign, then," he said.

"What did you have in mind?"

"A smear campaign—character assassination, that sort of thing. Plaster the store with 'owner hates cats' posters. Spread vicious rumors. Maybe he'll give in."

I smiled and nodded, trying to picture it. But no. "That's not my style and it's not yours, either. Is it?"

He shrugged. "I can get pretty dirty if the occasion calls for it."

"In business," I said. "But you're nice to everybody else."

"Anyway, it probably wouldn't do any good. Reese is the type of person who always comes out of that kind of fight clean and everybody else is covered in mud."

"Well, bless my eyes!" Mrs. Simmons' voice sang; she was nearly at our table, her arms wide, creamy-orange curls dancing as she shook her head.

Cal got up and let her wrap him up in a bear hug.

"I was beginning to wonder if I'd ever see you again. And you here with our Sophie. How wonderful."

"I'm sorry I haven't come by."

"Don't be silly, you're a busy man. But you're back now. And you two together."

Reese and Jake were both looking at our table and the entire restaurant could hear Mrs. Simmons.

I shook my head. "We're not together."

"You never know," Cal said with a sly grin.

"Tara's Theme" rang out and I startled. I dug my phone out of my purse. "It's Carrie." I was surprised, realizing it was the night of her big date with Noah. Had something gone horribly wrong? "My cousin, you remember her?"

"Go on and talk," Mrs. Simmons said. "I'm taking Cal to the kitchen for a bite of bread and butter pudding. You come along when you're finished."

I said 'hello' and Carrie said, "I can't believe you would lie to me like that!"

Chapter Thirty-eight

Oh, Carrie; I'm so sorry." I could hear Reese's voice in my head, telling me I shouldn't meddle in people's love lives. What had I done? "What happened? Are you home already? Was it awful?"

"Awful? Sophie, he's adorable. Honestly, you made it sound like I was going out with a socially awkward man-child who still lived with his parents and spent his days in his underwear playing Nintendo."

"And you're saying he's not?"

"Not at all. I don't have much time. We just finished dinner at Flambé—"

"Continental Flambé?"

"—and he's in the bathroom. We're going over to Tracks for drinks."

"So, it's going well?" *Astounded. Stupefied. Properly jealous.*

"I can't believe you thought he was a dork."

"Well...he sits in that flower booth all day wearing faded jeans." That says "dork" all over it, right?

"He's not wearing faded jeans now, I assure you. And the conversation! He's really smart and witty."

"Okay. Carrie. Are you sure you're out with Noah? The Flower Power guy?"

She laughed. "Who else would have shown up at my house to take me out?"

"Do you think he hired someone to be him?"

I heard her say, "It's Sophie. She thinks maybe you're not you."

"Carrie," I screamed. "Don't you dare tell him—"

"Thinks you hired a proxy," she said. "I have to go now, Soph. Oh, I forgot why I called. Noah and I wanted to say thank you for setting us up. We're having a fabulous time."

When I put my phone away, I sat back in the booth and stared straight ahead of me for a bit. I still wasn't sure she was actually out with Noah. I mean...Noah at Continental Flambé? Not in faded jeans? Carrie thinks he's adorable? Well, I did think he was...kind of cute...didn't I?

Instead of joining Mrs. Simmons in the kitchen with Cal—I'd been there before, and eaten way too much cheesecake one time—I waited at the table, trying to watch Reese and Jake without them noticing. I couldn't stop wondering what he'd done to Cal. Why would Cal think Reese was an awful person who tried to ruin his life? Then again, I realized I hadn't been fond of Cal—a huge understatement—for the past six months. Maybe they were both rotten and I was just taken in by their incredible good looks. That hardly reflected well on me, but there it was.

Cal kept me waiting for at least forty minutes—long enough for Reese and Jake to finish their meals, pay their check, flirt some more with Katie, and walk past me to the door. Reese nodded at me, a bit of a disenchanted smile on his lips. As if my being with Cal, someone he obviously thought was *so* much lower than the fabulous Reese Fuller, disappointed him. Finally Cal came back to the table and paid the bill, even though I insisted I should pay half. We walked back to Bookish where his sleek, black Mercedes was and I let him drive me home. When I slipped into the passenger seat, a rush of nostalgia wafted over me. It was as if my body remembered the curve of the seat, the funk of spilled milkshake and old French fries, and settled in comfortably.

"Don't walk me up," I told him before I got out of the car at Creek Overlook Apartments.

He got out anyway, and took my hands at the bottom of the steps. "Think about it," he said.

"You know Cal. I don't think I will. Not right now."

"Why not?"

"Because you just broke up with Lydia and her cat is in your apartment."

"I can get rid of the cat."

"No. That's not what I'm saying. You need time. If after, say, six months, you still think you want to go out with me again, give me a call."

He scoffed, dropped my hands and stepped back. "Six months?"

"You can't give a girl six months?"

His mouth opened and closed a few times. "Two weeks."

"Five months."

"One month."

"This is absurd."

"Six weeks, Sophie. Six weeks and we give it another go."

I sighed. "Six weeks and I *think* about it."

He smiled and took my hands again.

"I mean it, Cal. I'm not guaranteeing anything. You dumped me for my best friend, remember?"

"Aw, she wasn't your *best* friend."

"Like that matters."

"But you'll think about it."

"I will...in six weeks."

Before I knew what was happening, he'd slapped his hands onto my face, dragged me in, and kissed me. I stood there and let him do it, dazed and, although it's cliché... confused, and remembering everything about him—his taste, his smell, his laugh, that quirky way he'd dance while scrambling eggs in the morning, the message he left on my phone telling me he was leaving me for Lydia. His lips popped off mine like a cork out of a champagne bottle and I took a step back, forcing his hands off my cheeks. He stood there smiling at me like he'd just played rock to my scissors.

"Goodnight, Cal," I said.

I think he watched me the whole time I was on the stairs—probably waited until he heard my apartment door close and lock, thinking I was only joking and would come running back down to him. Because who could resist Cal Saunderson, right?

I stood inside my apartment and whispered to Willow, "Wait a minute, what?" Cal had said he could get rid of Lydia's cat. Just like that—as if it would mean no more than tossing out an empty soda can. "I can get rid of the cat," I mimicked, peeved.

Were there no devilishly attractive men who liked bookish girls and appreciated humanity's inferiority to the feline—our call to worship them!—anywhere on the earth?

Reasons I didn't want Cal to walk me up

1. It would be too much like a date if he did.

2. Pari might see us and then I'd have to talk about it because she'd wait for him to leave and then come over and ask me a million questions I didn't want to answer.

3. He would kiss me. Standing in the parking lot by his car could elicit a kiss—and it did—but it wouldn't be one of those 'at the door' end-of-date kisses—and it was not.

4. If he kissed me like that—like we'd just got home from a date—I would like it because I was sad about Reese

Fuller, and angry at Reese Fuller.

5. If I liked it—the answer to that point already a given—he'd want to come in. In fact, I was pretty sure that was why he wanted to drive me home.

6. ~~I might let him come in~~. I would have to fight him off, because no way would I let him in. Nope. No way.

So, all in all, everything worked out for the best. Except that Chloe, never the most attention-seeking cat, got one whiff of Cal's musky cologne on me and darted under the bed. When I thought of the nights I cried myself to sleep clutching one of Cal's left-behind t-shirts, with all three of my darlings hovering about me on the bed, worried, I couldn't blame her. Cats remember.

Chapter Thirty-nine

CrochetMom: *Reese! Don't listen to your father*

ReeseFuller: Good morning, Mom

CrochetMom: *I mean it. It wasn't a big deal. I just vomited a little*

ReeseFuller: Are you feeling better now?

CrochetMom: *Much*

ReeseFuller: He says you're not eating

CrochetMom: *I told you not to listen to him*

ReeseFuller: Sorry

CrochetMom: *Are you working today?*

ReeseFuller: Actually, I'm going to something called Nerd Fest

CrochetMom: *LOL. That sounds weird. Where's it at?*

ReeseFuller: Here in Strawbridge

CrochetMom: *Must be new. Are you a nerd?*

ReeseFuller: I don't think there will be a litmus test. But if there is, I'll turn my t-shirt inside out and fold up the hem of my jeans

CrochetMom: *Amy's here. She says it's not that new. Says it's packed. Something about jousting*

ReeseFuller: Yes, all sorts of medieval, fantasy type activities and a lot of vendors

CrochetMom: *Vendors selling what?*

ReeseFuller: I assume comic books and figures and stuff

CrochetMom: *Toys? It's for kids?*

ReeseFuller: Collectibles

CrochetMom: *I know. I'm teasing you. Is there a teasing thingie...?*

ReeseFuller: You can make a winkie face

CrochetMom: *How?*

ReeseFuller: ;)

CrochetMom: *That's the cutest thing I've ever seen*

ReeseFuller: I thought I was the cutest thing you've ever seen :O

CrochetMom: *You are. Amy, too, of course*

ReeseFuller: You have to say that because she's there with you

CrochetMom: *Did you find out anything about Sophie being with Cal?*

ReeseFuller: No. I'll ask her if I see her again. But it's not really any of my business

CrochetMom: *Still, I'd like to know. Even though it feels like gossip. I talked to Marty Collins*

CrochetMom: *She said he's doing well. A real estate broker*

ReeseFuller: Good for him, I guess

CrochetMom: *I confess, sweetie. I've always wondered if you felt guilty about it*

ReeseFuller: Not for one second. Ever. He deserved it

CrochetMom: *I know he did. But I also know you*

ReeseFuller: ?

CrochetMom: *I think you're more sensitive than most*

ReeseFuller: That's because I had a big sister who tortured me

CrochetMom: *Amy says LOL*

ReeseFuller: I love you, Mom. Gotta go

CrochetMom: *I love you. Call me later*

ReeseFuller: You know I will

212

Chapter Forty

The next morning, Hugh picked me up at my apartment for Nerd Fest. I was Black Widow—Carrie lent me her Mega Con costume. It was...tight. Black body suit, leather utility belt, holsters strapped to my thighs, leather boots. And Hugh was Hawkeye, also decked out in black. I think we made a great pair and Hugh said he had no doubt we'd meet up with Thor, Captain America, and Bruce Banner there. Maybe even Iron Man, but that wasn't the easiest costume to wear.

The festival was pretty crazy. Outside the Strawbridge Auditorium, they had an area set up for pseudo jousting. There were kids' games with a pirate theme and a bounce house of a sort where you could battle with huge air bats. Inside stood row after row of booths where we got to look at everything a person could imagine being remotely connected to nerds and gaming. The crowd was so thick Hugh and I lost each other a few times.

We hadn't finished looking at all the goods before it was lunchtime and we made our way over to the gaming room where the kitchen was and got hot dogs and chips. It was quiet there. People sat hunched and serious at folding tables playing Magic the Gathering, Warhammer—their seats surrounded by plastic bins filled with their collections—and Yu-Gi-Oh!

"Not the best lunch I could have offered you," Hugh said as we took seats across from each other at a large table with some other attendees.

"You take what you can get, right?" I said.

We ate in silence for a bit and I thought about what he'd said. It sounded like he thought we were on a date. "Hugh," I said, tentatively. "Gramps told me you would think we were dating...if I came here with you."

I was relieved when he smiled. "I don't think Nerd Fest, as much as I like it, would be my choice for a first date. And anyway, we're friends. Friends don't start dating. The relationship just morphs." He blushed. "Or not."

"Well, he seems to think you're interested."

"Sophie," he said and shifted in his seat, as if he was preparing to lecture me. "I like you. I do. But you're a crossover book and I'm not."

"What?" I chuckled.

"You know how it is. Some books are right where they have to be in the store. I'm a *Dungeons and Dragons Monster Manual*. I'm not going to be mistaken for a romance novel. Now, I might qualify as fantasy, maybe, but nobody's going to shelve me in fantasy by mistake. You see what I'm saying?"

"I think so." *What was he saying?*

"You, you've got 'cross genre' written all over you. Sure, you're pretty much shelved in the fantasy section with the rest of the nerds, by choice, I might add. But you could also fit nicely in poetry, literary, romance, even thrillers. You're one of those people who can step out of the mold society has you cast in and date better books."

"I don't know whether to be flattered or horrified."

"Why would you be horrified?"

"You're basically saying you could never date a girl like me, as if I'm too good for you."

"That's not what I'm saying at all. I could date you, if

214

you'd have me. And we'd probably have a great time, because we like the same things, get the same jokes. I'm saying the only types of girls who will be interested in me, are the ones who get shelved in my general area of the store: fantasy, sci fi, gaming. You get shelved there, too. But when someone like Reese Fuller comes in—"

"What kind of book is he?"

"He's a thriller, definitely. A Ludlum or a Clancy. Bond, James Bond. Anyway, he comes in and he gets to choose from all the books with crossover potential. I can't get a romance book or a literary novel. No way. For me, it's strictly fantasy. Maybe not even that. D&D only...and any girl who fits there."

"You're saying there are dating genres."

"Of course there are."

"I don't think we're supposed to admit that. I think we're supposed to believe love wins out; it transcends rules, tiers, and genres...surpasses even shallow physical attraction."

"Maybe it does, on rare occasions. Are you saying your attraction to Reese is shallow?"

"What makes you think I'm attracted to him?"

"Are you trying to fool me, or yourself?"

"Oh, all right. I'm having trouble getting him out of my head even now, knowing he's a cat hater."

"He's not a cat hater. He's got a business to run. Stray cats are not a protected species."

"Too bad."

"And what about Cal?"

"What about him?"

He stared at me, his eyebrows lifted, hot dog poised and ready for another bite, waiting.

"It was just dinner."

"Why would you go to dinner with him?" Big bite.

"I don't know. I spent two years with him. I thought I loved him. I probably did. You can't stop loving someone."

"Sure you can, when they treat you the way Cal treated you."

"I know you're right. He's a beast."

"Then why?"

"I don't know."

"Reese?"

I pushed my plate away, frustrated. "What would he have to do with it?" Again, he merely stared at me. "I hardly know Reese Fuller. I hung out with him at a couple of bars. I kissed him—"

"You did?"

"—I danced with him and that's it. It's not enough to go running back to Cal over, is it?"

"There's no reason good enough for that."

"Don't put me in the position of defending him."

"Why would you?"

"Fine. Have it your way. Cal isn't evil. He's a great guy. I loved him for two years. I saw my future with him. Every time you act like he's scum, you're saying I'm stupid for dating him, for loving him."

"I don't mean it that way."

"And I wouldn't be stupid for taking him back." *Uh, Sophie, what are you saying?*

"I disagree."

"He made a mistake. He broke up with me in the worst way. But it doesn't change who he is and why I loved him."

I could tell by the look of him, Hugh was fuming. And it was true enough that, as I was going on about all of Cal's assets, that little voice inside my head rose higher and sharper into a desperate shriek. I figured it was the voice of 'hurt and betrayed Sophie.' You'd expect her to try to hang on to the anger a while longer. But maybe it was time to let it go.

"Did you invite Cal to Nerd Fest?" he said.

"No. Of course not."

"Then why is he at the door waving at me? Why is he coming over?"

I turned and sure enough, there was Cal, looking completely un-nerdy in his jeans and tight t-shirt. He would have made a great Thor.

"Hey, Hugh, right?" he said, taking a seat next to him. "Is this thing wild, or what? And look at you. What are you, a ninja?"

"He's Hawkeye. I'm Black Widow."

"I never got into comics much."

"There aren't many words in them," Hugh said.

"What are you doing here?" I said, hoping to distract Cal from Hugh's insult. "I thought we agreed to wait..."

"We agreed to wait before getting back together—"

Hugh's mouth fell open and he closed it as fast as he could, but too late. I saw it.

"—but we didn't say we weren't going to be friends in the meantime."

"Still," I said, "why are you here?"

"I didn't follow you here. Don't worry about that." He slapped a thick hand on Hugh's shoulder. "No, I'm here with Angelo; you remember him? We wanted to check it out. But when I saw you, well, I think I might have an answer to your cat problem."

"You found someone who wants five cats?"

"Nobody wants five cats, Sophie."

"Then what?"

"I've got a buyer for that building. Somebody who won't mind the cats being on the property."

"But Reese has already made a deal."

"They haven't signed yet."

"But why would the owner go with someone else?"

"Money. A lot more of it."

"Wouldn't that be breach of contract?" Hugh said. "If the seller backs out after accepting Reese's offer?"

"It won't matter."

"Reese could sue," Hugh said.

"He could. But he won't."

"How do you know?" I asked.

"From what I know about the seller, and about Reese, he won't sue. He'll take the lump and walk away."

"Why would he?"

"I'm telling you, he will. And then you can keep your cats."

"You know for sure they would let them stay? And not tear up the parking lot?"

"For a fact."

"How can you be sure?"

"This particular buyer owes me more than one favor."

"You'd do that for me?" I said. The look on Hugh's face was frightening. I must have been gushing.

"Of course I would. I'll let you know when it's all set up."

Cal came around the edge of the table and kissed me on the forehead before disappearing into the crowd of the larger room. I was left to cringe under Hugh's disappointed glare.

"You're getting back together with him? But you said..."

"I promised to think about it, that's all. And I told him I wouldn't even think about it until he'd been without Lydia for at least six weeks."

"Six weeks! Six weeks and then you'll go back to the guy who dumped you for a back stabbing—"

"I only said I'd *think* about it."

"Why would you even do that?"

"Why wouldn't I? He's sorry about what he did."

"That's just manipulation. Exploitation. He's an operator, Sophie. He gets what he wants. Why do you let him do it?"

"If this is your idea of being a friend, I don't care for it."

"This is exactly what friendship is. Somebody has to

have your back."

"Only if I want it."

He shook his head, angry, as he gathered up our paper plates and cups and took them to the trash can. As we left the gaming room and entered the throng once again—me following behind like a scolded mud-covered puppy—we heard the announcement for the costume contest.

"Come on," he said. "Let's find us a Thor." He was not happy.

I said nothing. I was watching Reese Fuller with his friend Jake at one of the comic book tables.

Chapter Forty-one

We never found Thor. A girl with a cardboard television set on her head won the contest. Hugh took me home at five and thanked me for a fun day. He didn't mention Cal again, but I could feel the subject there between us. I had to admit I understood his fears. No one wants to see his friend make mistakes. But would it really be a mistake?

After peeling the Black Widow body suit off me, I ate a turkey sandwich in my pajamas, sitting on the sofa in front of the television, warding off meat-stealing cats, flipping through channels. When eight o'clock rolled around I was still sitting there, still flipping, and Willow had eaten the leftover bits of lettuce off my plate.

"What am I doing here?" I asked him. He meowed.

I fed the cats and got dressed—my jeans and a frilly-hemmed top from Fiona's—touched up my makeup, grabbed my wallet and makeup kit into a little over the shoulder purse and went to the door. Was I...? No! Was I going out? *I was.* I didn't want to wallow alone in my apartment. It was the strangest thing. I blamed Cal—he had turned me into a socialite or something. Seeing him again must have sparked it, poked at it. I didn't like it, but I knew I couldn't sit there until nine and then spend the rest of the night in bed reading. Not on another Saturday night. *No.*

As I walked toward downtown, I got on my phone and

called Melissa.

"Sorry, Bookish," she said. "I've got a date. I think the only one of us available tonight is Karen, and she said she wanted a hot bath, a pan of brownies, and a classic film."

Discouraged, I went on, determined to be out with humans. I took the breezeway and turned west, with The Fort in mind. I couldn't go alone. But who could I call? I thought of Cal. It would be so easy. Just dial him up and ask him to meet me. I stopped in front of Begotten, already closed and dark, and stood there, wondering what I thought I was doing. *Go crawling back to Cal?* No. Even if I did take him back, he'd have to work for it. And I couldn't go to The Fort by myself. *Who does that?* A great sigh left me, one of those 'almost crying, dejected, I'm a loser' sighs. I turned, defeated, to go back home, and there was Reese Fuller walking toward me.

"Hey," he said.

"Hey," I said. "What are you doing here? I mean, not like it's any of my business."

"I was following you."

"Why?" I admit, I was flattered. It was a complimentary following, not a creepy stalker following.

"I'm embarrassed to say."

I think I must have screwed my face up into a gargoyle because he laughed a little. I was trying to imagine what sort of following would be embarrassing for him. Had he been hit over the head, developed amnesia, was lost, and hoping I would lead him somewhere familiar?

"I'm on my own tonight," he said. "Thought I'd go have a drink or something, but I didn't want to do it alone. Thought you might be going somewhere."

"I was. But, yeah, I didn't want to go by myself, either."

"Is that why you turned around? Chickened out?"

"Hey," I said, insulted. "Are you pot or kettle?"

"I freely admit I was mooching off your daring. But we'll

never know if I would have chickened out, if you hadn't shown up."

We decided on Tracks. The subdued atmosphere of its front room was great when you had company, ego crushing if you were alone. We sat at a table for two in a corner and ordered beers. We got bottles and frosted mugs and had a little rivalry over who could get the best amount of foam, then argued about what the best amount of foam was. It was Salsa Saturday and Latin music had my feet dancing under the table.

After our first beer was done and we were on our second, I asked him, "When did you learn to swing?"

"Fifth grade, my dad took my sister to the parent-child dance in the school cafeteria. They had such a good time, I asked my mom if I could take her to the dance when I was in sixth grade. Of course, she accepted. A while later, she asked me if I'd be interested in taking some lessons with her. I didn't know it then, but she'd been a ballroom dancer. So we took lessons. And by the time the dance came around, we were a good pair, even if I was way too short for her. What about you?"

"My grandfather," I said. "After my grandmother died, he wanted to take the lessons they planned to take. We danced in a little dance off at the mall once. I was surprised I remembered the steps. I know you had to fudge a little."

"Only a little."

"But how could you remember, all the way from sixth grade? You must still dance."

"I did some in high school. In my sophomore year, my mother wanted to take part in a competition. That was when I learned about her dancing creds. Anyway, my dad could dance with a sixth grader, but he was no twinkle toes. My mom thought I'd do better."

"Aw. Was your dad hurt?"

He laughed. "I think it was his idea. Anyway, after that I

danced a bit at some spots. But it's been a long time."

We were silent for a bit and I tried to avoid looking at him. I wondered if I should tell him about the other buyer Cal found, but I shied away from the idea. What if Cal didn't manage it? Would I be causing trouble between them? It was clear they didn't like each other. And anyway, didn't I *want* Cal to do it? There was no way Mr. Z was going to let me have eight cats in my apartment. Wouldn't everything be so much better if Reese didn't buy the storefront?

I sighed.

"How do you know Cal Saunderson?" he asked.

I took a sip of my beer, delaying. I should have known he'd bring it up. "I dated him for two years." Why did I feel like I was apologizing?

"When? If you don't mind my asking."

"It's been six months."

He nodded. "I heard you recently went through a bad breakup."

"The downtown area sure does talk, doesn't it?"

"I'm finding that out."

"They didn't tell you about...the lagoon incident, did they?"

"I don't remember any mention of the lagoon. Tell me."

"Oh, no. Forget I said anything."

A wicked smile crossed his lips. "You have to tell me, now. If not, I'll be forced to ask around."

I sucked in a big breath and held it with a grimace, then deflated as I let it out. "Okay," I gave in. "It's like this. I... well, we'd broken up already, basically, and then he called me and told me Lydia was packing up to move in with him."

"Ouch."

"Totally. But worse, she was too cowardly to come across the landing and ask me if there weren't some of her things in my apartment."

224

"That's why he called?"

I nodded. "I hung up on him and just...freaked. You wouldn't believe it."

"I think I would."

I slapped at him playfully. "So, I went around and found all her stuff—nail polish, a scarf, a few shirts, a pair of sandals, her comb and some scissors—and went across the way. I fully intended to dump them at her door..."

"But?"

My mouth was open and I was shaking my head slowly, amazed at the memory of my insanity. "Somehow I ended up down at Manatee Park, on the boardwalk, holding each thing up, screaming 'I hate you!' and...tossing it into the lagoon."

He let out a shout of laughter.

"It gets worse," I said.

"Keep going, then."

His laughter affected me but I carried on as best I could. "At some point, I realized what I was doing. Luckily, I hadn't got to the nail polish. I mean...the pollution. Anyway, I'd tossed her comb at the very second I decided I shouldn't and reached for it...clawed more like it. Stumbled. And fell in."

His face was red by that point and he'd snorted a few times trying to keep from laughing at me but it was no use.

"There's still a video of a young man pulling me out, by my feet pretty much, floating around on Youtube...if you're interested."

We both laughed until it hurt and each time I thought we'd settled down, it would start back up again. Finally, we were back to mere smiles and sips and silence.

"So," he said, "you two are getting back together?"

Take a drink. That's right, a really long swig. "I don't know."

"Wary? I wouldn't blame you."

"Why do you say that?"

"When somebody does something that devastates you... it changes things. You lose trust."

"I guess I should be wary. But people can overcome their mistakes, can't they?"

"Maybe. Seems Cal has."

"Well, I haven't forgiven him yet."

"That's not what I mean. I mean...never mind."

"You don't like him."

"No. But, he must have changed. He couldn't be the same person I knew."

I smiled. "That's forgiving."

"Is it? I don't know."

I watched him, waiting for him to go on. He was struggling, I could tell, like he wanted to say something, but couldn't make himself do it.

"He told me you two had some kind of, I don't know... you didn't get along."

"To put it mildly."

"So, what happened between you?"

"I can't tell you."

"Why not? Is it classified?"

At least he smiled.

"No. But, it's not the kind of thing I should tell you. I mean...he has to have changed. You wouldn't have gone out with him for so long if he hadn't. Right?"

"How can I answer that? I have no idea what you're accusing him of."

"I don't think you're the kind of girl who would go out with the Cal I knew."

"You're making me really wonder now."

"Let's just say he wasn't a nice guy. But it was a long time ago."

"So, whatever it was...you're saying it was his fault?"

He didn't answer, but sipped his beer instead.

"This isn't fair," I said. "I told you about the lagoon

incident."

His face hardened and he took in a slow deep breath. "That's different."

I wanted to say, 'oh, really?' but I didn't. "I'm sorry," I said. "I shouldn't meddle."

"Let's dance."

Salsa has many moods. There's party salsa, upbeat and happy—often about salsa itself. There's droning salsa, usually about being drunk. And then there's sexy salsa—slow, rhythmic, hip-swirling, passionate. We drank a few more beers and danced every romantic salsa the band played, as if we were called to the floor with that first sensual beat. I thought of Cal much too often, but always in comparison to Reese. Cal didn't dance. Cal didn't look into my eyes or my face like that. Cal didn't stand so close without touching me, letting a bonding sort of energy race between us. Cal was a grabber; Reese was a smooth caress.

Reese walked me home late that night. It was muggy and warm and I was already hot from dancing, now covered in a thin layer of sweat that, for some reason, enhanced the mood. We stopped under one of downtown's fancy street lamps and he took his phone from his pocket.

"Smile," he said, and clicked a picture of us, cheeks together, drunk and giddy.

We crossed Mangrove and passed his new storefront on the corner.

"I'm really sorry about the cats," he said.

"I know."

"I'll ask everyone I know if they could take one. But it's not likely."

"Thanks. I'll probably end up taking them home with me. And getting evicted."

He squeezed my hand—didn't let it go until we took the concrete steps up to my apartment when he rested a supportive hand on my back. I turned to him at my door and without hesitation he pulled me to him, paused—our breath quick, hearts pounding—and kissed me. Cal never kissed me like that.

"Can I see you again?" he said.

"If you don't mind dating a girl with eight cats."

Chapter Forty-two

ReeseFuller: Mom?

ReeseFuller: I tried to call Dad back but it's busy

ReeseFuller: You up to texting?

CrochetMom: *Amy on phone with doc I'll be okay*

ReeseFuller: I'm coming up there

CrochetMom: *No. Tell me what's up. Take my mind off it*

ReeseFuller: ...

ReeseFuller: Okay. Well, I went out with Sophie last night

ReeseFuller: ...

ReeseFuller: Had a great time. Did some Salsa dancing

ReeseFuller: ...

ReeseFuller: You still there?

CrochetMom: *Keep going*

ReeseFuller: First I thought she might be getting back with Cal

ReeseFuller: But she seemed iffy. So, I asked her if I could see her again. She said yes

ReeseFuller: At first, you know, I had doubts. I mean, how could she have dated him?

ReeseFuller: Oh, I didn't tell you that part. Two years, they dated. Anyway...

ReeseFuller: ...

CrochetMom: *You tell her about him?*

ReeseFuller: No. My instincts tell me he must have

changed. I just can't see a girl like Sophie dating him otherwise

ReeseFuller: And it wouldn't be right to tell her about something he did when he was fifteen

ReeseFuller: I guess if I keep seeing her, I'll have to tell her. But not now. No need, really

ReeseFuller: Anyway, we're getting together this afternoon at Café Flamingo with her friends

ReeseFuller: Oh, and her cousin and Noah Holland

ReeseFuller: You remember him? You'll never guess what he's doing

ReeseFuller: I almost didn't recognize him when I saw him a while back...the day I met Sophie. Took me a while to place him

CrochetMom: *Flowers*

ReeseFuller: You know! He's hilarious. I've been over to talk to him a few times. He remembers Amy babysitting him

ReeseFuller: I asked him what happened...why was he selling flowers from a booth

CrochetMom: *Rude*

ReeseFuller: Yes! I apologized. But I was shocked. Did you know about it?

CrochetMom: *His mother told me*

ReeseFuller: He says his production went through the roof as soon as he opened the booth. He's got thirteen books already

ReeseFuller: Sits in the booth all day writing

ReeseFuller: And nobody knows because of his pen names. He says he likes it that way

ReeseFuller: I can send you his latest, if you want

ReeseFuller: ...

ReeseFuller: Have you been able to read much?

CrochetMom: *I'll be fine*

ReeseFuller: I love you, Mom. As soon as I sign the

papers, I'll come up
    CrochetMom: ...
    CrochetMom: Okay. See you soon

Chapter Forty-three

I went to Bookish the next morning...wait, I should say: I danced to Bookish the next morning. Floated, glided, tumbled. All of those things. I was smiling wickedly, so hard my face hurt. But I couldn't stop. It was as if Reese was still there. His hand on my back, our feet moving in sync, hips rotating, swiveling. I closed my eyes, relishing in the memory of it—so present and real. I nearly walked into Benjamin at Namaste. I gushed all over the boy. Took in deep breaths of his lavender incense.

"You're happy, today," he said.

I started singing that 'happy, happy, happy' song Octavia loved so much. I was decidedly off the cliff. Once at the store, Gramps wasted no time.

"Word on the street says you were out with Loverboy last night. Salsa dancing!"

"Who told you?"

"I got it from the Simmons. They were out front of MacAuley Awley's with Officer Palmer this morning and he told them he saw you there. Steamy. That's how he described the two of you." He whistled and smiled impishly.

"And they ran over here to tell you?"

"Waved me down when they saw me opening up."

"This town is awful, Gramps. The gossip!"

Mr. Cornell had come in just in time. "What gossip?"

"Sophie and Loverboy."

"Oh, I was hoping you'd heard something about the contest."

"It just ended," Gramps said. "Let 'em tally up the votes."

"What are you going to do if Trudy loses?" I asked. "Make her change her window?"

"You bet I am. And on my window, it will say 'Voted Best Antiques in Downtown Strawbridge.' That'll show her."

"Sure it will," Gramps said.

"And what if she wins?" I said.

"Impossible. Trudy's Treasures? In that old, creaky house? Ought to be called Trudy's Hoard."

"So, Gramps," I said, hoping to get it in before the Geezer started in on some weighty topic that would take up an hour of Gramps' time...like the color of chalk Officer Palmer used on the tires. "I'm supposed to go over to Café Flamingo this afternoon for something of a soirée. I know I jilted you completely yesterday."

"Go on, go on," he said, like I knew he would. "Soirée all day if you must."

"I'll only be a couple of hours. It's all the Divas. Like a party. Spur of the moment, though."

"A diva party!" Gramps sang out. "A big diva party. Big divas. Little divas. Red divas. Blue divas."

"You've been reading Seuss again," I said.

"All at a diva party! What a diva party!"

"Keeps him young," Mr. Cornell said.

I left my two favorite old geezers to the front and went about straightening up the store from the busy Saturday chaos. I never minded the mess. Gramps taught me to be grateful that people were reading. I was knee deep in the science fiction section when Hugh came in. He seemed suddenly shy.

"I heard you went out last night," he said.

"I did, kind of on accident."

"I was glad to hear it."

"You were?"

"I like your new thriller a lot better than your old horror book."

I punched him. Not hard. Still. "Cal is not a horror book. He's a thriller too. Just a different sort. You don't have to hate him because he broke my heart."

"Maybe it's more than that. Maybe I never understood what you saw in him. He's controlling and pompous."

"Is he?"

"And arrogant."

I brushed off my hands, having placed the last of my stack of books into its correct slot on the shelf and turned to Hugh. "I guess you're right. But maybe he had a right to be. He's successful in business, he's smart enough. And come on, he was always so kind to Alfred. Really, Hugh, once I get past what he did to me, I have to remember that Cal has a lot of good qualities."

"And you never once thought maybe he was showing a different side of himself to you than he shows to other people?"

"Are you saying he did? You'd have told me before, wouldn't you? Did he do something to you?"

"You were already dating him when we met. So...no. I wouldn't have told you something like that."

"I thought we were friends."

"Friends don't try to sabotage relationships by ratting on boyfriends."

"Wait a minute, now. What did he do?"

"Nothing, really. I mean...not anything bad enough to go running to you over."

"What?"

Hugh blushed and shrugged. He reached up to the shelf

at his shoulder and pulled out a paperback, absentmindedly, then slid it back. "He was kind of mean."

"What did he do?"

"Whenever he came into the store and saw me, he'd smack me on the head and call me Nerd Face."

"I never saw him do that."

"He never did it when you were around."

"So, you're saying that behind my back Cal was mean to people?"

He hesitated, shoved his hands into his pants pockets, bounced a bit on his heels. "Yep," he said. "That's what I'm saying."

I was stung, to put it mildly. After Hugh left, my mind darted from memory to memory, thought to thought, trying to find any evidence that Cal was not the charismatic, confident, boisterous, kind man I knew him to be. But so much was a blur. So much in my recollection was of me feeling somehow grateful to him, in awe of his attention to me, even while a couple of nights out with Reese Fuller showed me what real attention was. It was true. Too true. Whenever I was out with Cal, it was always about him and about the people around us. His attention wasn't on me, was it? It was on other people he wanted to talk to. He flirted with every female we came across. Young, old, married, single, didn't matter. And he talked sports with every male. Except Hugh. And Benjamin...and Noah. He looked right through them.

When Gramps approached me some time that afternoon, I was staring at the shelf of horror books.

"I think your party is starting," he said. "Reese is here."

"Okay," I said.

"What is it?"

"I was thinking about you and Grandma. How you two were always holding hands. Always smiling at each other as if you had a secret."

"I miss her, too."

I hugged him and got my purse. Together, Reese and I crossed the street to Café Flamingo. Carrie was already there with Noah, at the first table on the left. I was stunned by both of them. What happened to the cute, awkward nerds I'd come to know? Carrie was in a creamy yellow sun dress and floppy hat—adorable! I knew right away I was going to ask if we couldn't expand the Divas beyond the business woman parameter to include her. Floppy Diva, we could call her. And Noah...did he shave? Slim sunglasses? Dark, dress jeans? For a moment, I thought I'd managed to awaken that morning into some sort of alternate reality.

"Bookish!" Melissa called.

"Hombre Caliente!" Vanessa screamed.

What a diva party!

The next day, everything went straight to hell.

Chapter Forty-four

I opened Bookish Monday morning; I insisted Gramps take the entire day off, but he'd hemmed and hawed and shuffled. He at least agreed to stay home until after two o'clock. I liked having the store to myself, especially that day. I was changed. Not the Sophie I knew. Almost a stranger; but there was something familiar there. Singing, giggling, dancing a bit. Whenever a customer came into sight, I chatted with her, asking about her favorite reads, characters, moments. It was easy somehow, natural, as if I'd *always* been able to hold up a conversation longer than four exchanges. Of course, somewhere in my brain I was asking myself if my idea of a healthy conversation might be rambling and unnatural from the other person's viewpoint. From what I could tell, nobody backed away from me, nobody looked scared. Nobody left the store screaming. So...I think I might have truly been...social.

I'd made a decision the day before, sitting with Reese outside Flamingo. Cal was in the past. Whatever was there, was gone. And Reese... Well, whether or not anything came of that, he'd already taught me what a relationship should look like: two people *into* each other. Gramps and Grandma had that. They did nearly everything together and those things they did apart, they related to the other as stories. They were a couple, not two separate people. They took on life together. That was what I wanted. And I planned to find it.

When my phone played out "Tara's Theme," my heart skipped and tumbled. Reese!

"Hello," I said, a smile on my face so big it was stupid.

"Did you ask Cal to do it?" He was angry.

"Do what?" I couldn't, for the loving life of me, figure out what he was talking about.

Bookish brains work differently than others do. Ours stop operating properly when we detect any sort of attack. Instead of reacting appropriately, we're likely to pop off some quote from a novel we believe is fitting, but almost always turns out to be completely irrelevant. I can only say, in retrospect, how lucky I am I didn't allow myself to laugh and say, 'Do you know what happens to lads who ask too many questions?'* Because I was thinking it.

"Your boyfriend's been brokering a deal with the owner of the space I made an offer on."

Oh, that. No. Wait. Don't. "Oh, that," I said, despite myself. "He's not my boyfriend."

"Yes. That. Did you know about it?"

I shivered and nausea rolled around in my stomach. "Yes, but I wasn't sure he'd go through with it."

"Why didn't you tell me?"

"I don't know."

"Did you ask him to do it? Is that why you were at MacAuley Awley's?"

"No. Why would you even think that?"

"But you knew what he was planning. This is perfect for you, isn't it? Your cats are safe, and I'm gone."

"Isn't there another space downtown?"

He laughed—an angry noise. "I can't beat his offer. This is just one more headache," he said. "One more punch in the gut."

"I didn't mean for this—Hugh said it was breach of

240

contract. You could sue."

"Are you kidding? Sue Mr. Stahl?"

"You don't have to yell at me."

"I'm not yelling. And if you think Cal did this just for you, you're dead wrong. The new offer is ridiculously high; he's gone to a lot of trouble to take another shot at me."

And, of course, without thinking, I blurted out, "Maybe it was all he could think to do, after you tried to ruin his life."

Dead. Silence. Not even angry breathing.

Finally, he said, "Is that what he told you?"

"Yes." Way too haughty. It's what you do when you're being mean and you know you have no real cause to be— you dig yourself a 'how dare you speak to me that way, here's something to hurt you, even though I probably don't know what I'm talking about' trench. And later, of course, you get to bury yourself in it.

"I'd love to know how he managed to spin it in his favor," he said.

"Well, I..."

"I have to go."

And what was I supposed to say? It happened so fast. I was up on a cloud and then I was being battered, so I lashed out and now I had to let it go. Right? It's the domain of introverted, bookish girls. Weird things pop out of our mouths with no problem, but once we realize what we've said, our mind locks up on us and we can't come up with a way to fix it without a lot of self-flagellation and list-making. And those things take time.

So, I said, "Okay."

And he hung up, leaving me suddenly hollow, empty.

"Are you all right, honey?" a customer asked. Her face was pinched with worry.

I nodded. "I'll be fine."

That was it. Just like that. Apparently, I had cavorted

with the enemy. Dumped again. At least, I consoled myself, I hadn't devoted two years to Reese. Better that things ended quickly. That didn't keep me from entertaining that awful sickness in the pit of my stomach.

The day was a blur after that. At lunchtime I watched Melissa, Kaya, and Vanessa sitting outside Café Flamingo laughing and talking. I was glad I couldn't leave the store, glad I wouldn't have to see them, try to be upbeat, or explain what happened. I didn't think I'd be able to say the words without crying. I should have warned Reese. I should have told Cal not to do it. Maybe I shouldn't have gone to dinner with Cal in the first place. Gramps showed up at one-thirty. He knew immediately something had happened. I cringed, feeling like a five year old confessing to stealing a cookie, as I told him what happened.

"Oh," he said, "don't you worry. Everything will work out. Your Loverboy will find a new space."

"But he thinks I went behind his back to ruin his deal."

"But you didn't."

"And I said mean things."

"You were upset; people say things when they're upset. It'll work itself out."

I didn't believe him. He wanted to cheer me up. What was he going to say: "Right, Sophie, you've made a total mess of it, haven't you?" Grandpas didn't say things like that, no matter how true they were. But I knew the truth. I'd lost Reese's trust. It was over.

At about five o'clock, Gramps started trying to get me to go home. "You're tired," he said at first. Then it was, "You don't have to work all day, every day, you know." And finally, "Sophie, you're walking around the store like a wilted balloon. It's depressing. Go see your stray cats."

And you would think that would sound like a good idea to me. But the thought of having to explain to Weesie and Roger Dodger what a mess I'd made of things was unbearable. And don't think they wouldn't understand. Cats *know*. But I could tell them, at least, that it looked as if they'd get to stay put. I should have been happy about that. Before I could get out the front door, Cal walked in, all smiles, his charm as loud as ever.

"I knew I'd find you here," he said.

"I was on my way home."

"Great, I'll drive you."

I sighed and turned to Gramps to say goodbye. He had a stern look on his face, as if he wanted to scold me but held back. I walked with Cal over to Burgers and down the little side street where he'd parked.

"We did it," he said. "It looks like my client is going to get that storefront."

"I hear he made a ridiculously high offer."

"You could say that. But he owed me one."

"Sounds like this person owes you a lot of favors."

I dropped into the passenger seat of his car, weary and feeling old.

"Nothing wrong with dealing in favors, is there?" He smiled at me and turned the engine.

As he made a u-turn to head back toward Manatee and Creek Overlook Apartments, I said, "Did you do it for me, Cal?"

"Of course I did."

"You sure about that?"

"Who else would I have done it for?"

"For you."

He was quiet for a minute. Then he confessed. "I guess there was a little bit of vengeance in it."

"What did he do to you that was so bad?"

"I told you I didn't want to talk about it. Anyway, it was a long time ago."

"Then why would you feel like you have to get revenge now?"

He shrugged and pulled into the apartment complex. After parking and shutting off the engine, he turned in his seat. "You're not mad about it, are you? You should be grateful. Your cats are safe, right?"

"Reese isn't happy about it."

"I would guess not. Did he tell you about it? Are you two friends or something?"

"I don't know. We might have, maybe, dated, if not for this."

"Wait. What? You and Reese Fuller?"

"Not officially."

"You said you didn't like him."

"I didn't. It's complicated."

"But you said we would get back together."

"I did not."

He laughed and shook his head. "Uh, yeah, you did."

"I said I'd think about it. In six weeks."

"I thought you were just making me wait, trying to get me back for dumping you the way I did."

"Maybe I was."

"Sophie..." His face was pinched, worried. "You're not making any sense. Are you dating him or not?"

"I don't know."

"How can you not know?"

I started rambling. Sort of in the manner of my new-found social butterfly bookstore behavior earlier in the day...when I was happy. But then, much later and my mood deflated, it was more akin to a one-girl therapy session in front of an audience of one. I'm pretty sure I started from the beginning with the book tumble onto Reese Fuller's head. I know I said the word 'Loverboy' and can only hope it was in reference to Gramps' preference for the title. Several Divas entered into it at some point. And the cats. There was mention of Lydia and her comb and it ending up in the lagoon. And I definitely told him about Saturday

Night Swing. Too much about that. I think I blurted out, "Salsa!" I wound myself around and around and back until, I suppose, I had finally figured myself out and said, "I hated you, Cal. Hated, hated, hated. And you deserved it. And then I liked Reese. Until I found out about the cats. And then I couldn't let myself like him. I'd be betraying the darlings. So, I let myself think that maybe there was a chance for you and me. But then I saw Reese again and realized I really, really do like him, regardless of what happens to the cats."

At least his face had relaxed during all of that...into something of a mild expression of horror. He nodded slowly, as if digesting.

"So, you and Reese."

I shook my head and felt the tears welling up in my eyes. "Not anymore. He thinks I had something to do with the new offer."

"It was business. If he dumped you over that...his loss."

"And you won't tell me what he did to you?"

He shook his head and chewed on the inside of his bottom lip. "No. Maybe later."

"But why not?"

"Look, Sophie. I know how it works with Reese Fuller. I told you, he always wins. Always comes out looking better. That's what will happen if I tell you. Somehow, he'll make it look like it was all my fault. I'll be the bad guy."

"Okay," I said. What else could I say?

"If we get back together," he said. "After a while, I'll tell you all about it." He stared at me for a bit. "So, what do you say? Are we going to get back together?"

"I don't know."

Not knowing things felt familiar. It was Old Sophie— quiet, shy, bookish—telling me she was coming home.

*From Terry Pratchett's *Mort*. Read it. You'll love it.

Chapter Forty-five

ReeseFuller: Mom, you there?

ReeseFuller: I just called the house, but it's busy

ReeseFuller: I need to talk. Need some advice

ReeseFuller: Start texting or I'm calling your cell phone. I don't care how much you hate it

ReeseFuller: :)

ReeseFuller: Mom. Everything is falling apart. The new store. The deal

ReeseFuller: Sophie

ReeseFuller: ...

ReeseFuller: You

ReeseFuller: I called again. Still busy

ReeseFuller: Are you there? What's wrong?

ReeseFuller: Mom?

CrochetMom: *Reese*

ReeseFuller: Thank god. You scared me

CrochetMom: *It's Dad. I'm on the phone with your sister*

ReeseFuller: No

CrochetMom: *You need to come back*

CrochetMom: *Now*

Chapter Forty-six

Tuesday morning, I fed the cats and tried to be happy that I now had more time with them. There was no need to smuggle them into my apartment and risk eviction. But I had to face the truth: they needed permanent homes. I'd been feeding them at the abandoned storefront for my own selfish reasons. Every time I found a home for one or two, I missed them, and backed off on placing the rest for a long time.

"I'm sorry Weesie," I said. "Roger, Piddle, Diva, Pooper. I promise I'll find you homes. I won't stop this time, until it's done." Weesie purred and rubbed against my legs. "I'll miss you."

I was forced to lunch with with Melissa, Karen, and Kaya at Café Flamingo. Gramps was there when Melissa called. I tried to pretend it was someone else, but she was standing outside her restaurant waving at Gramps and me in the bay window of Bookish, where we were setting up our summer display.

"A Diva lunch," he said.

Before he could start mangling Dr. Seuss again, I agreed to go. I tried to stay upbeat, didn't tell them about the phone call and how I kept going over it and over it in my head, wondering whether or not I should call Reese and try to fix it, and asking myself if it was really over. And then Old Sophie would pipe up and say, 'Of course it's over; it was never going to happen with Reese Fuller in the first place.' I was desperate to ask Melissa if Jake had said anything to her—about me and Reese, about the deal—but I couldn't bring myself to do it. Old Sophie didn't want to know.

"So what's the deal—"

Deal? Did someone mention the deal?

"—with Carrie and Noah?" Kaya asked. "Are they inseparable, or what?"

Oh. That. "I think it's love. They keep thanking me."

"You? It was *my* idea."

"That's true," Melissa said. "Kaya's idea."

"Maybe you should be president of our matchmaking enterprise," I said.

"Yes, I heard about the Trudy Cornell thing," she said. "How about Divas' Dating...Directory? An online thing."

"Think of the weddings we'd get invited to," Melissa said.

"No thank you," Karen said. "I always get sat at the losers' table."

"Not at my wedding," Melissa said.

"Are you making an announcement?" Kaya said.

I sucked in a breath. Were they going to talk about Jake? Would that lead to mention of Reese? And me?

"No. I'm just saying..." she said.

Skunked again.

"How is Jake, anyway?" Karen asked her.

Jake, yes! Finally, there will be talk that could lead to mention of Reese. At that point, Old Sophie told me to shut up.

"Pretty busy. He said they're scrambling over the new store, whatever that means."

"It's business," Kaya said. "Get used to it."

After lunch I carried a small collection of Terry Pratchett novels for Alfred down Strawbridge Main, to the mall.

"There she is!" Octavia called, exiting her booth, arms

wide for a hug. "Girl," she said, "what have you done to Noah?"

"Nothing, why? What's happened?"

"He always spent more time cooped up in that flower booth than is good for a man, but he at least came out a few times a day for some conversation. Since you set him up with that cousin of yours, I haven't heard a peep from the boy. Not a one. He sits in there all day staring at his monitor. He only nodded at me today. Said he can't talk now. He's got work to do. What on earth is he talking about? Work! He sells flowers."

Worried, I pulled Octavia over to the Flower Power booth and peeked inside. She was right. There was Noah, sitting at his little counter, staring at his computer screen.

"Noah?" I said.

"Shh," he said.

"But, Noah..."

He rolled his eyes and pried his gaze from the screen. "What?"

"What?" Octavia bellowed. "Is that how you talk to your friends now? What'd she do? She cut you loose? You taking it out on us?"

Noah stood and stuck his fingers up under his glasses, rubbing his eyes. "No," he said. "Sorry. I'm just..." He pulled his glasses from his face and looked up at us; he was lit with excitement, glowing, if you asked me. "I'm inspired," he said. "Since that first date with Carrie, I can't stop writing. The words run from my head to my fingertips like a river—a rollicking, boisterous, downright fabulous first-draft river."

"What on earth are you going on about?" Octavia said. She grabbed him, pulled him to the front of his counter in the little booth and squeezed herself behind it as far as she could.

"No," he said, grabbing at her arm. "Don't."

But it was too late. Octavia was peering at the screen, her eyes wide, her mouth open. Then she read, "Carrissa, my darling, my darling."

"Please, don't," Noah said.

Octavia gave an aggravated shake of her head and continued, "His thumb rested on her throat; her pulse throbbed against it." She looked up at Noah and smiled. "Are you writing erotica in here?"

"Not erotica. Romance."

"Is it a book?" I said.

"It's what I do. Don't tell anybody."

"What do you mean, it's what you do?" Octavia said, still reading.

"You sell flowers," I said stupidly.

He chuckled, raised his shoulders and said, "The booth is my office."

"I don't understand." That was an understatement.

"My Mom owns the store downtown and we opened this booth up so I'd have a place to write. Something about being out of the house works better for me. I sell a few bouquets and write all day."

"So, you've written other stuff besides this?" I said.

"This will be my fourteenth novel. About half romance, the rest fantasy."

"Fourteen?" Octavia said. "Nobody writes fourteen books."

"Sure they do," I said. "Have you had any published?"

"They're all published."

"Why haven't you told us? Gramps and I could get some in our store."

"They're already there."

Octavia came around the counter and the two of us stood there gaping at Noah like he'd suddenly taken off his human mask to reveal his true lizard alien identity.

"You sell books in Bookish, and I don't know about it?"

"I write under pen names. I'm not ashamed or anything. It's just that, I think women prefer to read romance by women and with the fantasy, well, I don't know."

"And honey," Octavia said, "you don't want other men knowing what you're doing, either. They'd pulverize you."

"I don't think they'd...physically attack me," he said, as if he was only now considering they might.

"Does Carrie know about this?" I asked.

"Of course she does."

"Move out of the way," Octavia said, pushing past us to the door. "I'm going to get my Kindle. You're going to help me find your books."

"So, you're an author," I said when we were alone among the flowers. "A romance novelist."

"Why are you looking at me like that?"

"It's nothing," I said. "You're...surprising, that's all."

He grinned. "It's one of my best qualities."

I left Octavia and Noah together searching for his books on her Kindle and took my stack of Pratchetts out back to Alfred. He was still eating his lunch—a turkey sandwich wrapped in wax paper, and an apple. I took a seat on the bench next to him and gave him the books. He nodded approvingly and handed *The Hitchhiker's Guide to the Galaxy* to me.

"Did you like it?"

"Yep," he said. "Lifted my spirits."

"You'll like the Pratchett books, too."

"Looks like you could use some lifting up, yourself."

"I'm just tired."

"Self-discovery is hard work."

"What does that mean?"

"I know what you've been going through," he said. "Even if you don't."

"Oh, yeah? Enlighten me."

"Six months out from that disaster you call Cal—"

"I thought you liked Cal."

"—you meet your soul mate."

"I'd hardly call Reese my—"

"But you fight like the devil to keep yourself from falling for him. Fear. That'll do it. And then along comes Cal, sniffing around, trying to get back what he threw away. And there you are, ready to consider it, because the heartache you know, is better than the possibility of falling harder than ever. The risk of tearing your heart up, even worse than Cal could do, is maybe too much."

"That's quite an analysis," I said.

"I see things. I know what's going on. So, what're you going to do?"

"I don't know, Alf. I've made a pretty big mess of things with Reese."

"You mean the store?"

"You know about it?"

"I was around when Madaline told him. He took it a bit harder than I would have thought. I think that boy has something else on his mind."

"It's just business."

"Maybe, maybe not. You hang on and he'll come around."

Alfred was a lot like Gramps. Or was it that older people looked at life from the perspective of having lived quite a bit more of it? Everything would be all right, because I'd go on living no matter what happened. If Reese never spoke to me again, it wouldn't be the end of the world. I'd meet somebody else. And then I'd look back on it and think, 'Well, then, everything worked out fine, didn't it? What was I so upset about way back then?' Or not. I could still end up forty-seven, unmarried, and living with thirty-five cats.

All day, I tried to convince myself there would be sunshine at the end of all the rain—it's harder than you'd think—vacillating between calling Reese and trying to fix things and letting Old Sophie come home to stay. I'd certainly have a lot more time for reading if I put the Divas, Reese, and Cal out of my mind.

I considered, briefly, finding this Mr. Stahl and pleading my case. I'd pour out my heart to him. You know...a story of love and heartache and all that. Ask him to take Reese's offer. But, he was probably the same age as Gramps and Alfred. He'd shake his head and *tsk*, or pat me on the head and say, "I need the money, honey. Money talks." Anyway, doing that would mean I was crazy and I didn't want to be crazy.

For an even smaller moment, I thought maybe I could wheedle the name of the new buyer out of Cal and contact *him*. I could beg him to take it back. I could tell him what an awful storefront it was. And how it wasn't even on Strawbridge Main; business would be terrible there. But he'd probably laugh at me and say, "I owe it to Cal. Everybody loves Cal. You ought to know. You loved him, too. Isn't Cal wonderful?"

Hmph. Let it go, I told myself. It was over. I should be happy about it. The cats can stay and I can go back to the way things used to be.

Melissa called and asked me to go with her to The Fort for Lipstick Night. Jake had too much going on, she said, but she wanted a night out. I turned her down. I wanted to sit at home with the cats, watching television, reading a book. I wanted to be Sophie again. That was why, when Cal called, I let it go to voice mail. "No more of any of that," I said to Willow. *No more.*

Chapter Forty-seven

As the days passed that week, I was drawn into a spiral of acute self-loathing. I even loathed myself for loathing myself. At one moment, I'd be fine with it—I was getting my life back, such as it was, and who cared if Gramps didn't approve? But the next moment, I'd be scolding myself—I should have called Reese and apologized. But after a few days of stewing, I was no longer sure what I should apologize for. The conversation we'd had dissolved in my memory; it was now only a feeling, like that of falling into a hole I couldn't get out of it.

My downtown hellos and waves were less and less animated and I realized it wouldn't be difficult to sneak Old Sophie back into the world. People adjust, after all. Mr. Booker, at Stogies, would get used to only a nod. And if I stopped going to Poetry Night, he'd eventually forget I was ever there. The Rollings sisters at Sweet Suite would, in time, forget all the excuses I made for not buying a brownie. Melanie, over at Brunch would soon forget I loved her quiche, and Benjamin would get used to me not stopping to smell incense. It would just take a bit of training, of easing them out of the Social Sophie routine and into a 'that girl looks like someone I used to know but I can't remember her now' routine. The only person I would not shy from was Alfred. But if I stopped visiting him outside the back door of the mall, he'd come to Bookish looking for me, and that would be our new way of doing things.

When Reese finally called, on Thursday morning, I was walking to Bookish thinking all of those thoughts. Somehow, I knew it was him before I saw his name on my phone. I stopped, in front of Begotten, and the perky lady who owned the shop watched me as I looked around, as if I'd find Reese somewhere nearby, pranking me. I waited until "Tara's Theme" stopped playing and put the phone back in my purse. Then I went to work. Simple as that. Better to let it go quietly.

It had been the same with Cal. Six months ago, after he told me Lydia was moving in with him, he'd called a dozen times. I ignored him. I had to. For my own sanity. And when I finally listened to his messages, some six weeks after he left me, they were so disgustingly vile and self-absorbed,* they helped me move on from the 'I'm so worthless he dumped me' stage to the 'I hate him with all the venom I can muster' stage. So, in a way, he was very helpful.

I wouldn't need to wait six weeks to listen to Reese's message. He and I had barely known each other, right? I'd listen to it soon enough. And so, each time he called after that, I let it go. Cal, of course, was calling nearly every day that week, like he was unconsciously competing with Reese. I ignored him, too. As I entered Bookish for work, I turned my phone off. That would do it, I thought. For all of them. No more Social Sophie!

Easier said and all that, I'm afraid. When I didn't answer Melissa's calls, she and Karen showed up at the store the next day, demanding I join them for lunch.

"Did you forget to charge your phone or something?" Melissa said, looking around the bookstore as if it were a museum of ancient artifacts. I almost expected to hear an amazed "whoa" echo from her.

Karen was distinctly more at ease, being familiar with

the artifacts in question. "She even had *me* calling," she said, "thinking you were mad at her or something. And I hate the phone, Sophie. Don't make me use it."

"I turned it off."

"You what?" Melissa said. "Do they even have off buttons? Give it to me."

I stared at her.

"Go on," she insisted. "Hand it over."

Dutifully, I took my phone from the cashwrap counter and gave it to her. She turned it this way and that until Karen took it from her and switched it back on.

"There," Melissa said with relief. "You're back. Anyway, come on over, we're doing lunch."

And there was Gramps with that hopeful grin, nodding at me behind their backs. So, Old Sophie, temporarily subdued within Social Sophie's body, went with them to Café Flamingo for a full-out, all-Divas-present lunch.

Karen twirled about in her new white sun dress before taking her seat, and asked if she still looked frumpy. We all, obligingly, told her she never looked frumpy. "Librarians," Pari said, "are beautiful people."

Pari was, to our surprise, wearing bedazzled sneakers with her pencil skirt. And instead of the typical lacy or silk top, she wore a Captain America t-shirt. "It's the end of the world as we know it," Melissa said. Pari said, "I have decided driving an eighth of a mile to work and back because of delicate footwear and expensive clothing is not my style. Not anymore, anyway." It was Eric Lawson; we were sure of it. Karen, who I'd begun to believe was a private detective in disguise, discovered Pari's new boyfriend was something of an ecology nut.

Vanessa was hair-and-nail perfection, as usual. And Kaya sported new gold hoop earrings so enormous they grazed her shoulders. I felt bookish sitting there in my jeans and tee, but Old Sophie told me to suck it up—*I wear jeans and tees, let the world deal with it.*

We talked about the usual thing girls talk about when they're together. Work. Pari had a client who wanted her to tell stories about all the others, instead of talking about his own problems. Kaya had designed some of her own outfits and was planning a fashion show at a future Triple F. We were all duly impressed. And I told them about Noah—not that he wrote romance novels, he'd sworn me to secrecy about that. But I was allowed to say he was a successful novelist, writing under a pen name. I think he and I both knew the truth would come out soon enough. They were all surprised, but none of them were what I'd call avid readers, and so, didn't pester me for more details.

"I write stories," Karen said.

We all turned to her, eyes wide.

"What sort?" Pari said.

She smiled coyly and blushed. "Romance."

"Ooh," Melissa said.

"Why didn't you tell us?" Kaya said.

"I didn't want you to make fun of me."

"Are they dirty?" Melissa said.

"See?" Karen said.

"I'm not making fun, honest."

"You should talk to Noah," I told her and halted, fearing I'd given his romance secret away. "For some feedback, I mean."

"Maybe I will."

We were silent then, and while it was a nice break from what seemed an hour of nonstop chat, it began to feel uncomfortable—as if they all wanted to say something to me, but were afraid. I thought I was being paranoid.

"So," Vanessa said, "have you heard from your Hombre Caliente?"

So it wasn't paranoia—it's not paranoia when it's true, right? "Why do you ask?" I said, rather stiffly, I'm afraid. It didn't come off nearly as nonchalant as I'd intended.

"Jake asked me if he'd called you," Melissa said.

"Wouldn't Jake know?"

She shook her head. "Reese is in North Carolina. Jake said he didn't want to bother him about it, but he was hoping you two were talking, at least."

"Why would Jake care?"

"What's he doing in North Carolina?" Kaya asked.

"His mother is sick."

"That's right," I said. "He told me."

"What about the new store?" Karen asked. "Madaline said they signed on Wednesday."

"They were able to do it long distance somehow. I think that's what Jake said."

"The signing?" I said. "I thought there was another offer."

"There was," Melissa said. "They were really upset about that for a day or so. But it never happened. The papers were signed on Wednesday as planned. But now Jake has a lot more work to do with Reese out of town."

"What is it, Sophie?" Vanessa said. She put her hand on my arm. "Are you all right?"

"Yes, I'm fine. It's just, the cats. I need to get them to my apartment."

"You'd better," Melissa said. "They started the renovations yesterday. Jake said they were ready to go, as soon as the papers were signed."

"I have to go," I said, standing.

"You don't have to get them this second," she said.

But somehow I knew I had to get them as soon as possible. I got back to Bookish only to realize Gramps still had to get his lunch. He and Mr. Cornell had plans to meet at MacAuley Awley's that day. I was antsy the whole time he was gone. When my phone played "Tara's Theme," though I saw it was Cal, without thinking, I answered it.

"What gives?" he said. "You don't take my calls anymore?"

"I'm sorry. I've had a lot to think about."

"I'll forgive you, as long as some of it involves me."

"So, you and Lydia are still not back together?"

"No, not exactly. But that's not why I've been calling."

"What do you mean 'not exactly?'"

"Turns out that deal I tried to broker didn't work out."

"I heard. What did you mean by 'not exactly?'"

"I don't know. It means I've seen her, but I wouldn't say we're back together. At least, not if you'll take me back."

"So, you're holding her off, waiting to see what I decide?"

"Well...yeah."

"I have to go."

"You doing anything tonight?"

"Yes."

"You're not going out with *him* are you?"

"If you mean Reese, no."

"Someone else?"

"No. I really have to go now."

"Come on, Soph."

"Cal, I have to go."

"Maybe I'll call Lydia."

"You do that." I flung my phone across the cashwrap counter. "What a jerk."

"Let me guess," Hugh said, appearing from behind a bookcase. "Our friend Cal?"

"Where have you been all week?"

"Hello to you, too."

"Well?"

"Working. I finally got that position at SynthTec."

"Shouldn't you be at work then?"

"Wow. You're in a mood. I get every other Friday off."

"Oh. Sorry. I'm really out of sorts."

"So I've heard."

I let Hugh talk—about books, films, how he saw Carrie and Noah one night at the mall while he was shopping for shoes, about his new job—until finally Gramps returned. I told him I had to leave, promised I'd come back as soon as possible. He looked at me curiously, but let me go.

Instead of walking down Strawbridge, through the breezeway and down Mangrove to Manatee, I took a short cut home, down the side street next to Burgers, through the back lots behind shops. I got my cat box from the utility room and headed over to Mangrove. I'd have to do one cat at a time. In the daylight. Mr. Z was sure to catch me. But I had this terrible suspicion they would start hammering away at the concrete behind the store on Saturday. And no matter how many times I told myself nobody in construction works on Saturday, I didn't believe it.

I shuddered as I came up behind the store. The back door was propped open with a concrete block. I heard voices. Outside, against the building, there was a pile of lumber, a few old display racks, and an old cabinet without doors. What caught my eye and made my heart race were rolls of what looked like orange, plastic fencing. Of course, I thought. They have to enclose the property during the renovations to keep people—and cats—out.

I walked across the cracked concrete to the picnic table by the old moss-draped oak and stopped, staring. My heart pounded in my chest. My breath quickened. Where were they? No Weesie. He was always the first out of hiding to greet me. No Roger darting under the table. No Pooper or Piddle. No Diva. The noises of the preparations must have frightened them. I called. "Kitty, kitty, kitty." Nothing.

"Hey," a man shouted at me from the doorway and I turned. "This property's being closed up, hon," he said. "You can't be here."

"I came to get the cats." *I thought I'd be just in time.* "Where are they?"

"They already came and got 'em," he said. "This morning."

A frantic stab of fear came over me and I knew, if only
by the worried look on the man's face, that I was panicking.
He held up a hand, as if to stay an outburst.

"Them people," he said. "Uh, uh...rescue something. I
was told they were gonna take them away."

I stood there, trembling, sinking, shrinking.

"You okay, hon?" he said.

I turned and stumbled back home sobbing, without any
sense of embarrassment at all, and as soon as I closed my
apartment door, a dreadful calm washed over me. I carefully
returned the box to the utility room, took my phone from
the little kitchen table, and returned Reese's call.

*A sampling of the messages sent by Cal Saunderson to the girl he dumped

1. Oh, hey, Soph, did I leave my Metallica t-shirt at your
place? Let me know.

2. Oh, hey, Soph, don't worry about it. Lydia found it.

3. Listen, Soph, it's all for the best, isn't it? What? You
can't even talk to me?

4. Okay, okay, I get it. I shouldn't have blurted out that
I loved Lydia. I should have been more...caring. About it. I
should have told you she was moving in with me in person.
But, you know how it is, right?

5. Oh, hey, Soph, could you pick me up from work? I
lent my car to Lydia; hers is in the shop. Come on. Still not
speaking to me? Well, if you get this, let me know.

264

6. It really hurts me that you can't even answer my calls.

7. Okay, if that's the way you're going to be about it. You can't say I didn't try to leave things good between us.

Chapter Forty-eight

How could you?" I shouted at him as soon as he picked up and said, 'Sophie.' "You had them taken away, without telling me. I didn't even get to say goodbye."

Then he said 'Sophie,' again, with a bit of a question to it, like, 'is that you, under that sobbing hysteria?'

"I tried to call you," he said.

"That's not even the point!"

And I think I heard him say, "Then what is the point?" but that could have been my imagination...or my own voice in my head.

"You knew I wanted them. You knew I was going to take them home. But you went behind my back and *took* them from me."

"I...," he said.

"Stop calling me. Don't ever speak to me again." I smashed my finger against the 'end call' button over and over again but there was little satisfaction in it. I wished I lived in the days of black and white. Then I'd have one of those handsets I could slam onto its cradle with vicious righteousness. And I'd slam it again and again, probably breaking the phone. But it would be worth it.

I proceeded immediately to bake a double batch of brownies; you know the kind...one pan, two mixes, extra thick, nearly-done-in-the-middle scrumptiousness. And when they were done and I had a bowl of moist brownie love topped with a few scoops of vanilla ice cream, drizzled with Hershey's Chocolate Syrup—yes, I know how to mourn properly—I sat myself on the sofa and sobbed, and ate, and ate, and sobbed. It's not an easy thing to do; you have to watch out for gooey dessert spittle.

Reese had the nerve to call me back, but I didn't pick up. I figured he waited an hour, thinking the crazy would have worked itself out of me by then, enough that I could be 'reasonable' (visualize sarcastic finger quotes there) and I hated him for that. And I knew what else he'd say: It was business; nothing personal. Oh, yeah? Well, as Meg Ryan once said, "All that means is it wasn't personal to you. But it was personal to me." And yes, I knew that wasn't from a book, but it was from a movie about a bookstore, so it counted.

Not that I could have picked up his call, anyway. I was much too busy with the sobbing and the stuffing of my face with brownies and watching *The Fault in Our Stars*, in case someone came over and saw me in that state. I knew how the world operated. Breaking down over some stray cats was crazy—nobody was going to sympathize. But over *The Fault in Our Stars*? Of course I'd be face down in a bowl of brownies. And then I laughed at myself—this grotesque, sugar- and young-adult-drama-fueled hysterical braying. Because who was going to come over to see me? Bookish Sophie Childers had no friends. And she *liked* it that way. She liked it just *fine*. Of course, there was Hugh. He might come over. And Pari. She popped by once in a while. And Gramps. And Carrie. But did relatives count? I decided they didn't, because I was trying my best at self-pity. The result: no one stopped by and I made myself sick and depressed and suffered a day or two of hypochondria about the whole cancer thing.

In the weeks that followed, I changed course. In every way

possible. I stopped the Social Sophie walk down Strawbridge Main to and from work each day and instead, walked along Manatee, despite its lack of sidewalk, to Cocoplum, the little side street by Burgers. I stayed put at Bookish, like I used to, letting Mr. Cornell bring in salads or sandwiches. Or I packed my lunch in a proper antique lunch box I got from Trudy's, much to the Old Geezer's dismay—a Star Wars lunch box with Luke and his light saber on it, Leia and her buns, and Obiwan, gazing off into the deep, clearly thought-provoking distance. I avoided Café Flamingo. The Divas called, one after the other and did everything they could to persuade me to come out. I finally stopped answering. I stayed away from Poetry Night. I didn't set up a table at Triple F that month. I told everyone I'd be fine. Just fine. I think they all believed me, except for Gramps. I told him I was happy—just the way I was—but he moped.

I called every cat rescue group I could find, including the Cat Whisperer, and asked if they took cats from that property; no one knew anything about it. I considered putting up posters asking 'have you seen these cats?' But I was pretty sure if there was a deep end, doing that would put me way too close to the precipice. Gramps would have me at some kind of 'introverts suffering loss' recovery group if I didn't watch it.

I figured it would take a little while, but eventually, I'd get there—I'd get to that pre-Cal, Old Sophie state I wanted to find before I dropped books on Reese Fuller. I'd learn to accept that the darlings were gone and I'd convince myself they found loving homes where they'd be overfed and idolized. The only real problem I had was that first week, while walking home the back way. Burning tar pricked at my nose for a few days and I knew they'd put down the new parking lot behind Summer Sun Surf and Beachwear. I growled. I'm telling you, I heard myself growling.

About a week after I'd told Reese Fuller off, the scowl

on my face started to loosen up; I could tell because Hugh and Gramps, even Mr. Cornell, stopped walking wide paths around me and started to look into my eyes when they spoke instead of turning aside and baring their necks to the alpha she-wolf. One particular day, a Wednesday, I ventured to the front window behind the cashwrap again and again, and scanned Strawbridge Main. I wanted fudge. Peanut butter chocolate fudge. A lot of it. But to get it, I'd have to walk down the street. Expose myself, if you will, to Historic Downtown Strawbridge. And what if I ran into Reese Fuller? Was peanut butter chocolate fudge worth it?

"Why don't you go on over?" Gramps said.

I jumped and turned to find him behind me in the cashwrap. "What?"

He nodded toward the window and when I looked out again, I saw Melissa, Kaya, and Karen at a table outside Café Flamingo.

"Oh," I said. "No. I wasn't watching them. I was thinking..."

"About?"

"Fudge."

"Ah, yes. Fudge. It's a fudge kind of week isn't it?"

"Wouldn't you like some?"

"No, no, no. I've got to watch my figure." He patted his belly.

"Your figure is fine."

"Because I watch it. You, on the other hand, too skinny. Go get some fudge."

"Could you go for me?"

He shook his head and left the cashwrap, taking great, overacting, hammy care in lowering himself down the steps. "Sorry, Sophie. My bad knees."

"You don't have bad knees," I said, leaning over the counter.

He slapped his hip. "Lumbago's acting up."

270

"Do you even know what lumbago is?"

He hobbled into the maze of bookshelves. "Too dang hot, then. It's the middle of summer in Florida and you want to send your poor old Gramps out into it." And he was gone, secure in his book sanctuary.

The bell jingled and Mr. Cornell walked in. "Walt," he called. "I hear the results will be announced soon. Took 'em an age, didn't it?"

"He's hiding from me," I told him.

He scrunched up his face and gave me the antique-inspector's eye. "You don't look like you're still in a foul mood."

I laughed. "I'm not. I just asked him to go to Chocshop and get me some fudge."

"Sophie," he said with a sigh, "I'm going to say this with all the love I can muster for you, my favorite female book-seller."

"Oh, yeah?" I tried to look busy shuffling papers and office supplies around on the counter.

"You and fudge...not a great idea."

He was remembering The Fudge Vortex, as I liked to call it. You see, fudge isn't quite like brownies. Brownies are, for the most part, chocolate. No matter what you do to them, they're still squares of irresistible, gooey, mood-enhancing chocolate. Caramel, nuts, icing, chocolate chips, sprinkles. Whatever you put on them, or in them, the power of the chocolate overcomes it all. So, there's no brownie vortex—you can wallow in pans of brownies for only a certain amount of time before you decide you're done and ready to move on. But there are other comfort foods that create vortexes—swirling pits of sobbing, orgasmic, tortured, joyous hell that a girl can get sucked into and not manage to swim out of without a great deal of thrashing, scolding, extra pounds, and fruit detox. Ice cream, for example. You might get tired of the Rocky Road after a few weeks and a dozen

271

half-gallons, but you can move on to Mint Chocolate Chip. Then Moose Tracks. Then Chocolate Fudge Brownie and Cookie Dough. The thing about ice cream, though, is that it takes a lot of attention. Whether it's in a bowl or a cone, you can't shelve books, pick up after customers, and crawl around on the floor while eating it. Enter: fudge. It comes in a variety of flavors and you can chop it up into small bits you pop into your mouth at regular intervals, akin to a sugar IV drip, thus soothing all your troubles. A girl can get lost in fudge and come out weeks later, five pounds heavier, pimple-pocked, dazed, and a little nauseated. And that very thing happened to me six months ago.

It started a week or so after Cal left. I found myself in ChocShop, drooling, with no idea how I got there. Lori Walker, my dealer, hooked me up with a Caramel Pecan... always a free sample to get you started. I didn't come out of it until I woke up a few weeks later to find myself standing in the history section shoving squares of Mint Chocolate fudge in my mouth, wondering what I'd done with my life. Yes. Fudge and misery are a very dangerous combination.

"I'm not looking for depression fudge," I told Mr. Cornell. "This is just a craving. You like fudge, right?"

"Never trust a man who doesn't."

"How would you feel about going down to ChocShop and getting me some? I can't leave Gramps, his lumbago's acting up."

"I'm fine and dandy," Gramps called from somewhere in the store.

I looked at Mr. Cornell, hopefully, forcing myself not to put my hands together in front of my face *a la* prayer. But it was no good.

"Sorry, Sophie. We're not going to be your enablers." Off he went in search of Gramps to gloat about his upcoming 'Best of' award.

Great, I thought. *Just great.* I went to the door and looked out, up and down the street as far as I could see. I'd have to dart out and down the sidewalk fast enough to make it clear to the Divas across the street that I was *not* coming over, no matter how much they called. I could slink down Cocoplum, next to Burgers, then go wide around the backs of stores and cross Strawbridge Main west somewhere, near those medical buildings. Then go behind all the stores on the other side of the street, until I got to Morgan's Office Supply. I'd have to get back on Strawbridge Main there— *Oh, for crying out loud.*

I pushed open the door, waved at the Divas, and headed down the street. The fudge. It called to me.

Chapter Forty-nine

I got the feeling Downtown Strawbridge was giving me space. Everybody knew about the Great Reese Fuller Cat Eviction. And the fact that I'd taken shelter in Bookish, like a literary refugee, must have clued them in that I was not happy about it. So, when they saw me walking hurriedly down Strawbridge Main, arms wrapped around my middle, head down, my gaze firmly rooted to the pavement, they must have chosen to let me be. Nobody called out to me, nobody tapped on her front window. I lifted my eyes the tiniest amount once I'd crossed over to Morgan's Office Supply, but just to take a quick look at Grumpy Cat plush toys in the window as I passed. I made it safely into ChocShop, where I nearly fainted from the aroma of seductive therapy.

"Hi, Ms. Childers," the kid behind the counter said, smiling. He was scrawny. A curly mop of red hair was contained in a net and he smiled a silvery metal smile. Poor thing. I wanted to tell him it would get better. I could tell by his cheek bones. He'd come out of it okay in the end.

I pushed myself off their front door and moved forward, tried to act as if I was just on my way somewhere and thought I'd stop in, see if there wasn't something tempting. I didn't want to march straight to the fudge counter and put my hands lovingly on the glass. Not right away.

"Call me, Sophie," I said. This was the same kid who'd

been in when I came to ask Lori to take a cat. I was sure I'd told him my name was Sophie.

He managed a weird sort of neck and chin shrug and said, "It's a rule. You'd have to talk to Ms. Walker about it."

"About what?" Lori came from the back room, wiping her hands on a paper towel. She tossed it into a bin. "Sophie," she said. "What can I do you for? Bryan, go on back and clean out the sinks." She approached the counter and pushed a little tray of free samples forward. "In the mood, today?"

I never understood how Lori could run the chocolate shop and not be at the very least, plump. But she was thin. Perhaps lean is a better word. She had a few inches on me and her black, thick hair hung straight to her shoulders and was cut straight across her forehead barely grazing her brows. She reminded me of Elizabeth Taylor in *Cleopatra*, except not as mature...Lori's cheeks were just this side of great-aunt-pinchable.

"Why can't your employees call me Sophie?"

"He's seventeen. Where I come from, kids don't call adults by their first names."

"I thought you were a Florida Cracker, like me."

"Where I come from isn't a geographical setting so much as a frame of mind."

"Still, I'm only a few years older than him," I said. "He makes me feel old."

She laughed. "Be glad I don't go full Southern Belle on you and make him call you Miss Sophie."

"Okay, okay. I take it back."

"So, what'll it be?"

"Fudge. A pound of peanut butter chocolate, a pound of peanut butter, and a pound of chocolate walnut."

She looked at me sideways before pulling on her clear plastic gloves. Then she went to work collecting my vortex.

"I hear you and Cal might be getting back together," she

said.

"Really? Is that what people think?"

"Do you care what they think?"

"No." I said it too quickly, always a bad sign. "I shouldn't," I amended.

"So, you're not?"

"I don't know."

"So you are." She boxed my last huge hunk of love and brought the three bundles of joy to the counter near the register where she bagged them.

My answer came out as a deep, depressed sort of weary sigh. Lori stepped slightly away from the register and looked at me.

"What is it?" she said.

I shook my head. "Nothing."

"Sophie," she said, smoothing her hands out on the glass counter with its trays of assorted chocolates beneath, "consider this the girl bar, and I'm your friendly neighborhood bartender." She held up the tray of samples and said, "Tell me all your troubles."

I smiled, albeit weakly, and took a bit of peppermint bark. "Do you know how I met Cal?"

"Spill."

I chewed and talked. "He was in the bookstore."

"Cal Saunderson in a bookstore? Hmm."

"In the previously read fiction section—"

"Previously read?"

"If they can do it for used cars, I can do it for books. Anyway, he was pulling paperbacks from the shelf and flipping through them. I asked him how I could help and he asked me if this book was good or that book was good and what was this book about. I did my best and in the end he had an armful. But he kept asking questions about the top book in the stack. I don't even remember. Stupid stuff, like, was the author a man or a woman. I thought he was flirting with me, so after I took his money and gave him his bag of books, when he asked me out for coffee, I said yes."

"Well, that's a nice enough story, I guess," Lori said.

I nodded. "After we went out a few times, I asked him how his reading was going and he didn't know what I was talking about. I reminded him of the books he bought and he laughed. A lot. Turned out, he'd bought them for a book drive for a women's shelter. They were collecting books at his agency—he said it was one of his realtor's ideas. He wasn't a reader at all. Didn't see the point in it."

She gasped. "Isn't that, like, blasphemy to the avid reader?"

"My feeling exactly."

"But you kept dating him."

"I did." A guilty sigh.

"And now you wonder why?"

"I wonder if I loved him or not. I really thought I did. But now..."

"You don't love him still?"

I shook my head. "Not at all. He's charming, and smooth, and good looking. But..."

"No spark."

"I don't think there ever was a spark. I think I convinced myself that sparks were something people talked about but didn't really believe existed."

"Like Santa Claus."

"Yes." I took another piece of chocolate and nibbled it.

"So, you're not going to date him again."

"No. Why?"

She sighed. "Sophie, I'm going to tell you something about Cal Saunderson." She leaned over the counter, resting her elbows on the glass. "I guess you don't know that I went to high school with him and Reese Fuller."

"I didn't. They've both told me they didn't get along well."

"To say the least. The way I heard it, it started in elementary school."

"What started?"

"The bullying. Cal was a bully."

I didn't grasp what she'd said at first.

"By high school, when I met them, Cal and his friends had a group of kids they liked to torment. The usual stuff. Shoving them into lockers, calling them faggot and pussy. Always barely getting into trouble. But in tenth grade, it got way out of hand."

At that point, it had sunk in. *Cal was a bully.* I couldn't say it didn't fit. Not that I'd ever seen him be cruel. But when I pictured his face in my head, with that arrogant smirk of a smile, I could see it there, beneath the surface.

"There was this ballroom dance thing," she was saying. "Reese and his mother were in it and they got featured in the paper. They were decked out in fancy clothes and in this weird dance pose. Cal brought a bunch of photocopies to school and was plastering them around and teasing Reese. But it didn't take."

"What do you mean?"

"It wasn't so much that nobody cared, but that everybody *liked* it. Reese started up a dance club after school and the next thing you know it's, like, the best club ever and everybody wants in, including the girl Cal had been trying to date."

"Well, that's good, then, right?" I said. "The bully lost."

She chuckled. "Cal Saunderson doesn't like to lose."

I shivered. "What did he do?"

"He and his friends dragged Reese into one of the bathrooms, as I heard it. His friends kept watch while Cal beat him up. Really bad. Like, hospital bad. They say Reese crawled out, couldn't walk, *crawled*. He was out of school for a long while. Broken ribs, sprained wrist, concussion."

"Oh, my god," I said, a few times.

"Cal and his friends were expelled and Reese pressed

charges. There was a trial and Cal ended up doing some time in one of those juvenile detention places."

"Oh, my god," I said yet again.

We both stood there for a bit in silence, shaking our heads and eating chocolate samples, warding off the horror of it all.

"Why didn't you tell me before?" I said.

"Are you kidding? You don't go up to someone you barely know and blurt out that her boyfriend is a bully."

"You were always so nice when we came in for chocolate."

"It's been a few years," she said with a shrug. "People have to be allowed to go on with their lives. And anyway, maybe he'd changed. You seemed like a really nice girl— sane and all. A bit on the intellectual side for the likes of Cal Saunderson. I thought you must be good for him."

"Why tell me now?"

"Just the feeling that...you ought to know."

I thanked her, both for the story—told her Cal wouldn't give me any details and we shared some stories about him, a way of purging any good feelings we had left of the guy— and for the fudge—she gave me a discount.

"Why don't you ever come to lunch with the Divas?" I asked her.

"It's telling that I know exactly who you're talking about, isn't it?"

"They're really not like that. I mean, I thought so too, but they're fun."

"Next time you get together," she said, "give me a call and we'll see."

It was only after I left that I remembered the days of Social Sophie lunching outside cafés with the Divas were over. I walked back to Bookish confused and a little angry. Once inside the store, I found Gramps beaming at me, proud that I'd braved the gantlet of social interaction once again.

"This is all your fault," I told him.

Chapter Fifty

It was true. Or, at least, I wanted it to be true. I told Gramps I was perfectly happy to be bookish. Introverted. Not shy, but quiet. A homebody. There was nothing wrong, I assured him, with being alone, with always having one's nose in a book, a bookworm, an avid reader. The kind of girl who prefers to stay at home on a Saturday night with a good book and a few cats. Nothing wrong with it at all. But he was the reason I dated Cal. I was perfectly fine the way I was, but Gramps never let a day go by without commenting on my cousins and their relationships. Rachel has a new boyfriend. Will Debra be the first of the girls in the family to get married? Candy just met a veterinarian!

"I went out with Cal just to shut you up," I said. "And you did it again with Reese!"

The store was dead quiet. Every customer—thank heavens not more than six of them—stopped reading to listen. Mr. Cornell's eyes were wide as dessert plates and wouldn't, apparently, close. Gramps frowned and hung his head, thoroughly shamed.

It took me a few hours and about a pound of fudge to finally come to reason and apologize. I mean, honestly, I might have gone out with Cal the first few times as a sort of talisman against grandparental pressure, but I didn't date him for two years because of Gramps. And I didn't love him—which I had to accept was more like great fondness than true love—because of Gramps. And Reese...well, if I was going to be honest with myself, I'd have to admit Gramps didn't have much to do with that.

I was hopeless. And no one but myself to blame.

About a week later, when all the fudge was gone and I had successfully fought off the urge to take another walk to ChocShop, I glanced out the front window of Bookish and saw Reese Fuller, lounging at a table in front of Café Flamingo across the street. I froze, except for some tingling. It had been weeks since I'd seen him and that made him all the more potent. You know how you walk into the bakery and your senses are overloaded with the heady aroma of brownies and cakes and pies and you're a bit dazed by it? But if you stand there for a bit, all the prickling and intoxication settle down and you can think straight again. That's what it was like, seeing Reese. The heightened awareness of every curve of his face, the memory of his lips, my increased heart rate, the silkiness of his hair between my fingers, all flooded back to me and I could feel my face start working its way into that damsel-ish adoration gaze. Stop it, I told myself and tried gritting my teeth. Grimacing, I stared at him. He was sipping a smoothie, reading a book, and wearing thick-rimmed reading glasses. I sighed. He was... adorable. I think I might have drooled a little. When he looked up at me, pulling his glasses from his face, I stumbled backward and turned around.

"Everything okay?" Gramps said. He was digging books out of a box and putting them onto our metal rolling cart.

"Sure."

"Why don't you go on over?"

I shook my head. "Over where?" Surely he didn't mean I should go talk to Reese.

He nodded at the window and I turned back, briefly—didn't want to be caught goggling—to see Melissa and Vanessa had joined Reese at the table. In the short glance, I'd seen plenty: smiling, laughter, happiness. What was he, honorary Diva? He had enough to be happy about, didn't he? His shiny new store would open soon, cat free. Everything was working out fine for him.

"I don't feel much like socializing," I told Gramps.

"Well, how do you feel about taking that purchase order over to Morgan's?"

"Now?"

"You said you'd do it two days ago."

"But I can't walk out there now."

Gramps put the last of his garage sale purchases onto the cart and turned to me with a severe look. I was sure I'd never seen Gramps mad; he wasn't the type. But this looked about as close to anger as he might get.

"If being anti-social is such a great thing, Sophie," he said, "why do you care *when* you walk out the door? What do you care if they see you?"

I pouted. And felt like I was three years old. Tears stung at my eyelids. "Not *anti*-social," I mumbled.

"You won't go out because you're afraid. I never thought I'd see my Sophie afraid."

"I'm not afraid."

"Then go to Morgan's and get our order."

He was right, of course. I didn't fault him for it. Old Sophie was all talk, apparently. Well...I mustered up my courage...it was time to embrace her fully. I worked the purchase order off the memo holder (it has a clip, but Gramps loves to shove papers onto it as if it's a nail), muttered a sarcastic "fine," shoved my phone in my front pocket and was out the door. I could run the errands. *Of course* I could run the errands. Even pre-Cal Sophie was able to walk around in public. Still, once I made it inside Morgan's, I felt as if I'd braved a jaunt across hot coals while being pelted with bits of coquina rock by island natives.

"Sophie!" Karen came out from behind her cashwrap to offer me a hug. It was oddly comforting.

"Hi, yes, sorry. I've brought our purchase order." I was breathless and apologizing, like a nerd.

"I'll get Daddy to bring it up."

She returned behind the counter, picked up the phone and gave her father our order number, then set the handset back on its cradle and turned her attention to me with a smile. "How have you been? I haven't seen you in a while."

"I'm all right. Getting back into the swing..." Which reminded me of Reese. "...you know."

"I hear he's back in town."

"Who?" It was supposed to come out of my mouth naturally, as if I really didn't know who she was talking about. But it didn't work. It never worked when I needed it to.

"Madaline told me this story you wouldn't believe, about that deal, you know for his store. She says..." She paused.

"She says what?"

"You're not getting back with Cal, are you?"

"No. Why does everyone keep asking me that?"

"Are you sure. Because, it's bad form to rat out a girl's boyfriend."

"What did he do now?"

"He tried to sabotage Reese's deal with Mr. Stahl."

"I know about that."

"Oh, did you? Well, I have to say, I was appalled. And so was Madaline. I mean, to stoop so low...to use some-one's cancer...just boggles—"

"Wait, what? What about cancer?"

"Mr. Stahl," she said. "He has cancer. He was hanging on to the building, hoping one day he could open a little golf shop. So says Madaline. But his family needs the money now. Anyway, Maddy says Cal knew Mr. Stahl was dying and Reese's mother has cancer—"

"What?"

"Yes. And so he finagled some crazy scheme to lure Mr. Stahl into this other deal, where he'd get more money. And he knew Reese wouldn't do anything about it, you know, because of his mom, and...you know. Are you all right?"

I was not all right. I could feel the tightness in my face, the way it was pinched up toward an imaginary point just in front of my nose. My forehead was struck suddenly with a razor-edged ache and I thought I was going to vomit all over the glass case full of Cross pens. Mr. Morgan showed up and handed me my big box of office supplies. I managed to find my way out of Morgan's, promising Karen I was perfectly fine, better than perfect, actually. No problem at all.

As I crossed the little side street, my phone played out "Tara's Theme" and I shifted the weight of the box over to my left arm, wiggled the phone out of my right pocket, saw it was Cal calling and dropped everything. *Everything.* My phone, and the box—out of which tumbled Gramps' new stapler, four rectangular boxes of staples, six packs of colorful hanging folders (five per pack), four boxes of Bic pens (two blue, two black), a phone message pad, that cascading wall paper organizer he just had to have, a pack of twelve manila folders, a block of sticky notes, some sort of bizarre spinner that held pens, pencils and what-not, and one of those plastic cylinders filled with paper clips, which rolled out into crosswalk on Strawbridge Main.

My eyes were teary—from shock over Cal, I imagine, and the mess I'd poured out onto the street, and perhaps the general shambles I'd made of my life (I do get melodramatic at times)—as I scrambled to get it all back in the box, scooped the box into my arms as best I could and, still stooped, looked around for my phone, realized it was in the box, then stood up, knocking the top of my head into Reese's chin.

"Ow," he cried.

"Ow," I cried.

He flopped around a bit, losing the cylinder of paper clips he must have retrieved from the street, and his book. He bent to get them, chased the cylinder a few yards, lost his reading glasses from his front pocket, grabbed them, then stood and carefully—the box of clips grasped in his hand, out in front of him as a barrier between us—walked back to me. I took the clips and thanked him.

"No problem," he said. He put a hand to his jaw and walked on down the sidewalk.

Chapter Fifty-one

O n Friday of the third week after losing the cats, Hugh took me out on a proper date. Dinner and a movie. He claimed it wasn't a real date—said I was still a cross-genre kind of girl and he would stay on that sad, lonely shelf set aside for gaming manuals. But I thought it was worth a try. I thought, maybe mine wasn't going to be a 'mad-cap, bookish girl meets dashing prince of a boy and love ensues' kind of story. Maybe mine was the kind of story that doesn't get told—a 'bookish girl realizes her nerdy friend is the right sort of boy for her' story.

We went to Burgers and sat outside on the patio, at a table for two, where we could people watch while we ate. He did most of the talking, telling me he worked in a cubicle and he had this device that made a swishing sound every time someone came in, like the doors on the Enterprise. Told me he'd switched from oatmeal to granola for break-fast and that his mom bought a dance fitness DVD and was now romping about in the living room in a leotard and tights in the evenings. He said there was a rumor going around about Noah writing romance books, and he thought maybe he should start up writing scripts again, couldn't hurt. And anyway, there was a local film group now, and maybe, if he could work up the nerve, he would join, and did I want to do it, too? He knew I wasn't into acting or writing, just books in general, but he'd feel easier about it if I went along. Then out of the blue he said, "I bought a Kindle. Can you forgive me?"

I laughed.

"So you *are* listening."

"Of course I am."

"You haven't said a word since we ordered."

"I'm tired; that's all. So, you didn't really get a Kindle?"

"No, I did. And I would like your forgiveness."

"There's nothing to forgive. The book business is changing."

"*You* wouldn't buy a Kindle."

"I wouldn't?"

"You strike me as a holdout. One of those who loves the feel of a book and the smell of it, almost as much as the words inside it."

I shrugged. "There is romance about books, I guess."

"How long can Bookish stay in business?"

"Long enough for Gramps."

"What about you? What will you do if you have to close someday?"

"We might not have to. I own the building. Very low overhead."

"So, you'd sit in there all day with your books, alone? That's not creepy."

"You'll stop by to see me, won't you?"

"What, with my Kindle? That would be awkward."

"Well, I like retail," I said.

"Hence your business degree."

"Despite the whole customer service thing."

"You're good at it."

"Because it's related to books, probably. But, maybe I'd open a different sort of store."

"What kind?"

"What about nerdy collectibles and gaming?"

"I like that."

"Then you'd still come by nearly every day. Nothing has to change."

"Things change," he said. He was looking behind me. "They always do."

I turned to follow his gaze and saw that Reese had come onto the patio with Jake, Melissa, and another woman. He saw me and before I could even register what sort of look he'd given me, I turned away.

"He's coming over," Hugh said.

"What?" I tensed and couldn't breathe. Focused on my clasped hands on the table, I struggled. When I could feel him next to me, I looked up. *Breathe, damn it, breathe.*

"Hey," he said. He shook hands with Hugh and turned to me.

I nodded, still trying to get a breath in.

"I know I'm not supposed to speak to you, but...I wondered if your head was okay."

I nodded again.

"That was some collision. I would have called, but..."

I lowered my eyes to the table again.

"About the cats," he said. "Did you ever listen to my messages...from before?"

I nodded, which was a lie...if a nod can be a lie—I think it can.

"Not that it helps," he said. "But I did try..."

I sat there like a panicked, crisp piece of toast.

"Okay," he said. "I'll see you around."

When he left I finally took in air and trembled. Hugh reached across the table and took my hand. I held on tight.

"Are you all right?"

I nodded and breathed. "I acted foolish, didn't I?"

"A little bit eighth grade, yes."

"Oh, god." I propped my elbows up on the table and let my face fall into my hands.

"You really like him. I can tell."

"It doesn't feel like it," I said.

"You're just hurt about the cats. I bet, if you gave him a chance, you two could go out again."

I shook my head. "I don't think I could forgive him."

"You don't want to forgive him."

"I didn't get to say goodbye."

"Sophie..."

I looked up at him, and let my hands fall into my lap.

"I'm going to say this—it needs saying—and I want you to know I'm saying it with all the kindness and respect I have for you."

"You're scaring me."

He nodded. "They're just cats, Sophie."

I started to sob. Blurted out like a baby. Had to put my hands up to hide the ugly crying face. So embarrassing. And Hugh let me do it. That was nice of him. I wondered if he knew what it was all about—it was about the last two-and-a-half years of my life. About Cal and the truth. About Reese and the spark he'd lit inside me that I'd managed to douse. About the cats. About weariness, fear, loneliness. Old Sophie. Social Sophie. Was there any real Sophie at all and if there was, why couldn't I figure her out?

I'd settled down when our burgers arrived and sat staring at my plate like a weary four-year-old after a tantrum.

We ate for a bit before he said, "I was just saying..."

"Anyway," I said, shoving a fry in my mouth, "he's with a new girl, already."

Hugh looked over to their table and then back to me. "I think they're talking about you."

"I did just cry in public."

"You *are* acting a little crazy."

"That's it, then. I am now officially a Crazy Cat Lady."

"You're not going to become a hoarder are you? They say suffering a traumatic loss can cause it. I can see you now, in an apartment filled with cats, like that guy."

"I'd like that. I think that's what I'll do. I'll buy a house and become a cat whisperer."

At some point in the evening—I think it was during the lull between explosions in the film we watched—I realized if Reese did try to warn me about the cats—to give me time to get them, I was probably, maybe, *possibly* being too hard on him.

That night after Hugh dropped me off at home, I fortified myself with a brownie, sat on the sofa with Willow and Midnight—Chloe watching from atop the kitchen counter (yes, I knew I shouldn't let her do it, but I wasn't in the mood to fight)—and listened to Reese's messages in order of arrival in my voice mail.

1. Thursday morning. "Sophie, I...I had to go out of town. I'm sorry I didn't call before now. Something...something happened. I'll try to call you later."

2. Thursday afternoon. "Sophie... Sorry I didn't catch you earlier." Pause. Breathing. Click.

3. Thursday afternoon. "Sophie...listen. The contract went through, after all. Anyway, my sister Amy works with cats in Orlando. She said she would have her friends come get them. Your cats, I mean. Find them homes. So...you know. Don't worry about them."

4. Thursday night. "Hey...Sophie. I guess you're not going to call me back. I get it. Listen. I wanted to tell you... never mind."

5. Friday night—after I'd screamed at him. "I'm sorry. You're right. It's...scheduling and all, it was too much for me to deal with. Anyway. I'm sorry."

If I'd listened to his messages on Thursday night, I'd

have gotten the cats into my apartment. Maybe. Maybe not. Maybe I would have cried a lot and said goodbye to them. Because the whole point at the start was to find them homes and, well, Reese Fuller did it. And if I had listened to his messages, I could have said goodbye. It bugged me that I didn't have as much reason to hate him as I thought—made me look crazy, or at the very least, self-absorbed to the point of mean-girl-dom. Not that it made any difference. It was over and done with. Finis. Kaput. The End.

Chapter Fifty-two

I'd managed, over the few weeks since I lost the cats and my wits, to avoid the Divas, mostly. They commiserated, as best they could, about the break up—even though I told them that what Reese and I had could hardly be described as a relationship and so we hadn't technically broken up; it was more of a scuttled launch—and about the loss of my darlings. But I was becoming used to being alone again, without friends. I thought they'd finally accepted that I wasn't really one of them—my bout with Diva-hood, I reasoned, was analogous to my non-relationship with Reese: never really started and so nothing to mourn. I was wrong, apparently.

On Saturday, I got into Bookish early, thinking I was supposed to open, only to find Gramps already there, as usual. And Mr. Cornell came in behind me, the Downtown Strawbridge Gazette in his fist.

"Did you see it?" he said.

"I did," Gramps said.

"See what?" I made the mistake of saying.

He ceremoniously unfolded the paper, snapped it open, and read: "The recently hatched scheme of Old Geezer's Antiques owner Bill Cornell to enlist downtown shoppers to enter into his dispute with Trudy's Treasures over bragging rights has backfired."

"Well, it certainly has," Gramps sympathized.

"Venerable Trinkets!" the Old Geezer shouted.

"Inside voice," Gramps scolded.

"Venerable Trinkets." Mr. Cornell pulled a folded copy of the Historic Downtown Strawbridge Business Owners Management Board newsletter—The HDS BOMB News—out of his pocket and tossed it onto the counter. "It's a conspiracy, Walt. I'm telling you."

"You may be right," I said.

"What?" Mr. Cornell said. "You really think so?"

"You think anybody around here wanted to take sides? Or ask their customers to do so?"

"But you did. Didn't you? You two voted for Old Geezer's."

"Of course I did," Gramps said.

Mr. Cornell looked at me and I offered him a sheepish grin.

"Say it isn't so, Sophie."

"What are you going to do now?" Gramps asked him.

"Well, I'm not taking my window down."

"So all three antique shops will proclaim themselves best?" I said.

"You don't think Swanson'll put it up in his window?"

"Why wouldn't he?" Gramps asked.

"Everybody knows you lost," I said. "You'll have to put something else in the window."

He slammed his palm on the counter and said, "Dang it all!"

"Who got best bookstore?" I said.

Mr. Cornell rolled his eyes. "Yours is the only book-store downtown."

I smiled. "I know."

I'm certain Mr. Cornell mumbled, "traitor," as he left Bookish for his own store where he probably spent the rest of the day concocting his next plan to get back at Trudy. I took myself to the back of the store and the children's corner. I was on my hands and knees a few moments later, digging stray books from behind and underneath a bottom shelf, when I heard the front bell jingle; I listened for more ranting from Mr. Cornell. But I heard no shouting, so got back to work. At some point I realized there was a pair of feet to my right—slender, tanned, the toenails painted lavender, shod in dainty cream sandals. And there were more feet crowded with them in the aisle—a pair of sensible shoes, a pair of glitzy, bedazzled sneakers, a pair of cute pink pumps, not too high in the heel, and a pair of flats that laced up the shin with olive green ribbons. The Divas.

"You can't unfriend us," Melissa said when I stood up to greet them. "Downtown Strawbridge isn't Facebook."

"I've been really busy, that's all." I was lying like a mad woman and they knew it.

"Come on," Karen said. "You're coming with us."

I shook my head.

"It's a Diva intervention," Pari said. "And it's long overdue."

Melissa gaped at Pari. "It was *your* idea to leave her alone this long. You said she had to stew a bit with her emotions before we confronted her."

"I said a week or so, not three."

"I can't leave Gramps on a Saturday," I said.

"It's all taken care of," Vanessa said.

"Not only did we clear it with your Gramps," Kaya said (And I have to say, I found it endearing that she referred to him that way), "but we brought in a replacement."

"A what?"

"That's right," Melissa said. "A Sophie Bot."

They dragged me up front where I saw Gramps chatting with a blond girl who might have been fourteen. She smiled at me and—I swear—giggled.

"Looks more like a Melissa Bot," I said.

"This is my sister Donna," Melissa said. "She's going to help out here for the summer."

I raised an eyebrow at Gramps. "I wasn't aware we were hiring."

Gramps shrugged. "Go on," he said, with a dismissive wave. "You've got Diva things to do."

As they escorted me out the door, I said, "Are you sure she's old enough to read?"

"She's seventeen," Melissa said. "And don't worry, your Gramps would never replace you."

"Me, first," Vanessa said.

I protested as well as I knew how, but I had little experience with interventions and ambushes. I was taken, by force, to Glam it Up!, shampooed, wrapped, sat in a chair, covered with an apron, twirled around and made to stare at myself in the mirror.

"What'll it be?" Vanessa said. "Highlights? Full color? You'd make a fabulous dark cherry."

"No," I said...maybe shouted. "Trim, please."

Vanessa sighed. "Very well."

There were three other stylists in the salon. Two of them had clients—one cut and one perm, by the look and stink of it—and the other sat in her chair eating crackers and drinking a Diet Coke. Vanessa chatted as she clipped and told me everything I needed to know about her, her aunt Rose, Glam it Up!, and love. And her fellow stylists joined in with Amens and Praise Bes and You Tell Its. Latin music tickled the air, barely audible, but loud enough to get the gist of the beat; everybody, including me, tapped something, or wiggled something, along with the radio.

"You can't look for love," Vanessa told me. "It has to come to you. Usually when you least expect it. That's why we so often try to push it away—it's because we weren't looking, so we don't know what we've got. But you know the truth of it? If it's the right love, all the pushing away in

298

the world won't get rid of it."

"Amen."

"You tell it."

"And so, you'll see," Vanessa said. "What's meant to be will be."

"Praise be."

"*Que sera sera,*" I said.

"You speak Spanish?" Vanessa said.

"No."

As I was being blown dry, Kaya came into the salon. Once I was finished, tried to pay and was refused, tried to tip and was thrown out, I was escorted down the street to her shop, where Karen and Melissa were ready to dress me. I went into and out of the dressing room about fifty times until I was declared saved by the power of new clothes. I did feel pretty good. They'd chosen a frilly, top in cream, one of those with the sleeves that fit down to the elbow and then go wide—Kaya called it Boho—a pair of form fitting dark jeans, flared, and wedged sandals that laced up my calf—very much like Kaya's flats—with ribbons. I was deemed eclectic.

"My turn," Karen said. "Come on."

She hooked my arm in hers and walked me back up the street to Morgan's Office Supply, all the other Divas following.

"Is this the arts and crafts portion of my intervention?" I said once we'd entered the store and the air conditioning made me shiver.

We all followed Karen to the counter where she reached over and took a flat, brown package from it.

"This is for you," she said. "The frame is from me and the picture is from Melissa."

I felt silly, to be honest, standing there in the office supply store surrounded by Divas, opening up a present, so I was blushing before I got the wrapping off.

"Oh," I said, as the paper fell to the floor. It was an eight-by-ten photograph of the darlings at the picnic table behind Reese's new store. Weesie and Diva were perched atop the table looking at the camera, while Piddle Paddle stretched out on his back on the bench beneath them, his face toward the camera but his eyes on something behind it. Pooper Scooper sat next to Piddle, looking at him, head tilted as if confused, and Roger Dodger peered out from beneath the bench. "It's beautiful. How did you get it?"

"Jake," Melissa said. "He's into photography. He took it a while ago."

"He's the whole reason for this intervention, if you want to know the truth," Vanessa said.

"Last night," Melissia said, "when we saw how upset you were at Burgers—"

"Oh, that," I moaned.

"—he told me about this picture and suggested I give it to you."

"And when she asked me about a frame," Karen said, "I told her we should get together and get you out of your slump."

"Is that what I'm in? A slump?"

"We shall see," Pari said. "I'm next."

"Oh, no, no, no. I don't want to be psychoanalyzed."

"It won't hurt a bit," she said with a wicked grin.

Chapter Fifty-three

"This way."

Pari took my arm and led me out of the store, down Strawbridge Main and, instead of across the tracks to the Executive Suites building where her office was, across the street to Brunch, where Melanie already had our quiche of the day plated and ready to put down in front of us.

"Go on," Pari told the others. "We'll be with you in a few."

"That's a relief," I told her. "I thought you were going to hypnotize me or something."

"I'm not a hypnotist; I'm a therapist."

"You're going to therapize me, then."

"We'll call this a quiche session. Normally, I'd do it over a brownie—"

"I know what you mean."

"But it's lunchtime, so quiche it is."

I dug in. Spinach. Melanie's best quiche, if you asked me. "What do I do? Talk about my childhood? My mother made me wear a horrid dress with puff sleeves on picture day in sixth grade. I've never forgiven her. We could talk about that."

"We could. Do you feel it's relevant?"

I shrugged. "I suppose not."

"Why don't you tell me about last night. The Reese

sighting."

"I behaved badly."

"I heard about it. Why do you suppose you reacted that way?"

"I don't know. I've spent all these past weeks hating him and mourning the cats. And then I'd turn around and blame myself and then go back to hating him again. It's been... exhausting."

"What if you hadn't alienated yourself from everyone for so long?"

"Alienated?"

"Avoiding everyone, not just the Divas, slinking to work the back way—"

"I wouldn't call it slinking."

"—hiding in Bookish all day, talking only to Hugh and your grandfather."

"I like being alone."

"But look where it's gotten you. There's nothing wrong with enjoying one's own company, Sophie. But cutting yourself off the way you've done...it can only lead to self-absorption."

"Cruel." *So, she was a mind reader.*

"But true."

"So, you're saying I wouldn't have acted like a zombie with Reese last night, and as a result, burst into tears, if I'd stayed around, kept being friendly?"

She didn't say anything, just kept eating her quiche.

"I see what you mean," I said. "I guess. If I'd been an adult about it, I'd have already seen him around town and talked to him—broken the ice, as they say. Probably apologized for yelling at him. Things would have settled down earlier."

"Mm hmm," she said.

"But, I really do like being...bookish."

"No one's asking you to stop being you. We're not

saying you must become a social butterfly. But you can't keep pretending that not being a part of the world around you is helpful to you. At all. In any way."

"Okay," I said. "I get it." Seemed to me everyone had a dose of Gramps in him, when you got right down to it.

"Anyway, you're a Diva now. There is no process by which one can become un-Diva-ed."

After we finished our quiche, we stopped in to see Mr. Booker at Stogies and talked poetry (I had no idea Pari was a fan of Rossetti); met the other Divas at Sweet Suite where the Rollings sisters gave me a big box of their special deluxe brownies—caramel infused and pecan topped—and told me not to be such a stranger; went inside Begotten, introduced ourselves to the owner, one Carolina Davies, and perused her selection of fine inspirational gifts and baubles; invaded Namaste and oohed and aahed over all the earthy peasant tops and hippie paraphernalia (Suri said she just *had* to have a frilly Boho top like my new one, and Kaya told her it was one of a kind...probably); and ended up outside Café Flamingo, sitting at one of the wrought-iron tables—Melissa on my left and Pari on my right, with Kaya, Karen, and Vanessa across from me—where we sipped iced teas and ate the Rollings' brownies.

"Consider yourself back in the land of the living," Kaya said.

"Whether you like it or not," Vanessa said.

There was a pause—an awkward, weird stop in which all the Divas took hold of their iced tea glasses and began to sip conspicuously.

"So," Melissa said and punched her straw up and down in her glass. "Have you heard about the new Summer Sun shop?"

I stared at her. "Yeah." Like. *Duh.*

"The soft opening is next week. Wednesday, I think."

"So?"

"Is it true that Reese is back?" Pari asked.

"Finally," Melissa said.

"Why was he away so long?" Vanessa said.

"His mother has cancer."

There were appropriate responses all around, though it was clear they knew more than I did.

"Karen told me last week," I said. "And he told me she was sick a while back."

"She had a really bad reaction to her chemo a few weeks ago," Melissa said. "That's why he left so suddenly."

"But Mrs. Simmons said she's okay," Pari said.

"From what Jake says, there's good reason to think she'll be all right."

"What's wrong?" Vanessa asked me.

"You mean, that first week he was gone," I said. "She had a reaction?"

Melissa nodded. "They almost lost her."

I cringed.

"What is it?"

"I called him, that week, and yelled at him about the cats."

Vanessa winced and the others made 'that was probably not a good idea' faces at one another.

"I didn't know what was going on with his mother."

"Of course not," Pari said.

"No," Kaya said. "You couldn't have known."

"I told him never to speak to me again."

"Oh," Karen said.

"Well," Melissa said, "there are worse things."

"Are there?" I said. "I called the guy while his mother was fighting for her life and berated him about cats."

"Yeah, well," Vanessa said, "okay. That was pretty bad."

"No wonder you two are acting so weird to each other," Kaya said.

"I'm surprised he's said anything to me at all."

304

"So, you have spoken to him? Before last night at Burgers?"

"A little," I said. "After I banged my head into his chin."

"What's that about?" Vanessa said.

"I saw it," Karen said. "I'm sorry to say, it was hilarious."

She went on to tell them about my office supply episode as if it had been a cartoon, which, in her words, it sounded very much like. And they laughed and laughed. Okay, I laughed too. The image of Reese, falling backward from my head banging into him, his book launched into the air and sailing to the ground, and those damn paper clips rolling away yet again, was too much to bear stoically.

"See?" Pari said after we'd exhausted ourselves. "This will all be something to look back on and laugh about one day."

"You're still a Diva, right?" Melissa said.

"Of course she is," Kaya said.

"No more hiding?" Karen said.

I sighed. "No more hiding."

It wasn't the end of the world, I supposed. It wasn't as if I had taken a stand against friendship and socializing on principle. And anyway, they'd taken me out of Bookish, spun me around, dressed me up, clipped me, gifted me, psychoanalyzed me and sat me down again brand new— they'd turned me into Social Sophie.

"Anyway," I said, "I was told once you've been Diva-ed, there's no going back."

Chapter Fifty-four

CrochetMom: *Reese, hello*
ReeseFuller: How are you feeling?
CrochetMom: *Much better*
CrochetMom: *I wanted to tell you again how much I love the locket*
CrochetMom: *and the picture of you and Sophie inside is darling*
CrochetMom: *just darling*
ReeseFuller: I'm glad you like it
CrochetMom: *Amy tells me there is hope*
CrochetMom: *with Sophie*
ReeseFuller: You taught me there is always hope
CrochetMom: *Well, keep me posted*
ReeseFuller: I will, now get some more rest
CrochetMom: *I love you, sweetie*
ReeseFuller: I love you, too, Mom

Chapter Fifty-five

It was Monday afternoon, when Reese Fuller came into Bookish. I was peeved, to say the least. I'd spent Saturday night—it was no easy task convincing the Divas I was not in any way prepared to go out; I had quite a lot to think about, after all—coming up with reasons to go see him. Excuses, I mean. And speeches, lines...things to say. I knew I had to get past the weirdness of that first real talk...and I had to apologize. But I couldn't just walk over to his store and, out of the blue...no. There had to be a reason. Hence, my lists.

Excuses

1. Oh, hi, Reese. I found this book I thought you might like. I can hit you with it, if you want... (too cavalier)

2. Oh, Reese, there you are. I don't know if you know this, but I've suffered a bit of a brain trauma... (too insensitive)

3. Reese, hi, I was on my way to see how Trudy is handling her defeat... (could work)

Lines to memorize

1. I'm so sorry, I didn't know, if only I'd known... (cowardly)

2. No, really, I blame myself. All my fault... (brazenly sacrificial)

3. No, go on and say it, I'm the stupidest, rudest, most self-absorbed—Pari says so too, and she knows about these things—selfish person you've ever met. (True)

I talked it over with Willow, Midnight, and Chloe and they agreed I should stop trying to make it all up beforehand. It would be so much more natural if I just let it happen. Then I laughed out loud and chided them. *Were they crazy cats?* I was not Conversation Diva. Social Sophie was, let's face it, something of a misnomer. I'd learned to smile and say hello and such, but that was about it in my repertoire of smooth operator abilities.

I ended up, that Saturday night, on the sofa, channel surfing where I came upon—you'll never believe it—*The Terminator*. I only missed the first bit, so far as I could tell, and sat mesmerized, hugging a sofa pillow—because I'm not a big fan of scary things and the cats wanted no part of my clinging—watching it.

And all day Sunday, I kept trying to walk out the door of Bookish to make my way, bravely, head held high, down Strawbridge Main to the new Summer Sun Surf and Beachwear where I was sure to find Reese Fuller hard at work. I'd walk through the door, assuming it was unlocked, right up to him and say, "Reese..." That was as far as I got. I figured it would be better to wait until I could at least think of a way to *start* an apology.

Anyway, my point is I was supposed to go to *him*. Grovel and all that. I didn't hope for much, seeing as I'd done a clever job of painting myself as moody, childish, and a tad daft. But I could at least be the one to offer the flag of truce and possibly friendship.

I was up on the ladder, lost in thought—okay I was saying over and over in my head things like, 'oh, Reese, hi, I need to apologize'—pulling down a hard copy of *Harry Potter and the Sorcerer's Stone*, when I heard the doorbell jingle.

"Gramps," I called. "Last copy. You'd better start scouting for more."

I expected him to tell me he'd been scouting but they're hard to come by. There are just some books people don't like to part with. Instead, I heard a voice from below me as I took a step down the ladder.

"Hi, Sophie."

I jerked around and saw Reese standing there, his arms covering his head.

"I know I've been banned from speaking to you," he said. "But please don't hit me with the books again."

I laughed. "No worries," I said, making my way to the floor. "I've given up my book assassin's badge."

"Relief," he said. "Anyway, I heard the ban on conversation might be on the verge of being lifted."

"It has been lifted."

"Oh," he feigned great relief, "you've done me great honor."

I stood there smiling. *Say it, Sophie. You don't need an introduction to it. Just blurt out the words. I'm sorry.*

"I need your help with something," he said. "If that's okay."

"Sure, what is it?"

"It's at my new store."

I figured that was his way of getting me to come by...a softening of the tension between us, because I was pretty sure I'd never be able to walk past his store again without thinking of my darlings, and probably crying. But I knew it had to be done. Of course Gramps said I could leave. His summer helper was around somewhere anyway, doing all the heavy lifting of customer service so I could spend my time dusty and covered in books—or booksy and covered in dust?

We left Bookish and I felt like all of downtown Strawbridge was at its front windows gawking at us. And they were all chanting, "Okay, Sophie, this is it. You can do it." The pressure was nearly intolerable.

We both waved at Mr. Cornell. He was standing inside his store, peering out the front window. The sign read: Old Geezer Knows a Real Treasure When he Sees it! *And so the war rages on.*

"Reese," I started. "I wanted to tell you."

He was kind enough to walk quietly beside me, letting me speak, knowing I'd likely botch it.

"I heard about your mom. I'm so sorry...for calling you in the middle of all that." *There! I did it.* I sighed. *Such relief.* "It was so...so..." I'd lost it. What good were words if you couldn't remember them when you needed them?

"You didn't know."

"But that's just it." The ramble began. "If I hadn't been so preoccupied with myself, and my thoughts, my feelings, and the cats, and...well, everything. If I'd answered your calls or at the very least went out in public and talked to someone. I mean, let's face it, downtown Strawbridge is a hotbed of gossip. Everybody knows everything about everybody. If I'd not been so...bookish."

"Bookish?"

"I don't mean bookish, by definition. I mean...*Sophie.* If I just hadn't been so Sophie."

He laughed. "You didn't know. That's all that's important."

"And Cal!" I blurted. "I had no idea. Lori over at ChocShop told me all about it. I swear, I didn't know."

"I know you didn't."

"Anyway, I'm really sorry. About everything."

"You know, my mom likes you."

"She does? But she doesn't know me."

He smiled. "I told her all about you."

"You must have left out a lot."

"You're too hard on yourself."

"Or maybe not hard enough."

We nodded hellos at Benjamin, outside Namaste.

"Cinnamon," he said and waved the smoke toward us.

"I saw you had a date the other night," he said.

"With Hugh, yes. You, too."

Carolina Davies poked her head out the door of Begotten as we walked by and said, "Hello, Sophie. It was so nice to meet you the other day."

"You, too, Mrs. Davies. This is Reese Fuller. He owns the new Summer Sun."

They shook hands and we went on. One of the Rollings —I can't tell them apart even now—called us into Sweet Suite. "Samples," she said. "You've got to try them. Cheese-cake brownie balls." They were heavenly.

"No," Reese said, as we left, still chewing.

"No, what?"

Mr. Booker called to us. "Reese, Sophie. You're coming to Poetry Night this Friday, right? We all missed you last time."

"You didn't go either?" I said.

And we went on toward Brunch.

"So...no, what?" I said.

"No, I wasn't on a date Friday night."

"But you were with someone."

Melanie tapped on the front glass window at Brunch and pointed to the sign out front: Now Available—Take Away Quiche! I gave her a thumbs up and we walked on. I tried to think of some way to get Reese to go on. He wasn't going to leave it at that, was he? We turned into the breezeway.

"That was my sister Amy," he said. *Finally.* "I thought Melissa would have told you."

"No. But after she told us about your mom, we were...I really can't tell you enough how sorry I am. About your mom. About Mr. Stahl and the building deal. Cal. And me. I was rude and childish. I hope you forgive me."

"It's forgotten, really."

We left the breezeway, crossed the little alley over to Fiona's on Mangrove, and there was his store across the street.

"Wow," I said. "It cleaned up really nice."

We crossed Mangrove, but instead of going to the front, he walked me around to the back of the store. I had a twinge of resentment in my chest. I mean, sure, I figured he was trying to get me past it all, but to just walk me back there straightaway, to see the empty spot where the old oak used to be? Where the picnic table used to sit? Where my darlings used to live? Shouldn't he ease me into this?

When we rounded the building, I saw what he'd done with the place. The black paved parking area was smaller than I expected it to be, only four spaces up against the back of the building, and four across from them, up against the little dirt road that led to parking for Manatee Park. Beyond that, he'd left the old oak, and set out two new picnic tables, but the area was closed off from the parking area. I could only see the tables through the wide slats of the wood fence and the old oak towering above it.

"This way," he said.

We walked across the little lot and to the back end of the fence where there was a gate. He lifted the latch and let me go in before him. I stopped and stared. He'd created a park, a sanctuary, green and lush, with the picnic tables and a trickling fountain. Up against the store, on either side of the back door, he'd created little sand beaches, lined with rocks.

314

"You've turned it into a break area," I said, "for your em-ployees. That's...nice."

"Yeah, that's one thing," he said.

"I thought you were going to put beach sand *inside*."

"We decided against that. The mess of it for one thing."

"But out back? I mean, no one will see it."

"That's not beach sand," he said. "Look." He was pointing at the back door to his store. "See the door?"

"I see it."

I'd begun to think all the work of renovation, the trauma of his mother's illness, having to deal with a crazy bookish Diva, had taken its toll and he was having some type of episode, but I heard Gramps' voice in my head saying, "Now that's not very generous, is it?" I was about to compliment Reese on his lovely back door when I finally saw it. I saw what he was trying to show me. Not the back door to his store. The *other* door. The mini door at the bottom. A doggie door. Or a cat—

The flap lifted and a furry black feline peeked out.

"Weesie!" I cried. He meowed and I rushed forward, only to scare at least two lives out of him. He ducked back inside. "Is he in the store?"

Reese's face was lit with this childlike, adorable, Loverboy sort of joy. He nodded. "Let's go see."

A flush of tingling tremors raced all over me as he pulled out his keys and unlocked the door. We entered the back room, one side decorated with two desks, a bean bag chair, and paintings of the ocean, and the other stacked with boxes. Weesie jumped onto a short stack and meowed again. Diva lounged on a desk chair. Pooper Scooper was curled up on the bean bag, and Piddle Paddle skittered about, batting a packing peanut across the floor.

"And Roger Dodger?" I said.

"He's usually hiding up front, by the register."

I approached Weesie carefully, held out my hand so he

could have a good sniff. He purred and I went to petting and giving him a good scratch behind the ears.

"Reese," I said, tears spilling freely.

He shrugged. "When I saw you at Burgers, you were obviously still upset about it. I felt terrible and my sister told me I should keep them. Make them part of the store." He pinched his face up into a funny sort of smile. "So, I did."

"Oh, Reese." I grabbed him. Literally. And squeezed. "Thank you, thank you, thank you." His arms encircled me, squeezed back, and I took the opportunity to breathe in his scent and nuzzle his chest. *If only...*

"And look," he said when I finally let him go and wiped my face. He took a Morgan's Office Supply catalog from one of the desks and showed me a page. "They do plaques. I'm ordering this one, for the gate. I'm declaring it a cat sanctuary."

"What will it say?"

He was grinning at me, like a cat with a mouse under his paw. "I was thinking, The Sophie Childers Home for Stray Cats."

"The beach!" I said. "It's cat litter."

"Oh, yeah." He set the catalog down. "That's what I wanted to get your help with."

"You want me to...scoop?"

"It's going to be a big job. What? Don't look like that. I'll get you a uniform if you want. And a title. You can be Assistant Poop Manager."

"Only the assistant?"

"Well, now, I *just* hired you. You'll have to work your way up to Big Poop Boss."

"Reese," I said, with as much seriousness as I could muster. "Would you go to Poetry Night with me this Friday?"

"I don't know," he said, his gaze cast to the floor. "I read thrillers."

"I can get past that; it won't be easy, of course."

"I could keep them hidden, under my bed." He looked up with a smile.

"I think that would be best."

"Still," he said.

I frowned. "Come on. I'm willing to put up with the thrillers, and the sexism, and your proclivity for wearing lipstick. You *have* to go out with me."

"But...do you think you could fall for a guy with five cats?"

"That *is* crazy," I said. "You're well on your way to being a stray cat hoarder." I reached my hands to his head, played with his hair, kissed his jawline where there was a hint of a bruise from my hard head. "But, seeing as you've been thoroughly inspected and found free of lumps...I'll take a chance."

Epilogue

The plaque, in the end, read: Sophie's Darlings. I sat on the bench of one of the picnic tables in the sanctuary, ignoring Roger Dodger—it was the only way he'd come near me. I had water from a can of tuna on my fingers and he sniffed, licked, and purred before skittering away, in the face of some unheard, unseen terror, back through the door flap and to, no doubt, his treasured spot in a box under the cashwrap counter of Summer Sun Surf and Beachwear.

Reese laughed.

"One of these days," I said, "he's going to let me pick him up."

Reese stood over me and dispensed a dollop of sanitizer in my right palm; he pressed my hands together between his and together we rid me of cat germs.

"Off with you," he said. He kissed me, pulled me to my feet and kissed me again, longer, deeper. "Go on to your sexist meeting."

I punched at him playfully. "I told you to get yourself a group of Divos."

"Oh, no. No segregation for the Divos. We'll petition to be let into the Divas Lunch like equal partners."

"Well, until that time, you are forthwith banned from participation."

"Even if we wear lipstick?"

"You'll find any excuse to put lipstick on. Should I be worried about that?"

"You said you'd tolerate that particular quirk." He smiled... adorable.

I kissed him, ruffled his hair, and left him to his store so I could walk over to Brunch and meet up with the Downtown Divas.

It was then end of August, hot as hell, and muggy in that suffocating way that makes you wonder why Florida is even a thing, much less a place to live. Alligators. Have you seen their skin? That's all you need to know.

Most of us were expected for lunch that day. Reese and I had just returned from North Carolina where I was presented to his parents; the Divas required juicy details. I was ready to hand them over—Reese and I were not allowed to sleep in the same room (he was forced to the sofa in the living room); his mother was radiant and well on her way to health; his father pleasant enough, but nervous and overly doting to his wife who often, literally, brushed him off; and yes, okay, he did try to sneak into my room the first night—ew, no, not his father...Reese!—only to find his parents (my guess is the father) had managed to scruff the door hinges making them squeak and screech so loud he ran in the dark, tripped over the magazine rack at the end of the hall (we think it was planted) and nearly broke an arm. Funny we hadn't noticed the door moaning and groaning that way during daylight hours. Such is a visit to one's Southern parents.

When I arrived at the outside tables of Brunch, Pari was missing. Attending were: Karen, Bella Diva; Melissa, Pink Diva; Kaya, Vintage Diva; Vanessa, Glam Diva; Lori, Fudge Diva; Carrie, Nerd Diva (her idea, I swear); Octavia, Goddess Diva; and me, Bookish Diva.

Karen brought us copies of her first few chapters. "Now," she said, pulling her hair behind her left ear. She'd ditched the barrettes and the resulting hair in the face made her feel, as she put it, like a sexy librarian. "Just because the protagonists are Ryan and Sandra, I don't want you to think it's about you two."

Kaya snickered, looking over the manuscript pages. "Sandra works at a bookstore and Ryan is a surfer."

"Coincidence," Karen said.

"Mm, hmm," Octavia sang. "Am I in here?"

"There is a girl who sings a lot." Karen blushed.

Vanessa leaned against the back of her wrought-iron chair, her face—sunglasses dark as a spy's—turned to the sun, and whined, "*Demasiado caliente para el romance*."

"I don't know what that means," Kaya said, but you don't sound happy."

"When does winter start?" Melissa said.

"Winter?" I said. "There is no winter here."

"Ain't that the truth?" Octavia said. She whipped open a folding fan and fluttered it in front of her face.

We heard the honk of a horn and saw Pari's hand waving at us from the window of her Honda as she passed. A few moments later she'd turned around and pulled up in front of Brunch—a lucky spot. The door opened and Fashion Diva stepped out.

"What happened to Eric and bedazzled sneakers?" I whispered to Karen. "What happened to walking instead of driving a few hundred yards from work?"

She shook her head. "He criticized her—" air quotes—"irresponsible spending on shoes."

We all gasped, duly horrified and prepared to support Pari. One does not condemn a Diva's shoe budget.

"Divas!" Pari approached and hugged me. She waved and blew kisses at the group before taking a seat. "What's on the agenda, today?"

"Item one," Melissa said. "Bookish will spill on her trip with Reese."

I sighed. "I wish I could offer some fodder for Karen's novels but I'm afraid our lives here are much more worthy."

"Item two," Karen said. "You all have to give me feedback." She handed a copy of her chapters to Pari.

"Item three," Pari said. "I need help with a frustrating situation."

"What?" We all said it at once and leaned toward her like she was a magnet.

"Apparently," she said, "there is a ghost in the Executive Suites building. They've brought in some sort of Ghost Whisperer—thinks he's a psychologist for the dead."

"That's sweet," Octavia said.

"It's intolerable," Pari said. "The man's insufferable."

I nodded—couldn't keep the smile from my face—and turned to the others conspiratorially. Vanessa winked at me.

"Perhaps you could invite him to Tracks for Salsa Night," Kaya said.

Pari glared at her. "I'm serious."

"All right," Melissa said. "It's on the agenda. I'm thinking... Downtown Divas Ghost Tour."

Pari slapped at her across the table, but she was laughing.

"Item four," Vanessa said—more like sighed. "Carrie needs a better Diva name."

"What is your objection?" Pari asked.

"I don't think nerd goes with diva."

"No more than bookish does," Carrie said.

"As Fudge Diva," Lori said, "I say Diva-hood should be granted to nerds as well as fashionistas."

"All those in favor?" Melissa said.

"Aye," we sang out.

"Very well," Vanessa said. "And item five. Sophie, what is up with Trudy? Why has she not come in for her cut and style? She won't tell me."

"Yeah, I think it's time we thought more about the Great Antiques War."

"Downtown Divas Matchmaking Service," Pari said.

"And Officer Palmer needs our help, too," Lori said. "Pat hasn't been to another Saturday Night Swing and he's beginning to panic. He's getting too aggressive with the tire marking, if you ask me."

"That will be Sophie's job," Melissa said. "She and Reese do the Swing thing. Salsa, too."

"I think we ought to make them Diva outings," I said. "You should all learn to dance."

Karen let out a loud snort of a laugh.

"I bet you can dance," I told her.

"Honey," Octavia said, "I can dance, but my body will not be contained by style. I've seen that Swing stuff. Too many steps."

"I'd like to see you at Swing Night," I told her. "Just do your thing on the floor. Let's see what happens."

"I know what will happen—some joker will grab me and start flinging me around. Nobody wants to see that."

I chuckled. "I do."

"You're out a lot now," Lori said. "Even more than you were with Cal."

Everyone went quiet.

"Was I not supposed to mention Cal?" she said. "Or ...Sophie going out?"

"Don't talk about socializing," Kaya whispered.

"We don't want to scare her back into the bookstore," Vanessa said. "It took us forever to get her out."

"Very funny," I said. "Anyway, Reese and I just do the Swing and Salsa nights. Our weekends are still, for the most part, spent at home, curled up on the sofa reading together."

A collective "ah" went around the tables.

"Nonsense," Vanessa said. "You two are all over town day and night reminding me of my single status. I demand friends of Hombre Caliente for all of us."

Laughter.

"There's nothing wrong with being single," Lori lectured. "You don't need a man to be a Diva."

"Hear, hear," Karen said.

"Brunch Diva!" Kaya said.

Melanie nearly dropped her tray of iced teas, but managed to steady it before setting it on one of our tables.

"Welcome to the club," Karen told Melanie. "You're a Diva now."

"Fashion Divas," I said. "Fudge Divas, Nerd Divas, Bella Divas. All at a Diva party! What a Diva party!"

"Okay, now you've gone bonkers," Pari said.

"I'm not the one with the hots for a Ghost Whisperer."

My behavior *was* rather silly, I admit. But I was...happy. Giddy. I was Social Sophie.

Books by Dianna Dann Narciso

Mainstream/Literary Fiction by Dianna Dann
Camelia
Always Magnolia
Bury Me

Fantasy by Dana Trantham
Children of Path: The Kell Stone Prophecy Book One
The Wretched: The Kell Stone Prophecy Book Two
Mark of the Faire: The Kell Stone Prophecy Book Three
The Kell Stone Prophecy: Complete Trilogy

Story Runners
Shards of Kholkari (2018)

Paranormal Humor by D.D. Charles
Zombie Revolution

Children's Fiction by Dana Trantham
Wayward Cat Finds a Home
Zombie Cats

For more, visit
waywardcatpublishing.com